THE
WI E
KT-430-944
r Burke

ff
FABER & FABER

First published in the UK in 2018
by Faber & Faber Limited
Bloomsbury House
74–77 Great Russell Street
London WC1B 3DA
This paperback edition first published in 2018

First published in the United States in 2018
by HarperCollins Publishers
195 Broadway, New York, NY 1007

Printed and bound by CPI Group (UK) Ltd, Croydon, CR0 4YY



This is a work of fiction. Names, characters, places, and incidents are products of the author's imagination or are used fictitiously and are not to be construed as read. Any resemblance to actual events, locales, organisations, or persons, living or dead, is entirely coincidental.



A CIP record for this book
is available from the British Library

ISBN 978–0–571–32819–2

2 4 6 8 10 9 7 5 3 1

For the Puzzle Guild
Friendship and Whimsy Forever

In an instant, I became the woman they assumed I'd been all along: the wife who lied to protect her husband.

I almost didn't hear the knock on the front door. I had removed the brass knocker twelve days earlier, as if that would stop another reporter from showing up unannounced. Once I realized the source of the sound, I sat up straight in bed, hitting mute on the TV remote. Fighting the instinct to freeze, I forced myself to take a look. I parted the drawn bedroom curtains, squinting against the afternoon sun.

I saw the top of a head of short black hair on my stoop. The Impala in front of the fire hydrant across the street practically screamed "unmarked police car." It was that same detective, back again. I still had her business card tucked away in my purse, where Jason wouldn't see it. She kept knocking, and I kept watching her knock, until she sat on the front steps and started reading my paper.

I threw on a sweatshirt over my tank top and pajama pants and made my way to the front door.

"Did I wake you?" Her voice was filled with judgment. "It's three o'clock in the afternoon."

I wanted to say I didn't owe anyone an explanation for lying around my own house, but instead, I muttered that I had a migraine. Lie number one—small, but a lie nonetheless.

"You should take vinegar and honey. Works every time."

"I think I'd rather have a headache. If you need to talk to Jason, you can call our lawyer."

"I told you before, Olivia Randall's not your lawyer. She's Jason's."

I started to close the door, but she pushed it back open. "And you may think your husband's case is on hold, but I can still investigate, especially when it's about an entirely new charge."

I should have slammed the door, but she was baiting me with the threat of incoming shrapnel. I'd rather take it in the face than wait for it to strike me in the back.

"What is it now?"

"I need to know where your husband was last night."

Of all nights, why did she have to ask about that one? For any other date of our six-year marriage, I could have offered a truthful account.

I already knew from Jason's lawyer that this wasn't the stuff covered by spousal privilege. They could haul me in to a grand jury. They could use my failure to answer as proof that I was hiding something. And a detective was at my door with what seemed like a simple question: Where had my husband been the previous night?

"He was here with me." It had been twelve years since a police officer last asked me a direct question, but my first instinct was still to lie.

"All night?"

"Yes, our friend brought over enough food to last the whole day. It's not exactly fun to be seen in public these days."

"What friend?"

"Colin Harris. He brought takeout from Gotham. You can call the restaurant if you need to."

"Can anyone else vouch that your husband was here with you?"

"My son, Spencer. He called from camp around seven thirty and spoke to both of us." Words kept escaping my mouth, each phrase seemingly necessitated by the previous one. "Pull up our phone records if you don't believe me. Now, please, what's this all about?"

"Kerry Lynch is missing."

The words sounded funny together. *Kerry Lynch is missing.* This woman who had been batting us around was suddenly gone, like a sock that never makes it out of the dryer.

Of course it was about that woman. Our entire life had been about her for the last two weeks. My lips kept moving. I told the detective that we streamed *La La Land* before falling asleep, even though I had watched it alone. So many details, tumbling out.

I decided to go on the offense, making it clear I was outraged the police had come straight to our door when Kerry could be anywhere. I even suggested indignantly that the detective come inside and take a look around, but in reality, my thoughts were racing. I assured myself that Jason could answer questions about the film if asked. He had seen it on the plane the last time he flew home from London. But what if they asked Spencer about the phone call?

The detective was obviously unmoved by my exasperation. "How well do you really know your husband, Angela?"

"I know he's innocent."

"You're more than a bystander. You're enabling him, which means I can't help you. Don't let Jason take you and your boy down with him."

I waited until the Impala had left to reach for my phone. Jason was in a client meeting, but took my call. I had told him the night before that I didn't want to speak to him again until I had made some decisions.

"I'm so glad you called."

With one stupid conversation, I had conformed to the stereotype. I was complicit now. I was all in.

"Jason, Kerry Lynch is missing. Please tell me you didn't do this because of me."

# I

# RACHEL

# 1

The first piece of trouble was a girl named Rachel. Sorry, not a girl. A *woman* named Rachel.

Even teenagers are called young women now, as if there is something horribly trivial about being a girl. I still have to correct myself. At whatever moment I transformed from a girl to a woman, when I might have cared about the difference, I had other things to worry about.

Jason told me about the Rachel incident the same day it happened. We were at Lupa, seated at our favorite table, a found pocket of quiet in the back corner of the crowded restaurant.

I only had two things to report from my day. The handyman fixed the hinge on the cabinet in the guest bathroom, but said the wood was warping and would eventually need to be replaced. And the head of the auction committee at Spencer's school called to see if Jason would donate a dinner.

"Didn't we just do that?" he asked, taking a large bite of the burrata we were sharing. "You were going to cook for someone."

Spencer is in the seventh grade at Friends Seminary. Every year the school asks us to donate not only money on top of the extraordinary tuition we pay but also an "item" to be sold at the annual auction. Six weeks earlier, I opted for our usual contribution at this year's event: I'd cater a dinner for eight in the highest bidder's home. Only a few people in the city connected me now to the summer parties I once planned in the Hamptons, so Jason helped boost my ego by driving the price up. I convinced him to stop once my item had "gone" for a thousand dollars.

"There's a new chair of the committee for next year," I explained. "She wants to get a head start. The woman has too much time on her hands."

"Dealing with someone who fastidiously plans every last detail months in advance? I can't imagine how awful that must be for you."

He looked at me with a satisfied smile. I was the planner in the family, the one with daily routines and a long list of what Jason and Spencer called Mom Rules, all designed to keep our lives routine and utterly predictable—good and boring, as I like to say.

"Trust me. She makes me look chill."

He feigned a shudder and took a sip of wine. "Want to know what that crowd really needs for an auction? A week in the desert without water. A cot in a local homeless shelter. Or how about a decent lay? We'd raise millions."

I told him the committee had other plans. "Apparently you're a big enough deal now that people will open up their wallets for a chance to breathe the same air. They suggested dinner with three guests at a—quote—'socially responsible' restaurant of your choosing."

His mouth was full, but I could read the thoughts behind his eye roll. When I first met Jason, no one had heard of him other than his students, coworkers, and a couple of dozen academics who shared his intellectual passions. I never would have predicted that my cute little egghead would become a political and cultural icon.

"Hey, look on the bright side. You're officially a celebrity.

Meanwhile, I can't give myself away without getting rejected."

"They didn't *reject* you."

"No, but they did make it clear that you were the member of the Powell family they want to see listed in next year's brochure."

We finally settled on a lunch, not dinner, with two guests, not three, at a restaurant—period, no mention of its social consciousness. And I agreed to persuade one of the other moms to buy the item when the time came, using our money if necessary. Jason was willing to pay a lot to avoid a meal with strangers.

Once our terms were negotiated, he reminded me that he would be leaving the following afternoon to meet with a green energy company based in Philadelphia. He'd be gone for two nights.

Of course, I didn't need the reminder. I had entered the dates in my calendar—aka the Family Bible—when he first mentioned it.

"Would you like to come with me?" Did he actually want me to join him, or had my expression given me away? "We could get a sitter for Spencer. Or he could tag along."

The thought of ever returning to the state of Pennsylvania made my stomach turn. "The chess tournament tomorrow, remember?"

I could tell that he did not, in fact, remember. Spencer had little in the way of organized hobbies. He wasn't a natural athlete and seemed to share Jason's aversion to group activities. But so far, he was sticking with the chess club.

The subject of his intern, Rachel, did not arise until the waiter brought our pasta: an order of *cacio e pepe* split between two bowls.

Jason let it slip like it was nothing: "Oh, something a little odd happened to me today at work."

"In class?" Jason still taught at NYU during the spring semester, but also had his own corporate consulting company and was a frequent talking head on cable television. In addition, he hosted a popular podcast. My husband had a lot of jobs.

"No, at the office. I told you about the interns?" With the university increasingly upset (jealous, Jason thought) about his outside activities, Jason had agreed to start an internship program, where he and his consulting firm would oversee a handful of students each semester. "One of them apparently thinks I'm a sexist pig."

He was grinning as if it were funny, but we were different that way. Jason found conflict amusing, or at least curious. I avoided it at all costs. I immediately rested my fork against the edge of my bowl.

"Please," he said, waving a flippant hand. "It's ridiculous, proof that interns create more work than they're worth."

He smiled the entire time he described the incident. Rachel was in either the first or second year of her master's study. He wasn't sure. She was one of the weaker students. He suspected, but wasn't certain, that Zack—the associate he'd tapped with the job of selecting candidates—had included her for purposes of gender diversity. She entered Jason's office to deliver a memo she had written about a chain of grocery stores. She blurted out that her boyfriend had proposed over the weekend, and held up her left hand to show off a giant diamond.

"What am I," Jason asked, "her sorority sister?"

"Please tell me you didn't say that."

Another eye roll, this time slightly less exaggerated. "Of course not. I honestly don't remember what I said."

"And yet . . . ?"

"She says I was sexist."

"She said this to whom?" I was pretty sure the correct usage was *whom.* "Why would she say that?"

"She went to Zack. These are the kinds of students we're accepting these days—a graduate student who doesn't understand the hierarchy at the firm where she works. She assumes Zack has some kind of power, because he was the one who hired her."

"But why was she complaining?" I noticed a woman at the next table looking in our direction and lowered my voice. "What is she saying happened?"

"I don't know. She started running on about getting engaged. She told Zack I said she was too young to get married. That she needed to live a little first."

Was there something wrong with that? I'd never had a job in a formal office setting. It sounded rude, but not *offensive.* I told Jason that there had to be more to it if she was complaining.

Another dismissive wave. "That's how ridiculous these millennials are. It's considered sexual harassment even to ask someone about their personal life. But if she barges in my office and starts telling me about her engagement, I can't say anything without melting the special snowflake."

"So is that what you said? That she was too young and should live a little, or did you call her a special snowflake?" I knew Jason's harshest opinions about his students.

"Of course not. I don't know. Honestly, I was annoyed by the whole conversation. I think I said something as a joke. Like, 'Are you sure you're ready to get locked down?' Probably that."

It was a phrase I'd heard him use before, about not only marriage but anything that was so good that you wanted to hold on to it forever. "Lock that down."

We put in an early offer on our house. "It's priced to sell. We need to lock that down."

A waiter telling us that there were only two more orders of branzino in the kitchen. "We're good for one. Lock that down."

I could picture him in his office, interrupted by an intern he'd prefer not to supervise. She's babbling about her engagement. He couldn't care less. *You're still in school. You sure you're ready to lock that down?* Jason had a habit of making teasing comments.

I asked him again if that was all that happened, if he was sure there wasn't something else that could have been misconstrued.

"You don't know how sensitive these college students are." The words burned, even though he didn't mean them to. I had never attended college. "If Spencer turns out like these microaggression asshole whiners, I'll ground him until he's forty."

Seeing the expression on my face, he reached for my hand. Spencer actually is special, not a special snowflake. He's not like these kids who were raised to think they're extraordinary even though they're extra-ordinary. Jason said he was kidding, and I knew he was. And I felt guilty because I realized I—like Rachel the girl intern—was being too sensitive, was feeling too special.

"So now what happens?" I asked.

Jason shrugged, as if I'd asked what he'd like to donate to the auction. "Zack will deal with it. Thank God the semester's almost over. But screw her if she thinks she's getting a recommendation."

As I poured a little more wine into my glass, I really thought that was the only thing at stake in Jason's interaction with Rachel—whether a graduate student would get a recommendation.

It would be four days until I realized how naive I had been.

# 2

**New York City Police Department**
**Omniform System—Complaints**
**May 14**

**Occurrence Location:** 1057 Avenue of the Americas
**Name of Premises:** FSS Consulting
**Narrative:**
Victim states that suspect "encouraged" sexual contact during business appointment.

**Victim:**
Rachel Sutton
**Age:** 24
**Gender:** Female
**Race:** White
Victim walked into precinct at 17:32 and asked to file a complaint. She proceeded to report that a coworker, Jason Powell, "encouraged" sexual contact between them. Victim presented calmly and did not appear distraught. When I asked her what type of sexual contact, she said, "He suggested that I should be sexual with him."

When I asked her to explain what she meant by "encouraged" and "suggested," she did not respond. I asked if there had been any physical contact between them or if he had threatened her or forced her to do anything she did not want to do. She abruptly accused me of not believing her and left the station over my repeated requests that she continue her complaint.

**Conclusion:** Forward report to SVU for consideration of further action.

**Signed:** L. Kendall

# 3

The woman who called about Jason donating a meal to next year's auction was Jen Connington. I no longer use names when I tell Jason what is happening in the parts of our lives he doesn't see, because I know he won't remember them. Jen is mother to Madison and Austin, wife to Theo. A top-three competitor for queen bee of the Friends Seminary Moms and newly appointed chair of the auction committee.

When I picked up the phone, she said, "Hey there, Angie."

My name isn't Angie. To the extent I ever had a nickname, it was Gellie, and only my parents ever used it. I guess women who shorten Jennifer to Jen assume that Angelas are Angies. "Thanks so much for your offer to cater another dinner!!" Exclamation points added. "But we thought you might want a break next year."

*We*. I immediately wondered which of the other moms was involved in whatever change was about to be decreed. "Seriously, Jen, it's the least we can do." My use of *we* felt smaller.

I immediately imagined her telling Theo over cocktails that night: "How many times does she have to remind us that she used to cater to the rich and famous in the Hamptons?" It was the only real job I ever had. At the time, I was pretty proud of myself, but women like Jen Connington would never stop seeing me as someone who had peaked as the help.

"Well, call me a radical feminist, but we thought it was about time for some of the dads to do their equal share, so to speak." She laughed at her play on the title of Jason's bestselling book, *Equalonomics*. "Don't you think we should convince Jason to come out of hiding?"

I had told her I wished he were in hiding. I would see him more often.

Jason's trademark thing was how companies could maximize profits by making corporate decisions based on principles of equality. It was perfect fodder for liberal Manhattanites—keep your one-percenter perks and be a good, moral person, all at the same time. His book spent nearly a year on the *New York Times* nonfiction bestseller list before it was released in paperback to enjoy another forty-week run. In the time that passed, the media appearances to promote the book evolved into stints as a talking head, which led to the podcast. And at the suggestion of his best friend, Colin, he started an independent consulting company. I was happy for him—happy for us—but neither of us had adjusted to his newfound celebrity.

My catering prize would no longer suffice for our auction give. Jen tried to soften the rejection by returning to her theme of letting Jason do his fair share of the work: "Every year, the moms bust their butts for this auction. Next year, we'll let Dad do the work."

It was the second time she had referred to Jason as Spencer's dad. I didn't correct her. There was no reason to.

*

When Jason and I, to my surprise, started to become serious the summer we met, I could tell how hard he tried to include Spencer. He taught him how to duck-dive waves at Atlantic Beach, played tennis with him at the courts in Amagansett, and climbed to the top of the lighthouse at the end of Montauk, a summer adventure intended for onetime tourists, but which Spencer never tired of.

When autumn arrived, Jason asked us to move with him to the city. God, how I wanted to say yes. I was only twenty-four years old, and had only lived in two places: my parents' house and a house in Pennsylvania I would have never gone back to, even if the city hadn't torn it down. I had never really had a relationship with a man who had met me as an adult. I dated a couple of guys on and off who I knew from childhood, but nothing that would have ever led to marriage. The last thing I wanted was to be another generation of East Enders, barely scraping by in life, especially when I wasn't in love.

And Jason wasn't just a good man who loved me. He was educated, intellectual, and refined. He had a good job, an apartment in Manhattan, and apparently enough money left over for a Hamptons rental in the summer. He wanted to take care of me. I could finally move out of my mother's house. I could work year-round in the city instead of having to work my ass off every day all summer trying to squirrel away enough cash for us to make it through the off-season.

But I couldn't. I wasn't the main character in a fairy tale, ready to be saved by Prince Charming. I was a mother to a six-year-old who didn't speak until he was three. Whom the doctors said might be autistic, merely because of his silence and a tendency to avoid eye contact. Who required supplementary tutoring during kindergarten to "prepare" him for what I wasn't supposed to call the "normal" classroom, rather than the "special" one his kindergarten teacher was suggesting. He was now about to start first grade at a school where he had friends, in the only stable home he had ever known. I couldn't uproot him into the city for a man I'd known for three months. When I told

Jason I couldn't move, I was prepared to say good-bye, both to him and to our whirlwind romance. I tried to tell myself that other girls my age would have had a summer fling by now.

Again, Jason surprised me. He rode the train out from the city every other weekend, staying in the cheapest room at Gurney's, with a view of the parking lot. He helped Spencer with his homework. He even managed to endear himself to my mother, who doesn't like anyone. In December, I accepted his invitation to bring Spencer into the city to see the Christmas tree at Rockefeller Center. We went ice-skating. It felt like a movie. For the first time since Spencer and I came home to live with my parents, my son spent the night under a different roof.

Jason showed up unexpectedly the weekend before Memorial Day. The season would officially kick off in a week. I was already booked for twenty-seven parties. I was in the kitchen making hundreds of bacon-wrapped dates that I could freeze for future use when I heard the doorbell. He dropped to one knee on my mother's front porch, opened the ring box, and asked me to marry him. I screamed so loudly that a passing bicyclist almost swerved into traffic.

He had every detail planned out. We'd move into his rental for the summer. I'd hire extra helpers to work the catering jobs I had already booked, and would stop accepting others. We'd return with him to the city in the fall. He'd ask friends to pull strings to get Spencer into a good school. He wanted to get married at Gurney's this summer, if it wasn't too soon. Last October, he'd put down a deposit to hold a date in July.

"You're insane," I told him. "I know what that place costs. You paid a fortune, all on a bet."

"I don't bet. When you're an economist, it's called researching and playing the market."

"When you're a normal human, it's called being a dork."

"If it helps, they gave me a discount when I told them what it was for. They love you there. Almost as much as I love you. Marry me, Angela."

I asked him why it was such a rush.

"Because I don't want to see you every ten days. I want you with me every night." He wrapped me in his arms and kissed my hair. "Besides, I don't want some other summer guy laying his eyes on you at a friend's party and stealing you away from me."

"And Spencer?"

"I want him to have a father. I want to *be* his father. Jason, Angela, and Spencer Powell. Has a nice ring to it, doesn't it?"

At that point, Spencer had my last name—Mullen. There had never been any consideration of another option. Now that Jason was talking about marriage, I saw the benefits of becoming Angela and Spencer Powell, in a big, crowded city. He would still see his grandparents. He had adjusted to kindergarten and then to first grade. He'd be able to transition to a new school. The benefits would be worth it.

I still remember Jason telling me how much his parents would have loved me the night after I said yes.

We got married at Gurney's on the date Jason had held, but at my request, there was no ceremony, just a dinner party for twelve. No puffy gown, no veil, no announcement in the Sunday Styles section. A nondenominational minister I found on the Internet showed up for cocktails to make it official. Jason's lawyer and best friend, Colin, filed the paperwork to change Spencer's name the following Monday. Legal adoption would take longer, but Spencer and I were officially Powells.

*

Two years later, over a table at Eleven Madison Park, I asked Jason if Colin was still working on making it official. His face immediately fell, as if I'd interrupted dinner to ask him to take out the garbage. "Is this really what you want to talk about on our anniversary?"

"Of course not. It's just the date—it's a reminder." I wasn't a lawyer, but it didn't seem possible it could take this long. There was no other father in the picture. "Did Colin tell you what the holdup was? I can get police reports if he needs them. I'm sure Detective Hendricks could explain—"

Jason rested his fork on the plate next to his half-eaten duck breast and held up a hand. "Please," he whispered, looking around as if anyone had been listening. "You're always the one saying you don't like thinking about that. That the past doesn't matter. So can we please not talk about it on our anniversary?"

"Fine." It was a reasonable request. He was right. I'd seen a counselor a few times when I first came home, but nothing that anyone would call real therapy. It was almost like I started life over again at the age of nineteen. I didn't need counseling. The only thing I ever needed was for people to understand that I was fine. I *am* fine. The couple of times Jason suggested that I "talk to someone," I shut down the possibility, and not gently. For me to raise the subject in passing over the dinner table was unfair.

But I couldn't ignore my suspicion that something had changed. What sounded like a pile of annoying paperwork a couple of years ago felt like an actual hurdle now, a line Jason no longer wanted to cross. Maybe it had seemed easier to imagine being a permanent father to Spencer two years ago, when we both assumed we'd have another child, a little brother or sister for our son, together.

I got pregnant the second month after our marriage. Two

months after that, I wasn't. I had never seen Jason cry before. That night in bed, we said we'd try again. I was still so young. It only took four months to get another plus sign on the stick. Then after two months: gone. Two miscarriages in a year.

The third time lasted almost to the first trimester mark. I was starting to look forward to sharing the news. But then we lost him . . . or maybe her. The doctors remained optimistic, telling me that my chances for a successful pregnancy were still over 50 percent. But I felt like I had already flipped that coin too many times, and it was going to keep coming up on the wrong side. I, of all people, needed predictability. I needed to know what was going to happen, and because I knew that about myself, I really only had one choice—to give up. I asked for the insertion of an IUD so I could have control over my body again.

Jason did his best not to seem disappointed. He said that no matter what happened, we still had Spencer, and he was enough. But I could tell that he was trying to convince himself more than anything. And I noticed that I was the one holding him. I was the one doing the consoling. Because we both knew that in some ways, the loss was more his than mine, because Spencer would always be more mine than his. Jason didn't have a child of his own.

And now Spencer still wasn't adopted.

"I thought maybe we'd gotten an update," I said softly.

He reached across the table and held my hand. When he looked into my eyes, he was no longer frustrated. "I love our son. And that's who he is now—our son. You know that, right?"

"Of course." I smiled. "It's been two years since you locked this down."

"Best decision I ever made."

"Just figured we'd have locked down Spencer legally by now, too."

He gave my hand a squeeze. "Time flies when you're happy. I'll call Colin tomorrow. I promise."

He kept his promise. When Colin sat me down and explained the process, he said it would be easy. We simply needed to notify Spencer's biological father and get his permission to terminate his parental rights. "Or," he explained, "if he never had any real ties to Spencer, we can argue abandonment and potentially skip the notification if you think it's going to be a problem."

I tried to keep my voice completely neutral. "He's dead."

"Oh, even better." He immediately offered an awkward apology, and I assured him it was fine. "Condolences, I guess? Anyway, all we need in that case is a copy of the death certificate."

"But the father's not listed on the birth certificate." I didn't explain that he was already dead and that Spencer was already two years old by the time that birth certificate was issued, listing me as his only parent.

"Huh, okay." I could tell that Colin was waiting for a more detailed explanation, but I didn't offer one.

"Well, that'll be a little more complicated. The judge might ask if you know who the father is, in which case we could offer up the death certificate. They need to make sure there's not some guy out there getting his kid taken away. It shouldn't be too much of a problem."

I nodded, knowing that Spencer was never going to have a legal father. When Jason got home that night, I told him everything I had learned about the adoption procedure. That was the last time we talked about it.

The paperwork isn't important. Spencer knows who his parents are. We have Jason's name. As far as anyone is concerned, Jason is Spencer's father, and that's all that matters, right?

# 4

The day after Rachel Sutton walked into the Midtown South Precinct, Detective Corrine Duncan received a copy of a brief report filed by the desk officer. She found herself shaking her head as she read.

She skipped down to the signature line at the bottom of the page. "L. Kendall."

Corrine had no direct knowledge of Officer Kendall, but immediately formed a mental image of him. *Him*, almost certainly, not only because of raw statistical odds but from the details of the report itself. The judgmental quotation marks around "encouraged" and "suggested." The way he noted that she "presented calmly and did not appear distraught," as if everyone knew that good victims cry.

Corrine could already imagine the conversation that might have ensued had Rachel Sutton not left the precinct. *What were you wearing? Why were you alone with him?*

Old-school. L. Kendall may as well have written DON'T BELIEVE WHAT SHE MIGHT SAY across the top in all caps. This was how police took a report when they meant to signal to the prosecution not to bother. If nothing else, it would give a defense attorney ammunition if the defendant were ever charged.

Corrine wanted to think she had never written a report like that.

She didn't start out on the job with NYPD. Her first two years were as a patrol officer in Hempstead, on Long Island in Nassau County. Policing was different there. With fewer than 120 officers, the department expected officers to investigate their own cases, with the exception of major crimes. So she learned things like why a child abuse victim might accuse an innocent person (to protect a guilty parent), why domestic violence complainants often didn't want to prosecute (out of fear or even love), and why sexual abuse complaints had more layers than any onion. "Embarrassment" didn't begin to describe the dynamics.

But in the NYPD, a patrol officer like L. Kendall didn't need to know all that. He took the report and pushed the paper to a specialty unit for follow-up.

She had already googled Jason Powell. The name hadn't rung a bell in the context of a police report, but the search results immediately jogged her memory. According to his bio on New York University's website, he had a bachelor's and master's degree from Stanford, a PhD from Harvard, and was the somebody-something endowed chair in human rights investments and professor of economics. Despite the impressiveness of that résumé, it barely made the first page of Google hits. Powell was better known as an author and speaker. The first sentence of his Wikipedia listing: "Jason Powell is the *New York Times* bestselling author of *Equalonomics*, the chair of FSS Consulting, and a frequent media commentator."

Corrine preferred fiction, personally, but even she had heard of *Equalonomics*. About four years ago it had been one of those books that everyone read—or pretended to read, in Corrine's opinion—to seem well informed.

Now, according to Powell's website, he hosted a podcast bearing the same name as his bestselling book. His Twitter account—a combination of business news, liberal politics, and snark—had 226,000 followers. *Cosmo* had named him one of the ten sexiest "gingers."

She recalled seeing the author on *Morning Joe* a couple of years ago. The panelists fawned over Powell, asking whether he might be interested in running for office someday. It probably didn't hurt that he was nice looking—trim, clean-cut, but with a little edge. A bit too pretty for Corrine's taste, but to each her own.

Next, she googled "FSS Consulting." Fair Share Strategies. She clicked the "About" page. The company provided "human rights and social justice due diligence" to investors and investment groups.

She wiggled her mouse, clicked on "Our Team," and scrolled down. The list was short, only two names in addition to Powell's: Zachary Hawkins, Executive Director, and Elizabeth Marks, Researcher.

There was nothing more she was going to learn from her computer. She picked up her phone.

*

The voice that answered sounded apprehensive, even slightly annoyed. "Hello?"

Corrine asked if she was speaking with Rachel Sutton—she was—and then identified herself as a detective following up on the complaint that was filed yesterday.

"Oh, of course," Rachel said apologetically. "I'm so glad you called. It seems like no one is listening to me. I was positive the officer at the precinct was going to file it at the bottom of a dumpster."

"It's all on computers, so . . ."

"Right. So now what happens?"

"Now, if you don't mind, you get to repeat everything you

already told Officer Kendall to me. We'll go from there."

Rachel laughed softly. "Are you going to roll your eyes and interrupt me every few seconds, trying to make it sound like I'm lying?"

"Was that your experience at the precinct?"

"The guy was a jerk. I mean, I sort of expected that when I reported it at FSS because Jason's the boss. So I wound up at the police station, but that managed to be worse—"

"Okay, we'll talk all about it, but in person." Most detectives arranged interviews at the precinct, which for the special victims unit meant a station house on 123rd Street in an area of East Harlem that many victims were afraid to enter. Corrine, however, believed she learned a lot about people by seeing where they lived. And sitting down in a victim's living room was a way to begin earning her trust. "Are you home now?"

"Yeah. Give me an hour to get cleaned up."

And already Corrine had learned something about Rachel Sutton. She was the kind of person who tidied up before talking to a detective about a sex abuse claim. That fact meant nothing on its own, but Corrine made a mental note of it, because Corrine liked to think she noticed everything.

*

Rachel's apartment in Chelsea was one of those generic new buildings popping up across Manhattan, all floor-to-ceiling glass. Ticky-tacky fishbowls, Corrine called them. Corrine, on the other hand, had a house—an actual hand-to-God house, with a yard and a driveway—because she'd bought in Harlem before hipsters decided Harlem was cool. A five-minute walk to work was only one reason Corrine had asked to come back to SVU after working homicides for four years.

She told the doorman she was there to see Rachel Sutton,

gesturing toward the badge hanging from the chain around her neck. Years ago, after only two weeks as a plainclothes detective, Corrine had opted for that placement. No one had confused her with a nanny or a housekeeper when she wore a blue uniform.

Rachel answered her apartment door in cropped boyfriend jeans and a black tank top. Her long dark-brown hair was pulled into a ponytail at the nape of her neck, and she had applied her makeup in that way that made it look like she wasn't wearing makeup. As Rachel gestured for her to take a seat in the living room, Corrine noticed a smear of ink on the back of Rachel's hand, like a temporary tattoo, a couple of inches from a Tiffany-cut solitaire that Corrine guessed was a full two carats.

"Nice place," Corrine observed, even though to her it seemed like a photograph from any modern furniture catalog.

"Thanks. My mom did everything." Her shrug seemed to acknowledge her good fortune. "I haven't told her about Jason yet. She's going to freak. And no way will she let me keep working there—"

"At FSS?"

"Yeah. It's an amazing opportunity for me. Jason's basically the leading voice at the cross section of finance and international human rights, and now this. I don't want to blow up my whole professional life before it's started."

Corrine suggested that they talk first about what happened before they discussed what actions might follow.

Rachel explained that she was getting her master's degree in economics at NYU and had an internship for credit at Jason's consulting firm. She'd entered Jason's office to deliver a memo she had drafted. "I didn't see him at his desk, but he must have heard me walk in, because he called me into his spa room."

"His what?" Corrine asked.

"That's what the interns call it. He's got this huge private bathroom with a shower and a little daybed to the side. Sometimes he closes the door, and we think he takes naps in there. A couple of the interns joke that he might actually live at the office. Anyway, I walked in there, and his pants were undone. I started to turn away, and he said it was nothing I hadn't seen before. Then he kept talking to me, like it's normal. But he was like touching himself the entire time."

"His genitals were exposed?"

Rachel shook her head. "No, or at least I didn't see. His hands were in his pants. I can't describe it. And it was so fast, and I was sort of freaked out. So then he looked at the memo in my hand and saw my ring. He said something about whether it was a conflict diamond."

Rachel must have seen the confusion on Corrine's face, because she paused for an explanation. "They're diamonds that come illegally from war-torn areas. Same thing as 'blood diamonds.'" Corrine nodded to indicate she was following along.

"I told him I really didn't know. I held my hand up like an idiot, telling him how I got engaged last weekend."

"Congratulations," Corrine said.

"Well, as if he'd care. I was nervous, trying to find something to talk about. He took the memo from me, and I started to turn around to leave, but he kind of grabbed my other arm. Not hard, but just sort of held it, like he was keeping me from walking off. I thought maybe he was going to skim my memo and ask some follow-up questions while I was there. But then he kind of pulled me back toward him, and his belt buckle was still undone. He told me I was too young to get married. I hadn't had enough *fun* yet. It was clear to me that he was about to put my hand against his—you know. I jumped back immediately."

Corrine asked what happened next.

"Nothing. I kind of stepped backward and pulled my hand

away, really abruptly. I didn't know what to say. And then he turned away, fastened his belt, and started flipping through the memo, like it was no big deal. He told me he'd let me know if he had any questions. And then I left."

Corrine asked Rachel whether she'd spoken to anyone about the incident.

"I told Zack Hawkins. He's the executive director, officially the person in charge of the interns." Corrine recalled the name from the FSS website. "I was so shocked," Rachel said. "I found myself in his office, telling him what had happened."

Corrine asked if Zack said what he was planning to do about her complaint.

"He said he'd talk to Jason about it—that he was sure it was some kind of misunderstanding." Her dismay that there could be any confusion about Jason's conduct was clear in her tone. "It was still eating away at me after work, so I went to the police precinct."

"Did you talk to anyone else about the incident? Maybe your fiancé?"

Rachel looked surprised by the mention of a fiancé. "I'm still getting used to that word," she said, admiring her ring. "No, I didn't tell Mike, for the same reason I didn't tell my mother. I don't want to make a big deal of this—"

"I'm a police detective, Rachel. Are you saying you don't want to press charges?"

"Like I said, I don't know, but I didn't feel right not saying anything. What if I let it go, and he ended up doing something worse to another woman? I guess I just wanted to file a report so it would be there. Do you know if this is the first time he's done this?"

Corrine told her that the NYPD had no prior complaints.

Rachel's lips pursed. "There's no way for me to prove what

happened, is there? It's my word against his. The classic he-said, she-said."

Yes, Corrine thought. And even if she had the entire incident on video, it wasn't obviously a crime. According to Rachel, Jason never touched her on an "intimate" body part and didn't clearly expose his own to her. After a few follow-up questions, she confirmed that Rachel's allegations—if she could prove them—might be considered an attempt to commit an "offensive physical touching." A Class B misdemeanor. Theoretically, a maximum sentence of six months, but much more likely to lead to probation and some form of counseling.

"And that's assuming we can prove that his intention was to place your hand on his genitals," Corrine added.

"So I should have lied and said he did it?" Rachel asked.

"No, because that's not what happened, right?"

Rachel shook her head and wiped away a tear. "Sorry, I'm frustrated."

"Have you thought about reporting it to the university? Isn't your internship through the school?"

"Technically, but it's more like a job, and Jason's basically a rock star at NYU. Plus he's got tenure, so I assume they won't do anything. To be honest, my guess is that a lot of the female students wouldn't have pulled away. I'm not sure I want to be 'that woman' on campus." She looked down as if pondering her fingernails. "So does this mean you're not going to do anything?"

"My next step would usually be to talk to any witnesses, but you say there weren't any. I'd speak to Zack to confirm that you reported the incident right afterward—ask him about your demeanor. And I'd usually speak to the suspect before concluding my investigation. That's *if* you want me to proceed. I can't promise he'll be charged—that's up to a prosecutor—but at least the reports will be there."

Rachel nodded.

"Is that what you want?"

When Rachel answered, she no longer sounded like a confused, conflicted student, worried about unwanted attention and a detour from her carefully planned professional track. Her voice was calm and decisive. "Yes, I'm positive. I just want him to admit what he did to me."

As Corrine walked to her car, she thought about all of the reasons no ADA would ever touch this case for prosecution. The delay in reporting. Rachel's defensiveness with Officer Kendall. The fleeting nature of the interaction. The absence of any type of force. Not to mention the stamp of ink on the back of Rachel's hand, left over from a club, possibly from the previous night, only hours after the incident.

The complaint wasn't quite right. But they never were. That was a truth that every sex offense investigator would admit if it weren't wholly unacceptable. You're not supposed to say that victims never tell the complete truth, because it sounds as if you're calling them liars. They're not liars. They're protecting themselves. They're preparing not to be believed. They're anticipating all the ways that others will attack them, and are building a protective shield.

All things being equal, Corrine believed that something had happened to Rachel yesterday—or at least Rachel *believed* it had happened. The main reason Corrine thought Rachel was telling the truth? Because a liar would have made up something far, far worse.

*

She called her lieutenant from the car. He didn't understand why she was calling him about a stupid misdemeanor until she explained who Jason Powell was. He responded with an annoyed obscenity.

As expected, he played hot potato and told her to call an assistant district attorney.

She called the New York DA's Office Special Victims Bureau and asked for the supervising ADA, Brian King. He answered after three and a half rings. "Hold on a sec. Sorry. I'm inhaling lunch before a sentencing hearing. I wasn't going to pick up until I recognized your number."

"I'm honored." She told King everything she knew so far about Rachel's complaint.

"Schadenfreude," he said. "Every time my ex-girlfriend saw him on TV, she used to turn up the volume. Have you questioned him yet?"

"No. We thought we'd get you roped in early. Make sure we do this right. One way to play it is to pop in and have a little chat. Get his side of the story. Maybe he admits something . . ." She let her voice trail off.

"Or maybe he kicks you out, calls a lawyer, and brings in a hazmat team to scrub down his sex den."

"Lots of men have private bathrooms in their offices."

"I don't see this thing going anywhere. You know that, right?"

"Won't be the first time. I just work the case. My guess is Rachel won't want to press charges if it's his word against hers, but I won't know until I at least ask the question."

"Fair enough. I'm thrilled to be involved early on," he said sarcastically.

Corrine was a few blocks away from the FSS offices when her cell rang. She had only dialed Rachel Sutton's phone number once, but she recognized it on the screen.

"Detective Duncan," she answered.

Rachel identified herself, apologized for bothering her, and said she remembered something. "His underwear. They were white boxer shorts with red candy canes. It was so ludicrous, I almost laughed. Does that help at all?"

In a case of he-said, she-said, "she" had just racked up one small point on her side of the board.

# 5

**Detective Corrine Duncan**

**Interview:** May 15, 1:55 PM
**Location:** 1057 Avenue of the Americas, FSS Consulting
I went to location to contact Jason Powell regarding a complaint filed by Rachel Sutton. I was told that Powell was not in the office. I then asked to speak with Zachary Hawkins, executive director of FSS Consulting.

I identified myself as an NYPD detective to Hawkins and informed him that an intern had reported an incident allegedly occurring the previous day. Hawkins nodded as if he knew what I was referring to. He said that Jason Powell had left earlier in the day for a business trip to Philadelphia, even though I had not indicated to him yet that the intern's complaint concerned Mr. Powell. I asked him directly, "Do you know why I'm here?" He said without hesitation, "This is about Rachel, right?"

Hawkins reported that he studied under Powell at NYU and began working at FSS after a few years at a hedge fund. He explained that this is the first time FSS has supervised student interns, under pressure from the university because Powell is still a professor while pursing outside business endeavors. Rachel Sutton is one of four interns, spending approximately 6–10 hours per week at FSS, primarily researching potential investments.

Hawkins indicated that Rachel Sutton went to his office the previous day, asked to speak to him, and closed his office door. She reported that Jason Powell had "sexually harassed" her. She stated that Powell had "been inappropriate" with her. According to Hawkins, when he pressed Sutton further for details, she responded, "He's the one who should explain himself."

I asked Hawkins what he did in response to her complaint. He admitted that he has no training in responding to workplace complaints, and that FSS is too small to have a human resources department. He said that he spoke with Jason Powell, who appeared "completely shocked and even outraged" by the question. Powell indicated that he could not think of any explanation for the complaint except for a brief conversation regarding Rachel Sutton's recent engagement.

I asked Hawkins if he had any other information to provide regarding the incident, and he said he did not. He said he was "stunned" and "disappointed" that the police were involved, indicating his belief that there was a misunderstanding between the two parties.

After leaving FSS, I telephoned Jason Powell at a cell phone number provided by Hawkins. I identified myself as an NYPD detective (I did not specify SVU) and told him that I wanted to speak to him about a complaint I had received. He immediately stated that he would not answer questions unless he was in the presence of counsel.

**Action:** Reports forwarded to ADA King, New York DA's Office Special Victims Bureau.

# 6

*Three Days Later*

This is how I found out.

I am used to waking up alone, depending on which moment you count as "waking up."

The first time is usually around three in the morning. Jason doesn't know about these restless minutes. No one does. I tell myself they don't matter, that they're not real. They have nothing to do with my life as an adult—in this house, with Jason and Spencer. These lost blocks of time belong to the person I used to be. It's as if sleep carries me into a time machine and I emerge briefly as my younger self: terrified, lonely, but more than anything, flat. That is how I used to feel all the time. Now, it's only how I wake up—the first time, in the middle of the night, after an awful dream. I force myself to close my eyes and follow the "alphabet game" that Jason taught Spencer when we first spent the night under one roof together.

Spencer was nearly seven years old at the time. He was used to falling asleep on Long Island to the sounds of ocean wind and the hum of cicadas. Jason's guest room was fifteen floors above Seventy-Fourth Street, but Spencer could not adapt to the staccato eruptions of sirens and honking horns.

He stepped into the living room in his Batman pajamas,

rubbing his sleepy eyes. I looked apologetically to Jason and started to get up to take Spencer back to bed, but Jason pulled him onto the sofa between us.

"Start by thinking of something you like—a cartoon, a TV show, a subject in school."

I wasn't surprised when Spencer chose Harry Potter. He was an advanced reader for his age, but I suspected that the movies—and my mother—had helped him work his way through the books.

"Excellent," Jason said. "Now close your eyes. Start with the letter A. Do you know your letters?"

Spencer smiled and nodded, eyes still closed. He had begun reading when he was only four.

Jason explained the game: Start with A and think of something related to Harry Potter. "Aunt Petunia."

Then to B. "Broomstick."

I could tell from my son's face that he was no longer scared of the street outside. His mind was busy, inside a Harry Potter story. It was the first time I felt sure that Jason was going to love my son, not just me. Jason promised him that if he went back to bed and played the game, he'd be asleep again by the time he made it to Z.

This is how I spend those middle-of-the-night minutes, working through the alphabet—our family's non-pharmaceutical Ambien—usually in the world of a familiar television show like *Scandal* or *Friends*. Something to make time pass. Anywhere except inside the dream that woke me in the first place, back in that house in Pittsburgh.

The second time I wake up—barely—is when Jason's alarm goes off at precisely 5:30 a.m. By the time I met him, his schedule called for getting up early so he could work on the book he hoped to publish someday. Once that plan had worked, the timeline was set in stone.

As for me, the day doesn't actually begin until my seven o'clock alarm, at which point my daily routine kicks in. I start with my iPad. Check e-mail. Browse Facebook. Skim the headlines. But I give myself fifteen minutes max, followed by a two-minute plank and a couple of stretches to get the blood moving. I swing by Spencer's room to make sure he gets up, then it's down to the kitchen to make breakfast. Boring? Yes. But I'm a firm believer in routine. Predictability is comforting. It's safe.

I first learned Rachel the Intern's last name from my iPad. From Facebook, to be precise. Jason hadn't brought up the incident since initially mentioning it at dinner. He'd spent two days in Philadelphia. By the time he came home, I had actually forgotten about it. I assumed that if an intern's complaint had moved beyond Zack, Jason would have mentioned it.

On the right side of the screen—beneath the name of an Oscar winner who was in the middle of a contested divorce and that of an athlete I barely recognized—were the words *Jason Powell.* My husband was "trending." For a split second, I felt excitement, but then I clicked on the link.

After a quick skim of the article, I reached for the remote control on the nightstand and turned to *New Day*, where Jason was scheduled for a segment this morning. They were on a commercial break.

I clicked over to MSNBC, where Jason was also a frequent contributor. The *Morning Joe* panel was interviewing some congressman I'd never heard of. No mention of Jason on the crawl beneath the program.

I flipped up three stations to the channel that focused on finance issues. Nothing.

One more click up to the leading "conservative" station. A photograph of Jason appeared in the upper-right-hand corner, not far from the face of the attractive blonde who was speaking his name. And then I saw the letters in a banner across the bottom of the screen. *Progressive Celebrity Economist Accused of Intern Sex Abuse.*

*

The article was from the *Post*, and 3,000 Facebook users had already shared it. The paper had pulled a photo from Jason's listing on the university's website. Jason looked so young. His long face was fuller then, and he wasn't yet sporting the short-stubble look he'd adopted a few years ago. His green eyes seemed to stare straight through the camera, and he was smiling as if he had thought of a joke.

The article itself was only two paragraphs long. It said that an unnamed college intern had accused "economist turned pundit and political lightning rod" Jason Powell of "involuntary sexual contact."

"An inside source tells the *Post* that the dirty professor keeps a secret room with a shower and a bed adjacent to the ritzy off-campus office where he has been earning a mint telling investors how to spend their money according to his liberal politics. The same source reports that the NYPD is close to making an arrest and that we will soon be learning more about the various uses to which the renowned economist has been putting the bed in question."

I had to stop myself from throwing the iPad on the floor. When we first moved downtown, Jason missed being able to run in Central Park every day. Splurging for that shower when he opened FSS had been a way to get back to his old running routes. And the bed wasn't an actual bed. It was the daybed we used to have in the hallway alcove of our old apartment. I had been the one to suggest moving it into the room we jokingly called his "suite" at the office. With no windows, the room was perfect for a quick catnap when Jason's early-bird grind caught up to him in the afternoon.

I tried calling Jason's cell phone, but it went straight to voice mail. "Jason, call me as soon as you get this." I sent a text with the same message.

I scrolled down the page on my iPad to see the Facebook comments accompanying the *Post* article. It was going viral.

I knew his good-guy shtick was an act.
The police are about to arrest? Is he still teaching undergrads? WTF?
I know a girl at school who interns with him. She's the only female in the program. It has to be her. Name is Rachel Sutton. She's hot.

Several comments followed that one, scolding the author for "doxxing" the woman who was single-handedly ruining my husband's reputation. Apparently it was okay for Jason to be named, but her privacy was to be protected. I made a mental note of her name and continued skimming the comments.

What kind of professor meets with a student alone . . . in a bedroom?
OMG. His son goes to my daughter's school! He always seemed so nice. I'm crushed.

The author of that last comment was a woman named Jane Reese. I clicked on her profile picture and recognized the teenage girl next to her from Spencer's choir performances. According to Facebook, Jane and I were "friends." And she was the one who was "crushed." I clicked the unfriend button.

Spencer.

Jesus, Spencer. I had protected him from so much, but I was powerless to shelter him from this.

I googled my name and Spencer's—using both Powell and Mullen—searching for any mentions within the last twenty-four hours. No one had dragged us into the story. Not yet, anyway.

But if some random Internet user had already posted the name of Rachel Sutton, how long would it be before people who thought they knew something about me jumped into the fray?

*

Spencer had a pillow pulled over his head to block the light seeping around the window shade. He let out a moan when I sat at the foot of his bed. My son had a way of treating each morning as a theater audition.

"Do I need to remind you that little girls in other parts of the world have literally died trying to get an education? Time for school, mister."

He squinted up at me from beneath his shaggy hair. "Normal moms say, Get the fuck up before I kill you."

This is my precocious son's idea of "normal." "I prefer guilt trips to death threats. Get up. But we need to talk for a second. Some kids at the school might be talking about Dad." Spencer had started calling Jason Dad after our first anniversary. We never asked why. We were just grateful.

"Loretta's mom has an Academy Award, and Henry's dad is literally like a musical genius. Trust me, no one talks about Dad."

Ah, the joys of a private school in Manhattan.

"There's a story going around the Internet. Someone accused him of something. It'll get cleared up, but I need you to try to block it all out today at school."

"What do you mean, he was *accused*?"

There was no way I could keep the details from my son, not with the 24/7 media cycle. "It's a student from the university.

College students can overreact, Spencer."

I started babbling from there. I told him that sometimes extremely troubled students found their way into the university. That his father had done nothing but try to help her by supervising an internship. That teachers have conflicts with students all the time, but Dad had the additional complication of being a public person. It was possible the student was looking for attention at his expense.

"So what are people going to say?"

I searched his pale brown eyes, which peered out beneath wisps of hair that should have been cut two weeks ago. My son was too old to be treated like a child, but he was young compared to his peers. His friend Henry, for example—son of the "musical genius"—had two nannies, a driver, and a bodyguard at his disposal, and saw his parents twice a month. These kids would pull no punches.

"That a student accused your father of inappropriate behavior."

"What? Like . . . sex?"

I said I didn't know exactly. That it was a misunderstanding. That I only told him in case someone mentioned it at school.

"And this is, like, *online*?" He started to get up, probably heading for the phone I made him dock downstairs in the kitchen,, one of the phone-related Mom Rules, along with divulging his passcode, asking permission before sharing photographs of others, and, most controversially, all phones in airplane mode while the car is moving.

I tried not to think about the other parents whispering in their kitchens right now about my husband. Or the NYU students texting links to one another during class. Or the people I used to know on the East End, gloating that my perfect life in the city hadn't worked out quite so well after all.

"This young woman is obviously troubled, Spencer. Deeply. And your father's been trying to help her, okay?" I was hinting at facts I knew nothing about, but needed to offer some kind of explanation for what was happening. Troubled girl gets fixated on successful mentor seemed, sadly, to work.

"Mom, I can't go to school. You have to let me stay home."

I walked to the bathroom in the hallway and turned on the water in the shower. It took forever to heat. "You can't stay home, or people might assume he's guilty. He's your father, Spencer, and you're not a child anymore. We have to protect our family."

# 7

While Spencer was in the shower, I tried Jason again. I hung up when I heard the familiar "You've reached Jason Powell . . ." I'd already left two voice mails and three text messages.

I flipped on the small television hanging beneath our kitchen counter, keeping the volume low to make sure I'd hear Spencer on the stairs in time to turn it off. I flipped to *New Day*. Jason initially became a semiregular on the show due to our friendship with one of the hosts, Susanna Coleman. Now that Jason's commentary was widely sought after, he still appeared about once a month, primarily out of loyalty.

Susanna and her cohost Eric were in the studio's kitchen, flanking a chef I recognized from one of those cable cooking shows. The chef was saying, "See? Perfect al dente," while Susanna and Eric attempted to sample the supposedly perfect spaghetti strands with grace.

Susanna was nodding in agreement until her mouth was free to speak. "You're my hero. I always overcook my pasta."

Had Jason already been on the air this morning? What was he supposed to talk about today? He had brought it up the night before, while I was trying to read Spencer's paper about James Baldwin's *Go Tell It on the Mountain*. My son was only in the seventh grade, but some of his homework was already more sophisticated than anything I had ever done in school. I had stopped reading to look up the word *circumlocution* on my phone when Jason mentioned his plans for the TV segment.

Now I remembered: seven retailers who were changing the world in small ways. It didn't take an economist, let alone one with Jason's credentials, to hype footwear and blankets, but these were the compromises he made for the sake of expanding his "platform."

Had he really gone on air and talked about guilt-free splurges without acknowledging the claim against him? No way. The Twittersphere would have been merciless. These days, the public thinks they're owed an immediate explanation.

I reached for my phone and googled "Jason Powell New Day," then narrowed the search for posts within the last hour. I found the answer to my question on a website that covered celebrities from a feminist perspective.

> *Seven minutes into* New Day*'s opening, cohost Eric Jordan abruptly interrupted one of Susanna Coleman's stories about her beloved dog. "I'm sorry, Susanna. But no one wants to hear about Frannie. Let's talk about the elephant in the room." He identified the elephant as the* New York Post*'s report that morning that a college intern had accused Dr. Jason Powell—"our own Dr. Jason"—of "inappropriate conduct."*
>
> *The irony of a man interrupting a woman to insist that she discuss allegations of sexual misconduct did not seem to be missed by Coleman. "You're telling me what I can and can't talk about right now?"*
>
> *Jordan proceeded to read what appeared to be a prepared statement. "As journalists, we know that every individual is presumed innocent until proven guilty beyond a reasonable doubt in a court of law. But as a television program,* New Day *is also aware that*

*the offscreen actions of on-air personalities can be distracting from quality content. As such, the segment we announced yesterday featuring Dr. Jason Powell for today has been canceled."*

*The program went to commercial and proceeded as business as usual from there.*

In other words, everyone's presumed innocent unless we think it will hurt our ratings.

Hearing Spencer's heavy steps on the staircase, I clicked off the television and placed my phone on the counter, screen down.

"Chocolate-chip pancakes?" he said drily as I placed three perfect round discs onto a plate. "I thought you said I shouldn't 'eat like a little kid anymore.'"

I hated the voice my son used when he impersonated me—so pinched and harpy. I let it slide for that day, and didn't mention the context for that particular lecture: his picking at his dinner the night before, only to order pizza two hours later.

I shrugged and handed him the plate and a bottle of syrup. Pancakes were not part of the usual rotation of weekday breakfasts.

"If some skank accuses Dad of murder, will I get a car?"

"Don't use words like that," I said, pointing a stern finger, though I was smiling as I said it. Finding humor was my son's way of dealing with the most unhumorous situations, and he knew how that kind of talk got under my skin. "Besides, I'm in denial that you'll ever be old enough to drive."

He didn't complain when I followed him out the front door after breakfast. At his request, I had stopped walking him to school this year, but I still found days when I was "going that direction anyway."

Jason had been adamant about paying for Spencer to go to a "good school." I thought the Springs School had been perfectly good. It was the same grade school I attended. It was the grade school that most kids in East Hampton attended—not the uber-rich sections of East Hampton, but the way-north-of-the-highway area where the normal people lived. People like my family. People like Spencer and me before I met Jason.

Manhattan was different, Jason explained. We couldn't drop Spencer into any random school. Parents who had to rely on public education chose their zip codes based on the quality of grade schools, and kids had to compete from there for spots in the best high schools. Families who could afford to opted for private schools, hiring consultants to assemble application packages and cozying up to potential references. The whole process sounded nauseating, but Jason knew more about education than I ever would, so I toured the "go-to" private schools. Friends Seminary had been the only one where I could picture Spencer being comfortable. Yes, there were children of rock stars and Oscar winners, but there were regular kids too. And it was Quaker. That had to mean the people were good, right?

I expected Jason to balk at the price tag, but the bigger issue was the school's Sixteenth Street address. The trip from his apartment on the Upper West Side to the Village was only three miles, but it was a long haul given Manhattan traffic at peak hours. Jason decided we would move downtown.

"But what about the park?" He had opted for the apartment on Seventy-Fourth Street for its access to Central Park, where he could enjoy open space and maintain his twenty-five-mile-a-week running regimen.

"I'll be the weirdo who does twenty laps around Washington Square. Besides, it's walking distance to the university. I should've moved a long time ago."

We could barely afford the rent on a two-bedroom on Waverly when we first made the move to the Village. Now, thanks to

Jason's extra income, we owned our own home on Twelfth Street—an actual carriage house, complete with a street-level parking garage—less than a ten-minute walk from Friends.

I could feel Spencer's pace slow as we neared the school. As usual, his eyes were glued to his phone.

"Catching Pokémons?"

"So two years ago, Mom. And you know what I'm looking at."

"It's going to be okay, Spencer. You know your dad wouldn't do something like that, right?"

"Well, yeah. But that doesn't matter. Police set people up all the time. People go to prison for, like, their whole lives, and then it comes out they were innocent the whole time. There's a place called the Innocence Project. Haven't you heard of it?"

My son is starting to figure out that I'm not as educated as the other adults in his life. I hate the feeling of disappointing him.

"Yes, I've heard of it, but that's irrelevant. Your father's not going to prison. It's all a misunderstanding. Absolutely nothing happened." Once again, I tried to sound like I knew more than I actually did. "Your dad's going to be fine."

"Yeah, I know," he said. "We're rich." I hate that my son knows so much already about the world. "Besides, this isn't nearly as bad as what some other kids went through. Seth's dad's been in rehab for basically all of middle school. And Karen's older sister made a sex tape with Little Pony."

"My Little Pony?"

"No, Mom. *Little Pony.* Geez, he's a rapper."

"Not my fault his name's stupid." We were at the corner before the school entrance, the farthest he let me walk him these days. He did allow me to give him a big hug. When I opened my eyes, I saw Jane Reese standing next to a black Escalade in the middle of the block, watching us. She quickly turned away. I wondered if she had noticed yet that I had unfriended her.

"Thank you, Spencer. You're a good kid. Remember: When they go low . . ."

"We go high." I gave him a quick fist-tap for good measure. "Are *you* going to be okay? I mean—what if people find out about . . . you know, us? I don't really care, but—"

I felt a catch in my throat. My son, facing school to pretend he wasn't scared that his entire world was falling apart, was worried about me.

"The police will have this cleared up in no time. It's all going to be fine." I looked away so he couldn't see the uncertainty in my eyes. Even he had no idea how much I distrusted the police, or my reasons.

*

I was almost home when my cell phone rang. My screen read "AMC." The American Media Center, the network that runs *New Day.* Maybe Jason was calling from the green room.

"Jason?" It was about time.

"No, it's me." Susanna was whispering. "I'm calling from the set during a commercial break. Are you okay?"

"No, I'm not okay. I didn't know anything about this. I found out online. The show felt the need to read a statement? Based on the word of some—" The word *skank* came to mind, planted in my frontal lobe by Spencer minutes ago. "Student?"

"Don't get me started. That was obviously the studio going to Eric behind my back. They probably knew I would've thrown down to defend him."

Television personalities have come and gone during Susanna's tenure at *New Day*, and few women sustain careers into their forties, but Susanna was practically an institution at AMC. She briefly served as lead anchor for the evening news several years ago, but decided she enjoyed the banter of entertainment programming instead. She was approaching sixty years old and was still beloved. On the other hand, no woman was immune from reality. The network had the decency to present Susanna and Eric as equal cohosts, but Susanna happened to know that Eric was twelve years younger, earned twice as much, and was treated as the heir apparent to the network brand.

I'd spent the whole morning pretending that everything was normal for Spencer's sake, but now that I was alone, listening to my friend's panicked whisper, my whole body began to shake.

"Did you see Jason this morning?" I asked. "He's not returning my calls."

"For a millisecond. I popped into the green room to say hey, but couldn't stick around. He seemed totally normal. Then I heard some crew members yenta-ing it up outside my dressing room. That's how I found out about the *Post* article, but I literally had *no* time before going on air. The next thing I know, Eric's throwing him under the bus on live television. Is it possible Jason didn't see the news before he got to the studio?"

It was more than possible. Jason's morning routine was a paragon of efficiency. No time for newspaper or web browsing.

"I don't know. And I have no idea where he is right now. I'm trying not to completely lose it." I could hear someone speaking urgently in the background.

"Shoot. I gotta go, but I'll call you when I'm off air."

I took a cue from my son and kept myself from crying by searching for something funny to say. "By the way . . . You told that chef you *always* overcook your pasta?"

"Hypothetically, in my imagination. Ciao!"

I happened to know that Susanna never cooked anything. That's how we first became friends. And it's how I met Jason.

# 8

Full-time work on the East End is hard to find. To the extent that farming and fishing have been replaced by the construction of new mega-homes, it's still work I don't know how to do. The retail shops and restaurants are packed in the summer, but only hire part-time and often close altogether in the off-season. I was looking for a job at the age of nineteen with nothing to boast but a recently obtained GED—a "high school equivalence" degree in name, but apparently not in perception. And it didn't help that my reason for not finishing regular school was the three years I had spent away from the East End. When I finally came home, I heard the not-so-quiet whispers about the "hell" I'd put my parents through.

I was finally hired at Blue Heron Farms, a third-generation family business where the men fish and farm, and the women cook and sell the food. What started as a side-of-the-road farm stand had grown into a posh summer market. Before the term "farm to table" became fashionable, Blue Heron had been providing delicious fresh food to Hamptons visitors eager to avoid cooking.

I started at the cash register. After suggesting a few recipes I'd played around with in my parents' kitchen, I was added to the cooking staff. It was my idea to launch a side business of setting up homes for weekenders. Mom would clean the house.

I'd make sure that it was freshly stocked with food and drinks. To find customers, I left flyers on the windshields of the fanciest cars at Main Beach.

Susanna was my first regular. By the middle of the summer, she was so happy with the food that I was preparing that she gave me a shot at catering a small cocktail party. I picked up more clients from there. And somewhere along the way, Susanna and I became something like caretakers for each other. I looked after her home. She looked out for me. She even offered the use of her guest cottage for the off-season.

Mom and Dad made it clear they didn't want me to move. At first I wondered if they had their own motives. It was only natural they wanted to keep Spencer and me safe under their wing. And Dad was having what we thought were back problems, making it hard for him to work. We'd only find out later, after he died of a stroke, that the problem wasn't his back at all. It was clogged arteries in his legs. But at the time, my extra income was helping to cover expenses.

In the end, Mom talked me out of it, saying it would make me too "dependent" on Susanna. "You can't have your son growing up in the backyard of a stranger's house, like Dobby the house elf." She had a point.

I was used to guests hitting on me during catering gigs. I was in my early twenties, wore my dark-blond hair in long, beachy waves, and had the perfect tan for those little black cocktail dresses that the Hampton set prefers for their party staff. When they asked me what I was doing when I got off work, my go-to response was "Going home to my son." Nothing like a kid to get rid of a man looking to hook up.

But Jason was different.

It was Susanna's Memorial Day party, her biggest bash of the year. Two of my staff—a bar-back and a kitchen helper—had no-showed, one of the risks of hiring summer Hamptonites as supplemental workers. Their first priority was to party, and it was the kickoff weekend of the season.

The icing on the cake was the delivery guy from the party rental company, a local who didn't like me for "acting uppity" since I came home. When he saw that I was the one running the fancy party, he decided to dump all the chairs and tables in the driveway, forgoing the usual custom of moving and assembling them for a tip. I did the work myself instead of telling Susanna that not everyone in town liked me as much as she did.

I was scrambling to make sure I didn't let her down, but keeping up proved less impossible than I had feared. I'd turn around, and the platter of shrimp cocktail that was running low would suddenly be replenished. The stack of tasting plates accumulating next to the bar would be cleared. I assumed that one of the two girls I had hired to pass trays for the party had been pitching in, until I walked into the kitchen to find a man reaching into the refrigerator for a plate of deviled eggs topped with caviar.

He looked surprised to see me when he turned around. "Busted." His grin suggested a combination of pride and guilt.

"I was about to get those. Sorry." When you work summers in the Hamptons, you get used to apologizing for things you have no reason to be sorry for.

"For what? So far, you're the best thing about this party." I thought it was the beginning of yet another pass until he pulled the plastic wrap from the plate and popped an egg in his mouth, one full bite. "This food is heaven," he said once his mouth was clear, "and these people are assholes."

"And yet you're here."

"True." The grin again. "So everyone here who's *not* in the kitchen is an asshole. *Except* Susanna. Her . . . I love. I'll be a good boy and won't tell her I hate these people—well, except for the nice woman who's working her butt off to feed all of us."

He pulled the special deviled-egg tray from a stack of platters on the kitchen island. "I assume these go here?"

"Absolutely nothing else could possibly go there."

We began moving the eggs over, two at a time, in silence. When we were finished, he grabbed the tray and left, giving me a little wink as he backed through the swinging kitchen door. "No one has spotted me yet. I feel like a ninja."

When the party died down, he reappeared in the kitchen as I was packing up the leftovers for Susanna's freezer. He even helped me carry my equipment out to the pickup truck I had parked behind Susanna's guesthouse.

"Cool ride," he said. I didn't tell him that I had borrowed it from a man named Matt Miller. Or that Matt and I were kind of a thing.

When the work was done, he closed the truck door for me, and that was almost it. I had backed out of Susanna's driveway and was halfway down the block when I saw him in my rearview mirror, walking toward one of the last cars parked on the street, lighting a cigarette. I reversed back and rolled down the passenger window. "I assumed you were one of Susanna's weekend guests."

"Nope. Just stayed late."

He was in the driver's seat and about to shut the door when I said, "I'm Angela, by the way."

"I'm Jason. Thanks for the nice party."

I broke down and asked Susanna for his last name two days later. She told me he was an economics professor at NYU. "He's single, you know. I called him last year for background on a story we did about global trade, but then I happened to mention my house out here. He was looking for a rental.

Anyway, he's terrific. Want me to matchmake?"

I didn't want to put Susanna in the position of suggesting that her college professor friend date a mom with a GED, so I made her promise not to say anything. "I was curious, is all."

By the time Jason called me a week later, he was all I could think about. To this day, both he and Susanna swear that she never meddled.

# 9

When I got back from walking Spencer to school, I called out Jason's name, but the house was silent. I sat on the living room sofa and flipped open my laptop.

If you search online for "Jason Powell wife," you find out that her name is Angela Powell. You'll find exactly one photograph of us together—at a fund-raiser for a mayoral candidate. Jason posts no pictures of me or Spencer on social media, and my Facebook page is under the name Angela Spencer and used only to be in touch with the other moms at the school. If you search for Angela Mullen, you'll learn she was credited as a sought-after caterer in a few articles about summer life on the East End, but no mentions of her for the last six years.

If you dig hard, you might find some archived news articles—nothing national, only from the *East Hampton Star* and *Newsday* on Long Island, right around the time *google* became a verb—referring to a missing girl by that name. The police said there were no signs of foul play, and unnamed "sources" speculated the girl had left on her own, but her mother, Virginia Mullen, doggedly blanketed Suffolk County with flyers and swore she would never stop searching for her daughter.

But, at least with my online skills, you wouldn't know for certain that the girl and the caterer were one and the same, or that Angela Powell used to be both of those girls, or where

Angela Mullen was while she was missing, let alone why she might actually be of interest.

How long could Jason's "scandal" make the rounds before someone started to wonder why his wife kept such a low profile?

I tried Jason's cell once again. It was still off. *Is he on the subway? Has he been arrested? Is he with someone—another woman, maybe?* My imagination ran through every scenario. I wasn't going to be able to do anything else until I heard from him.

When my phone finally rang, I swiped right to accept the call without reading the screen. "Jason?"

"It's Colin. I've been trying to reach him, too. Do you know about these reports I'm seeing? Does he need a defense lawyer? I've got some names for him."

In addition to being Jason's closest friend, Colin Harris is also an attorney and the kind of person who likes to fix problems. Five years ago, when I had my medical issues, he bombarded me with recommendations for specialists who could help. He was not going to rest until my troubles were solved. That's what Colin is like.

"He's not answering his phone," I said. "I mean it, Colin, if Jason's not in jail, I might be, for killing him."

"Did he know this complaint was coming?"

"I have no idea. I mean, he told me that a female intern complained he said something sexist. He sounded annoyed by the whole situation, but he didn't mention the police. He left this morning for a segment he was supposed to do on *New Day*. They canceled it as if Jason were Ted Bundy or something. He didn't call you?"

"No," Colin confirmed.

I tried to find comfort in that fact. Colin was a well-connected insurance defense lawyer at a big law firm that represented big corporations. If Jason thought he was in legal trouble, surely he would have called Colin.

Now that I was on the phone with another person, I felt tawdry for scanning Rachel Sutton's Facebook page. She probably had no idea that one of her classmates had outed her name in an online comment, and that others were now repeating it on various less-than-reputable websites.

Graduated with honors from Rice University in Houston, head of the Environmental Society. Volunteer for People for the Ethical Treatment of Animals while pursuing her graduate degree in economics at NYU.

There was a photograph posted a week ago of two hands entwined on a tabletop. The female hand bore a solitaire diamond ring. The caption read, "I said yes." Seventy-two comments of congratulations followed for Rachel and the groom-to-be, who was apparently named Michael Logan.

Colin was asking if I had tried calling both of Jason's offices, at the university and at FSS.

"He didn't answer," I said, scrolling down to scan more photographs of Rachel. She had dark brown hair, pale skin, and pretty almond-shaped eyes. She looked like she could be mixed-race. She looked nothing like me.

"Did you call Zack?" Colin asked.

I realized that Colin knew Jason's professional friends better than I did, the consequence of my avoiding his work-related shindigs, where I inevitably felt out of my element. I have no interest in socializing with grown adults who always seem to launch a first conversation with "And where did you go to school, Angela?"

When I told him that I hadn't reached out to Jason's protégé, Colin said he would call Zack and let me know if he heard anything. Before he hung up, he told me to let Jason know that he had the name of a "hard-core crim shark" ready to go. He also promised that everything would be all right.

I found myself staring at a photograph of Rachel with two other gorgeous twentysomethings, one male, one female. According to the "check-in," the photograph was taken at some place called Le Bain, apparently a rooftop bar at the Standard Hotel. Swanky.

I clicked on the name of the male friend tagged in the picture—Wilson Stewart. He had perfect white teeth and floppy, sandy brown hair. He was a frequent poster: politics, food reviews, lots of photographs. At this point, I was hitting my laptop's touchpad at random to keep my mind occupied.

I was reading about the online persona created by this stranger—Rachel's young, good-looking friend, Wilson Stewart—when my cell phone rang again. The screen told me it was Jason.

"Where are you?"

"At school. Shit, you heard already, didn't you?"

"It's all over the news," I said, "online, at least. And Susanna called. So did Colin—he has a lawyer he wants you to contact. What the hell is going on, Jason? Rachel's claiming you assaulted her? You told me it was an offhand comment."

"It's complicated, okay? I didn't think it would come to this—"

When he mentioned it at dinner right after it happened, he'd sounded amused by it. Now it was complicated.

I heard him sigh on the other end of the line. "A cop called—a woman—while I was in Philly. I told her I wasn't talking without a lawyer. I was ready to call Colin if she pressed it, but she didn't. I assumed she was dotting her i's because Rachel blew it out of proportion. Now this."

I told him again I'd been trying to call him all morning. "Where have you been?"

"The dean's office. His secretary was dialing my cell before

I'd left the television studio. I felt like a child being hauled into the damn principal's office. He said the university's initiating its own investigation. If they try to use this to fuck with me, it could derail everything."

I knew he didn't literally mean *everything*. He would still have me and Spencer, and he'd told me how hard it was to revoke a professor's tenure. Jason was referring to everything else that was important to him right now—his newfound role as a public intellectual, his plans for the future.

His voice trailed off. I had seen my husband go from the dean's beloved academic wunderkind to an outsider in a handful of years. After the *Wall Street Journal* reported that Jason got a seven-figure deal for his book, his colleagues accused him of being a sellout. They liked him better when he published heavily footnoted articles that no one read.

"Jason, are you sure there isn't something else I should know?" I shut my eyes, afraid of the answer. Maybe there was a flirtation. A moment between an admiring young student and her attractive professor. I pictured all the girls daydreaming about Professor Harrison Ford in *Raiders of the Lost Ark*, "love you" etched on a set of eyelids.

I fell for Jason at about the same age. Why wouldn't they?

He answered immediately. "I swear on my mother's grave, Angela, nothing happened. It was—damn it, when she walked into my office, I was changing clothes. She must have thought—"

I held my free hand to my face. "Jesus, Jason."

"What? I ran at lunch and had taken a shower. It's not like I was naked. I was tucking in my shirt, I think. I was almost done when she walked in or I would have told her to come back later. This girl's crazy. And damn it, I want a fucking cigarette."

"Don't even." When Jason asked Spencer what he wanted for his thirteenth birthday, Spencer had asked his father to quit smoking. *I want you to live forever, Dad.* Jason resisted at first, joking that he liked the look on strangers' faces when they saw him light up after a long run. But he finally quit on New Year's, successfully substituting gum for the cigarettes he'd taken up while finishing his PhD dissertation.

I didn't realize I was still scrolling through Wilson Stewart's Facebook page until I stopped suddenly on a photograph. He was drinking from a highball glass—something dark, maybe scotch. His eyes were glazed, trying to focus on the screen for the selfie he was taking. A thin arm was draped around his waist from behind. A head of dark shiny hair was visible over his shoulder, pale skin pressed against his neck as two lips found the lobe of his ear. No ring, not yet. It was Rachel Sutton.

I clicked "About" on this friend of Rachel's profile page. He was also a graduate student at NYU. Current work: Fair Share Strategies.

"Jason, do you know someone named Wilson Stewart?"

"He's one of the interns. Why?"

*

I rushed to the door when I heard keys in the lock. Jason wrapped his arms around me so tight that I felt a pinch beneath my ribs. I thought I heard him choke back a sob. When he finally let me go, he pressed his forehead lightly against mine and cupped the back of my head with his palm. "Don't worry, babe. Everything's going to be okay."

I could tell he didn't quite believe it, and was only saying it for my benefit. He knew all I ever wanted was a nice, quiet life together.

# 10

When I opened the front door for Colin forty minutes later, he gave me a quick hug. "How are you holding up?"

I shrugged.

"Where is he?" Colin asked, his eyes moving up the staircase.

"Kitchen. Eating ice cream." That was usually my nervous habit, not his.

"How about Little Man?"

"I sent him to school this morning, thinking it would look bad to keep him home. Now I feel selfish."

"You did the right thing. No use in him sitting around the house worrying about his parents."

In the kitchen, we found Jason at the breakfast table. He greeted Colin with a "Hey, man" and an extended carton of peanut-butter-cup ice cream.

Colin declined the offer. "A defense attorney named Olivia Randall is on her way over."

I had already googled her. Based on the number of newspaper articles about her celebrity clients and high-profile trials, she seemed like a heavy hitter.

"Does it make Jason look guilty to hire a lawyer so fast? Especially a big-name criminal defense lawyer?"

Jason apparently had the same concern. "It looks like I'm admitting I did something wrong."

"Some girl's trying to destroy you, Jason, and you're sitting here with Häagen-Dazs like you're in a *Cathy* cartoon."

"Ack ack," Jason said as he got up to put his ice cream away.

"You're in denial, friend. This girl started a war with you. She needs to be swatted down like a bug. Olivia Randall will do it."

I had seen photographs of Olivia online. Dark hair, intense. Pretty. Not entirely unlike Rachel Sutton. I pushed the thought away. What mattered was that she was a good lawyer, and that's what Jason needed right now.

She arrived fifteen minutes later, dressed in a fitted black skirt and a bright green silk blouse. After quick introductions and professional handshakes, she skipped the chitchat and went directly to business.

"I'm sorry about this, Angela, but you can't stay—"

Jason immediately interrupted. "I've already told Angela everything."

"It's not a matter of trust. To protect attorney-client privilege, Colin and I need to speak to Jason alone. And, no, it doesn't matter that you're his wife. In fact, having Colin or me around while the two of you speak destroys the privilege each of you shares with the other."

I already felt like the stupidest person in the room. I opened my mouth but nothing came out.

Colin placed a protective hand on my shoulder. "Angela's the one who found something online about this Rachel girl that might be helpful. Why don't we go over that first, and then the three of us can speak privately."

I opened my laptop from the coffee table as we all got seated. Wilson Stewart's Facebook page was already pulled up. "This is one of Jason's other interns at his consulting practice. I found him by clicking on a recent photograph he was tagged in on Rachel's page."

Olivia was leaning in for a closer look.

"The photo on Rachel's page was nothing special—the two of them and a female friend. Strictly professional appearing. But on *his* page, I found this." I scrolled down to the photograph of him holding up a cocktail and getting kissed on the neck by someone who looked an awful lot like Rachel Sutton. "He didn't tag her, so she may not even know that he posted it. But this was only two weeks ago, and supposedly she has a fiancé now. That's how this whole thing came up—Jason said something that offended her when she told him she was engaged."

I saw something flicker behind Olivia's eyes. An idea. Something good, as if she were connecting my information to a fact only she knew. I had been worried that a female attorney might be offended at the thought of trashing the so-called victim, but she seemed pleased by my discovery.

"Okay, that actually helps a lot. Now, I'm sorry, but I'll need you to leave us for a bit. I promise, Angela, I'm going to do everything I can for your husband."

I felt like a child being sent away while the grown-ups talked. As I passed Jason, he mouthed a silent thank-you and grabbed my hand for a quick kiss. His lips felt warm against my fingertips.

*

Twenty minutes later, I heard footsteps on the stairs. I opened the bedroom door to see Colin reach the landing.

"Hey, I thought it would be Jason."

"They're still talking. I figured I'd come check on you. Crim law's foreign to me anyway—"

"Am I being stupid?"

He looked at me, clearly confused by my question.

"Believing Jason. Am I being stupid? I mean, he says he

made some sarcastic comment about her getting married too young, and she turns that into a sexual assault allegation? What am I missing?"

I felt myself begin to shake. He stepped toward me but stopped short of touching me. "You're not stupid. Jason did not do this, okay? I think there's an explanation."

He glanced back downstairs. He didn't want to tell me too much.

"Look," he said, lowering his voice. Colin's close-cropped dark hair was beginning to gray, but he still had the same clean-cut, heart-shaped face that had led me to nickname him Boy Scout when we first met. "Olivia made some calls before she came over. She basically found out that there's no evidence except this girl's say-so, and what she told the police sounds worse than what she supposedly said to Zack right after the incident."

"Well, that's good, right?"

"It's *very* good, but apparently the girl said something about being able to describe Jason's underwear. Candy canes or something."

I held up a hand to my mouth. "He said he was tucking in his shirt."

"Wait," he said, trying to calm me. "That picture you found of her sucking on that kid's neck might be a better explanation. Jason said there are urinals in the men's rooms at the econ department."

I was able to connect the other dots myself. The interns get drunk. Rachel and Wilson hook up. Wilson says something about spotting their hero's unexpected boxer shorts in the men's room. Rachel uses that fact to strengthen a flimsy accusation she made for God knows what reason.

"So is that what happened? Did Olivia call Wilson already?"

"We don't need him to say anything. Jason doesn't have to prove his innocence. They have to prove his guilt. This gives us an alternative explanation for what she claims to have seen in his office. It gives us a legitimate reason to make an issue of that picture you found."

A *legitimate* reason. But we all knew the *real* reason that photograph had been a good find. It made Rachel look like "that kind of girl."

I heard the staccato clicks of high heels on the hardwood of the first floor, and then spotted Olivia Randall looking up at us.

"We're almost done, Angela. Sorry, again. Colin, you want to come down for a quick talk before I go?"

I returned to our bedroom and opened the top left drawer of our dresser. A pair of crisp cotton boxer shorts adorned with bright red candy canes were folded neatly at the back, behind a uniform row of Jason's go-to black boxer briefs. The candy canes were a gag gift, something to fill space in his Christmas stocking. I remembered the first time I saw him in them as he was climbing into bed. He said I was shaking both the mattress and his manliness with my laughter.

I lifted them from the back of the drawer and placed them in the bottom of my gym bag. I would find a garbage can on the street tomorrow.

# 11

Corrine Duncan was making her fifth call to ADA Brian King since she'd seen the first story about Jason Powell that morning. Once again, no answer.

King had declined the case almost immediately after Corrine submitted her reports. Corrine had hoped that he would deliver the news to Rachel himself, but apparently he hadn't. When Rachel called her yesterday, looking for an update, Corrine had delivered the message: it was one person's word against another in a system where the government had to prove guilt beyond a reasonable doubt. It was a speech she had recited hundreds of times.

Rachel's response still burned in her mind. "So is there no way to prove such a thing?" she asked, her voice jumping an octave. "Instead of pulling back, I should have waited until he raped me so I'd have scientific evidence?"

Corrine had to admit, the woman had a point. In a world where DNA evidence could make or break a case, sex offenders could grab and grope and grind and gratify, as long as they didn't leave behind physical evidence.

In theory, handfuls of people could have leaked the complaint against Jason Powell. Records clerks. Her lieutenant. Friends of Rachel. Rachel, of course. But Rachel had already called Corrine twice this morning, wondering how the *Post* found out about her complaint.

Corrine had another theory.

It was the way she and Brian King had left their last conversation. After King concluded they didn't have anything close to enough evidence to take to trial, Corrine had suggestions for investigating further. King had rejected every one of them. "You'd be wasting your time," he insisted. "We know how this plays out. It's her word against his, with no way of meeting our burden. Not with her word alone."

*Not with her word alone.*

That was the phrase she remembered when she saw Jason Powell's name pop up on her phone's *New York Post* alert this morning.

She tried King's number again, and this time he picked up.

"King," like he didn't know who was calling.

"You could have given me a heads-up," she said.

There was silence on the other end of the line. She was used to this—ADAs who liked to play boss over the police. There was something about Corrine—black, female, grown-up, straightforward—that threw them off their game.

"You're not mad at me, are you?"

"Two days ago, you sounded perfectly willing to let the case go."

"I called a law school friend of mine who works in the career services office of NYU law school. She asked around. No official complaints, but there are rumors."

"Of?"

"Something off. Maybe he's just the hot professor who students dream about, but some people get a bad vibe off him. A little too cute, a little too flirty. A guy on the prowl."

Corrine thought about King's initial comment about his ex-girlfriend's celebrity crush on Powell.

"You heard from anyone yet?" she asked.

"It's only been a few hours," he said.

She'd seen this before when weak charges were filed against someone with the profile of a potential serial offender. King had let the police report leak in case any other women might want to come forward about incidents they had written off as "misunderstandings."

"Any calls on your end?" King asked.

Thanks to an offshoot series of *Law & Order*, an increasing number of sex offense victims contacted the special victims unit directly.

"Nothing yet," she confirmed. "I guess I better call Rachel back—and, no, I won't tell her it was you. I'll make sure she knows to stay in touch. It's possible that Powell will try to silence her."

King didn't respond, and for a second, Corrine wondered if she'd lost the connection. "You there?"

"Yeah, sorry. I got an e-mail from Olivia Randall." Corrine recognized the name of one of the biggest pain-in-the-ass defense lawyers in the city. "She says she represents Jason Powell and has information I might be interested in. That sounds fun."

"You're the one who wanted to stir up some trouble. Looks like you may have found the wrong kind."

"Whatever. Let me know if you hear from other women."

# 12

I was doing my monthly shuffle of the dry cleaning—from wire hangers to real ones—when Jason found me in the bedroom.

"The lawyer's gone?" I asked.

He nodded. "I didn't want to explain who she was to Spencer." He'd be home any minute.

I had hung Jason's final shirt when I said, "Did you know that when you google Jason Powell, the fifth suggested search is 'Jason Powell wife'?"

"That's normal. People get curious about author bios. They want to know if I'm married or not."

I shook my head and closed the closet door harder than I needed to.

"I'm so sorry, Angela. I promise, I'm not going to let you get dragged into this."

If only he had listened to me four years ago when he decided that he couldn't simply be a professor with a bestselling book. He had to extend the ride, and I had no choice but to go along.

"What if they find out? People will print anything these days. Maybe not the *New York Times* or the real papers, but one blogger. That's all it takes. I mean, the *Post* didn't print Rachel's name, but it's all over the Internet anyway. It only took me a couple of minutes to find out she was cheating on her boyfriend with that other intern. Pretty soon the trolls will start looking for secrets about you and me."

"Would that really be so bad?" Jason asked. "I know your parents had their reasons for protecting you, Angela, but it didn't have to be that way. You've never had anything to be ashamed about."

I gathered up the wire hangers and left the room without saying a word. I'd given him my answer the last time we talked about this, and I wasn't going to change my mind now.

*

It was four years since the last time Jason had encouraged me to "come out of the closet." *It might help you to talk about it. Maybe go to a therapist. Or go big and write that book Susanna offered to help you with. Or give her an interview. You could help other people, Angela, including yourself.*

I was surprised he brought it up. At the time, I even wondered if he was thinking more of himself than me. Being known as the man who married that "poor girl" could only help book sales and his growing public image.

I had made my answer—a resounding no—crystal clear. I didn't need help, and I certainly didn't need to help anyone else.

I also can't change the world.

Every time I read an article about a child missing or a woman abducted, I am reminded of all the reasons that my parents decided that it was better to protect my privacy when I came home than to tell the town that I hadn't run away. Admit it. When you hear about a missing kid, or a murdered woman, you scour the article for clues. Not clues about the perpetrator. No, we search for clues about what makes that woman or child different from the women and children we know and love. Mom was having an affair. Kid was using meth. We need an explanation, something to reassure us that the horrible things that happened to them could never happen to us.

In my own case, you wouldn't have had a hard time finding facts to comfort you.

I started cutting class here and there in the ninth grade. My teachers and parents blamed my best friend, Trisha Faulkner, because it was easier that way. Various Faulkners were in and out of prison. They sold drugs, drove drunk, and picked fights in public over the slightest offense. Just like you feel better when you find out that the missing kid kept bad company, it was convenient to think that the Mullens' beloved daughter had "changed" because of the influence of a troubled girl from the most troublesome family on the East End.

I wasn't an exceptionally bad girl. I got As and Bs in school, despite my occasional detentions. I was sent home twice for back-talking teachers, but had justifications that I stand by to this day for both outbursts. When I first got my learner's permit, I got stopped in my dad's car with beer in the trunk. The cop was nice and let me pour it all out, can by can, at the side of Old Stone Highway rather than call my parents.

Any signs of my rebellion were basically under the radar until one summer night when Trisha and I were in the car with some guy from the city who crashed his BMW. Dad made it seem like I was some kind of hostage, under the control of a cokehead who was "only after one thing." The reality is that Trisha and I thought the guy was a joke. He bought us wine and let us blast music he had never heard of and told us stories about closing deals and making money. He was more like a drunk uncle for the night than any kind of predator.

After my parents were called down to the police station, my father was determined to keep me from getting into any more trouble, and that's when things got really bad. Because here's the thing: the fact that adults made the BMW guy seem like the bogeyman made me believe there was no such thing as the bogeyman. It was the boy who cried wolf, flipped on its head. Instead of a child sounding too many false alarms, it was my parents. Because that one guy had been harmless, I assumed the same of others who were happy to goof off on summer weekends with some local girls. And because my father prohibited me from hanging around with Trisha, she took on a new importance in my life. We became inseparable. If she cut class, I did too. If she rode the train into the city, I followed. But where Trisha was willing to run off for days at a time, that was a line I never crossed. Missing curfew by hours was one thing; sleeping at a stranger's house because anyone was better than your own family was another.

Ironically, the reason I was alone the night I was kidnapped was because I declined Trisha's invitation to crash for a few days with a friend she'd made a few weeks earlier in Brooklyn. On a summer weekend, it wasn't hard to find something to do without her. I showed up at the beach with a joint and found a bonfire party to join. Usually I'd end up running into someone I knew, but not that night. They were all city people. I left once the sun was down and it was starting to get cold.

As I was walking to the bus stop, a white Lexus SUV stopped and rolled down the passenger window. "Need a ride?"

"I'm good," I said. The 10B ran a loop all the way through Springs. It was practically door-to-door service.

"You sure? Walking on the road in the dark's not exactly safe."

He had a point. Only a few weeks ago, a minivan had swerved to pass a turning car and run right into Corey Littleton on his bike. He was going to spend the entire summer with a cast on his leg.

He offered another gentle nudge. "Plus . . . no bonfire." He made a brrrr motion.

It was the first of many clever things he did to work his way into my brain. To this day, I don't really know whether I actually recalled seeing him around the fire. But that comment sealed my impression that he had been there, too.

I got into the car, and just like that, I was gone.

I don't know why no one from that bonfire remembered seeing me. Maybe they had all left town by the time my mom started blanketing the South Fork with my photographs. Or maybe I just wasn't that memorable.

But because my parents didn't know I'd been at the beach that night, they didn't know what time I went missing. All they could tell the police was that I was gone when they came home from work. It didn't help that when the police called Trisha's to see what she knew, her mom said she hadn't been home for three days. Once Trisha did return, she said she "didn't think" I'd run away without telling her, because that was the kind of thing Trisha would say.

I didn't come home for another three years, and when I did, I had not only my reappearance but one-year-old Spencer to explain. My mother went from the woman searching for her missing daughter to the lady who told everyone it was "none of their beeswax" who Spencer's father was. The Mullens had made their decision—better I be seen as yet another single teenage mom than as a freak show for life. As I had explained to Jason too many times, they were protecting my privacy. But they were also protecting me.

I smoked pot. I was partying. I was bad. I got in the stranger's car. And then I stayed in that house with him for three years.

If some intrepid blogger decided to out me, I knew how that story would read; I know it's only human nature to blame the victim. After all, wasn't I the woman who was helping my husband's lawyer paint Rachel Sutton as the "kind of girl" who would lie about her professor, even as a pair of Jason's boxer shorts was hiding in the bottom of my gym bag? I, of all people, knew I did not want to be the Rachel in the story.

# 13

When Jason's alarm pierced the silence at 5:30 the next morning, I wasn't sure whether I had ever managed to fall asleep. Every time I turned to face Jason, he was dozing peacefully, but I had no way of knowing whether it was from a lack of worry or the sleeping pill he took before turning off the light.

He hit the snooze button, rolled onto his side, and pulled me into a tight spoon position. "You're awake," he whispered. "Did you sleep at all?"

"I think so. You're getting up already?" I assumed he would want to stay home under the circumstances.

"I'm not letting some twit turn me into a recluse. Colin seems to think that lawyer will be able to shut this whole thing down fairly quickly. In the meantime, we have to go on with our lives."

Knowing his mind was made up, I told him that he was right. But unlike most days, he stayed in bed with me for two full snooze cycles. When the alarm sounded a third time, he kissed the back of my neck, told me he loved me, and made his way into the shower.

I was on my iPad, googling his name, when his phone let out a single staccato buzz on the nightstand. I never look, but that morning I did. It was his calendar reminding him of an appointment at noon. The event was entered simply as "Kerry."

*

He was buttoning his shirt cuffs when I pretended to wake up again. "You're still home," I said with a sleepy smile.

"Sorry for the noise."

"No, I like knowing you're here. So what do you have scheduled for today?"

"Not much. I'm going to make a point of going to campus. If those petty fuckers think I'm in hiding, they'll start circling like wolves. They need to know that I have every intention of fighting back if they try to get rid of me."

I suggested he find a way to remind the dean that at least three of Jason's senior colleagues were married to former students. "Anything scheduled, or do you think you might be able to come home early?"

The pause that followed felt long, but could have been completely imagined, like what I perceived as a quick glance at the cell phone that had buzzed minutes earlier. He popped a piece of Nicorette from his nightstand into his mouth.

"Just a lunch meeting with someone from Oasis."

The name sounded familiar, but he could tell from my blank expression that I was having trouble filling in the details.

"The world needs water?" he said as a prompt.

Their slogan.

Jason's early academic scholarship applied principles of moral philosophy to corporate governance practices. I made a habit of reading his articles, but had a hard time understanding them. The book that made him famous was a pop version of his ivory-tower work, weaving together liberal politics, corporate scandals, and stories across history and cultures to demonstrate a correlation between economic health and equal treatment of citizens. His consulting group, FSS, was an outgrowth of his academic work. In theory, he was an adviser to corporations, teaching them how to maximize profits by following guiding principles of morality and equality. But he also paired corporate clients with financial clients, essentially endorsing private, for-profit entities to investors who supported his theories.

As I understood it, Oasis specialized in bringing clean water to different parts of the world. A few months earlier, Jason had been working nearly full-time, counseling and finding financing for Oasis until something happened to give him pause.

"Is the meeting about that problem you mentioned?" I asked.

"Did I mention that?"

"Well, not in detail."

He looked up from the belt he was buckling. "You're actually interested?"

"Of course."

He sat on the edge of the bed. "They may not be as kosher as everyone thinks."

"Well, that's not good. Water sort of needs to be clean?"

"Yeah, but it's not the water itself that's the problem. Oasis is a major up-and-comer on the CSR lists because of the substance of what they do: treating and transporting water. They're on the cutting edge of developing systems for global water security—basically, making sure the entire world has access. It's truly transformative stuff. But as usual, too many of the CSR gatekeepers are idiots."

I was following so far. The CSR lists ranked companies based on their "corporate social responsibility." Jason's book and podcast had brought those lists into the mainstream, exposing the general public to their existence, but also demonstrating how companies can manipulate the CSR rankings for marketing purposes. A retailer, for example, might tout its "green" operations—reusable bags, organic foods, energy-saving operations—while capping employee hours to avoid paying for health benefits. Jason had made a name for himself by publicly shaming several Fortune 500 companies and the so-called analysts who supported them without due diligence. Jason's stamp of approval was now the gold star of the CSR world. His consulting company helped companies develop CSR policies and paired worthwhile firms with major financial backers.

"So what did the others miss?" I asked.

"The technology itself is worth nothing if it's not implemented where it's needed most," he said. "Getting clean water to Arizona is great, but getting it into farms and villages in remote parts of the world is the game changer. Needless to say, the potential for corruption in that process is huge."

"And you found corruption?"

He raised his eyebrows. "I'm not sure. But yeah, I think so. The books don't look right. Inconsistent payments to local vendors that don't line up to actual work or equipment. It reeks of massive kickbacks—basically bribing the power brokers to get into the territory."

"Is that really all that bad, if it means the locals get water?"

"Except my entire life's work is about not making those kinds of compromises. We don't pollute the planet to create jobs, or use slave labor to bring the Internet to developing nations. Sorry, I'm ranting. In this particular case, it's not only the usual tradeoffs. Given the region I'm talking about, that money might have gone to terrorists and warlords."

Jason was more animated than I'd seen him in days.

"So what are you going to do about it?"

"I don't know. I can't prove my suspicions, but I also can't turn a blind eye. Basically, I've got a conflict of interest. Oasis is my client, but so are the investors I paired them with. Plus, there's my own reputation."

"Your 'brand,'" I added with air quotes, because I knew how much the word irked him.

"Precisely. And most importantly, at the end of the day, I need to be able to look at myself in the mirror and believe I've done the right thing. So, yeah, if anything's been weighing on me, it's been this clusterfuck, not the nonsense with what's-her-name."

Rachel Sutton, I said to myself. She had a name.

"I'm hoping the lunch meeting I'm having today might help. I've been trying for a month and a half to get one of my contacts at Oasis to come clean and do the right thing."

I told him that I was sorry he had so much on his plate at one time.

"Don't be sorry. I'm the one who decided to take all this on. You of all people warned me." He kissed me on the head. "You smell so *good*." He kissed me one more time on the cheek and stood up. "I'll try to be back home by the time Spencer gets out of school. Maybe we can pick him up together, stop at Agata on the way home for lamb chops?"

"Sounds great." I pictured the two of us standing outside Spencer's school, holding hands in front of all the gossipy moms. He had a point about going face-to-face with the circling wolves. He had his pack, I had mine.

When I heard the front door close, I tapped the top of my iPad screen and typed in "Oasis Water Kerry."

Within a few clicks, I confirmed that the vice president of marketing for Oasis Inc. was a woman named Kerry Lynch. That was my husband's lunch meeting, exactly as he had told me.

I felt silly for checking.

# 14

Spencer was already scrambling eggs in the kitchen when I walked downstairs. He had two small plates on the counter, plus a jar of salsa.

I remember the first time I realized that my son was a stronger person than I'd ever been. He was in half-day kindergarten. I'd mistimed the baking of a batch of mini quiches for a client's cocktail party and couldn't leave. Mom was cleaning a house. As I had way too many times, I asked Dad if he could pick Spencer up from school. His legs were killing him by then, and he moved so slow. He showed up probably seven minutes after I would have.

When the two of them returned, Spencer tossed his backpack on the kitchen table, declared that he was ready for "taste-testing duty," and then rated my latest creations "five-star nosh." He disappeared to our room—the one we still shared at my parents' house, the one I'd grown up in—as if everything were normal.

Dad broke the news. When he pulled up in front of the school, he saw Spencer on the ground, two boys standing over him. He managed to get out of his car in time to hear the gist of the boys' comments. Why did he have the same last name as the one his mom grew up with? Why didn't he have a dad? *Everyone knows your mom ran away and came back with a bastard baby.*

The boys took off when they saw my father headed their way.

"I thought you should know," Dad told me. "I still think we made the right decision, but it's always up to you. Oh, and for what it's worth, I recognized the biggest kid as Tony Faulkner's boy. I'm half tempted to drive to that hellhole of a house and have a word with him."

"That's a bad idea, Dad."

Dad shook his head, but said nothing else. The hellhole in question was a multi-acre lot off Three Mile Harbor where multiple generations of Faulkners resided. The Faulkner family was despised throughout the East End, but the topic of their family was especially touchy in our house. Mom and Dad still believe that my entire life might have been different if it hadn't been for my association with "that girl," as they referred to Trisha.

Tony Faulkner was Trisha's youngest uncle, which would make the kid bullying Spencer her cousin. Based on what I knew about the things Faulkner men did to children, it did not surprise me at all that his son would already be screwed up.

When I asked Spencer about it that night, he shrugged and insisted it was no big deal.

"If you want to tell other kids where you were born, and why your last name is Mullen, you can."

Against my mother's wishes, I told Spencer the truth about the circumstances of his birth the first time he asked me, on his fifth birthday. I also told him that my parents had made the decision for me at the time not to share the details with anyone. All they said to those brave enough to ask was that I was back home, and they were overjoyed to have their baby grandson, Spencer, at the house, too. Filling in the blanks, most people assumed I had run away, gotten pregnant, and then come home again. It was a way to protect my privacy—to let me start over without people asking me about "what happened" for the rest of my life—but none of us had stopped to think how it would eventually affect Spencer. At the time, I was the child who needed protecting. Spencer was just an extension of me.

"They only went after me because of Luis," Spencer said.

"Who's Luis?"

"He's a Mexican kid in our class. They were telling him that his parents work for free and that they're taking jobs from all the people who were born here and that they don't speak English right and stuff. So when I was captain of the kickball team, I picked Luis first and refused to pick any of them. It matters a lot when you get picked."

My six-year-old son, after everything he had been through, had stuck up for another kid.

"Besides," he added, "it's not their beeswax." He sounded exactly like my mother.

"True, but it's yours. I didn't want you to think that you have to keep a secret or tell a lie. All I ask is that if you tell anyone, make sure that I know too, okay?"

I'd been home for five years by then, and in that time I had told only one person where I'd been those years, and that was Susanna. If Spencer's decisions were going to change that, I needed to be prepared.

"It's not a secret or a lie," Spencer said. "It's not anything, because I don't remember not living here. And I don't care where the other half of me came from. I'm a Mullen. I'm from you. And Grandma and Granddaddy." He added with a smile, "And I was about to kick those kids' asses before Granddaddy saved them."

Seven years later, as he carried a plate of eggs and the jar of salsa to the table, Spencer looked over my shoulder and caught me reading a website called Rate My Professors on my iPad, where there's a chili pepper next to my husband's name, indicating "hotness."

Spencer had to know why I was looking. It was now day two, and the *Post* had a follow-up story. With nothing new to report, they ran a "Who is Jason Powell?" piece, complete with quotes from online student reviews. *"Distractingly smoking." "Seems like he might be gettable." "Sexy AF. I'd let him teach me anything he wants!"*

We've all read this book and seen this movie before: a potentially great man struck down by the lingering shadows of a scandal. Would-be presidents tarnished by extramarital affairs. Celebrities unable to find work after tape recordings emerge of their most hateful comments. Businesses boycotted for being on the wrong side of the cultural tide.

I imagined Jason floating beside the other castaways. I pictured unsold copies of his book being returned to the warehouse, the loss of clients at his consulting company, and the university trying to strip him of tenure. What would happen to Spencer and me? What would everyone say about us?

But if Spencer was worried, he wasn't letting on. "Dad's innocent," he said. "Everyone else will realize that soon enough. And then everything will go back to normal." There was not a shade of doubt in his voice.

I squeezed his hand and said "I know," then waited until he left for school to continue reading.

*

I was alone when I heard a knock at the door an hour later.

I looked through the peephole to see my mother glaring at our hideous brass knocker, the one I called the Vomiting Gargoyle, the one I'd meant to replace since we first closed on the house three years earlier. It took me a second to process that she was actually there, standing on my stoop. Ginny Mullen does not show up on doorsteps in Greenwich Village.

I could count on one hand the number of times she had visited me in the city. Though they weren't officially related to any of the original Bonacker families of the seventeenth century, she and my father were born and bred Islanders, with at least four generations settled in the Springs on both sides. But where their great-grandfathers were able to work with pride as fishermen and farmers, my parents worked service jobs (handyman for Dad, housework for Mom) for wealthy summer vacationers in the hopes of squirreling away enough money to make it through the rest of the year. My mother associated the city with the people who treated her as something less than human. She famously declined the opportunity to accompany my sixth-grade class to a Christmas show at Radio City Music Hall, explaining that all of New York City smelled of sweat, urine, garbage, and dirty money. When I told her I was marrying Jason, she told me, in this order, that she was happy for me, that Jason was a good man, and that "you better not let my grandson turn into a little asshole."

As I untumbled all the locks, I had no doubt that her sudden appearance in the city was directly connected to the unreturned messages she had left on my phone since Jason became viral fodder the previous morning.

"Hey Mom," I said as I swung the door open. "What are you doing here? Did you take the train?"

She was in the foyer before I finished my questions. "No, I had Jeeves the butler hire a goddamned limousine."

"Why did you come all the way into the city?"

"Oh, please, Angela, you're not the center of the universe. I have an appointment. A specialist. Figured I should at least stop by and see my daughter while they're ripping off my Obamacare."

For a second, I wasn't sure what to believe. Was she lying

about the doctor's appointment to check on me, or had she been calling about a health problem, only to have her only child ignore her calls?

"What kind of specialist? What's wrong?"

"I'm old," she said, the words themselves serving as a shrug. I took her response as confirmation that nothing serious was wrong with her health. She was only sixty-five and had never referred to herself as "old" until my father died five years ago. The medical appointment was either fabricated or minor.

"I take it you heard about the incident with Jason and his student?" I led the way into the kitchen and popped a Nespresso pod into the machine, waiting for her to mock the absence of a real pot of coffee.

"So did he do it?"

"Of course not, Mom. He made an innocent comment about her being too young to get married. She took it to be a pass, and then everything got exaggerated."

Mom took the tiny cup of caffeine from me, complete with an eye roll, then made her way to the refrigerator for a dash of the whole milk I keep around for Spencer.

"Even innocent comments can be loaded," she said. "In my day, it was called innuendo."

I did not want to think about my mother engaging in what she considered to be "innuendo," but without prompting, she did me the honor of an impromptu performance. "You're *much* too young to become a *bride*," she said in a masculine voice. "You might be right, Dr. Powell," she said in a ridiculous femme fatale delivery. "Why don't you show me what I'll be missing?"

"And . . . scene. 'Thank you very much, ladies and gentlemen. Tip your servers. We'll be here all night!'"

"Angela, you're smarter than this. I have no doubt it was a misunderstanding, but misunderstandings don't happen when a situation is black and white. They only happen when there are shades of gray, when there could be two different versions of the same damn thing. What did Jason do with that girl?"

"Nothing, Mom. Nothing happened."

She took a sip of the coffee that, from the look on her face, still wasn't to her liking. "Are the two of you—okay?"

"Mom, please."

"A man his age has certain needs. I know you don't like to talk about it—"

"Jesus, Mom. I am not having this conversation with you. Jason and I are fine. I can't believe you are blaming this on me. Do *not* make this about me."

By the time she reached for me, my hand was trembling as I slammed a fresh purple pod into the Nespresso machine. "You can always come home if it's too much. He's already been pushing you to the brink."

Other women would be proud of Jason's accomplishments. But my mother knew that, as much as I didn't want to be yet another cog in the East End service culture, I never wanted a spotlight either.

"I don't need to come home, Mom. Colin hired a lawyer for Jason and says everything's going to be fine."

"Maybe so, but that's why I'm here, okay? You need to take care of yourself and Spencer. The two of you come first. If Jason made this mess, he can deal with it on his own. I've seen how these people blame everything on anyone else—"

We spent the next twenty minutes arguing about whether Jason could be clumped in with "these people," during which she invoked several examples of what she perceived to be Jason's sense of entitlement. When I couldn't take it any longer, I asked her whether she had a doctor's appointment or not.

"Yes, I have an appointment, like I said."

"Is it something serious? Can I come with you?"

She carried her ridiculously tiny Nespresso cup to the sink, rinsed it out, and rested it on a dish towel on the counter. When she turned around, her broad, flat face was filled with a smile. "My appointment is for a manicure, and you're coming with me. And Jason's going to pay."

"Well, that sounds absolutely lovely."

"I'm serious, Angela—if he fucked up, he really does need to pay."

I told her once again that everything was going to be fine. She didn't look convinced, but stopped pressing the point for the time being. "Look on the bright side: the last thing you wanted was him running for office. Doesn't seem like you'll be needing to worry about that anymore."

I shook my head and smiled, but part of me realized she had a point. Assuming this crisis passed, Jason would have a good reason to stay out of the public eye for a long, long time.

# 15

The woman was probably in her midthirties, with straight, shoulder-length dark hair and full lips. Dressed elegantly in a simple long-sleeved navy dress and heels, she glanced around nervously, as if she knew how out of place she looked.

Corrine rose to shake her hand and gestured toward the chair next to her desk.

"You're the detective in charge?" A civilian clerk had helped the woman find her way to Corrine when she showed up at SVU, asking about Jason Powell. "Are you still investigating that case with the intern?"

"I can't comment on that, I'm sorry. Do you know something?"

The woman shook her head.

"So how can I help you?" Corrine asked.

The woman looked down at her hands folded on her crossed legs, obviously contemplating something. When she finally spoke, she looked up to make eye contact. "Six weeks ago, he raped me and I did nothing. Today he came to my house and offered to pay me a hundred thousand dollars if I promised not to say anything. I assume he's afraid I'll come forward, now that someone else has."

"Okay, let's go talk in private. I'm Detective Duncan, but you can call me Corrine."

"I'm Kerry. Kerry Lynch."

# II

# KERRY

# 16

Jason's attorney worked fast.

Within thirty hours of her leaving our house, a left-wing gossip site ran the photo I found of Rachel Sutton kissing her fellow graduate student and intern, Wilson Stewart. Beneath it was the picture she had posted days later, showing off her engagement ring. The website had blurred her face, but the comments that followed repeatedly mentioned her full name, now easily searchable online.

By that evening, an entirely different narrative emerged. One website ran a quote from Rachel's fiancé, saying that he was "hurt and confused" when he saw the picture of Rachel and Wilson together. More helpfully to Jason, the fiancé told a reporter that Rachel had never mentioned her complaint against Jason, and that she only called him about it after the news went viral. When asked whether the couple was still engaged, the fiancé said, "I doubt it."

The fiancé wasn't the only man distancing himself from Rachel. The following morning, Wilson appeared on *New Day* with none other than Susanna Coleman to confirm he had a "brief and casual relationship" with a fellow intern—still officially unnamed—that developed after a night of drinking on the rooftop bar at the Standard Hotel. "She told me the first night we hooked up that she thought Jason—Dr. Powell, I mean—was 'sort of hot.' I got the impression that she was into him. A lot of the students are. But he lets it be known that he's happily married."

Making every attempt to appear objective, Susanna asked Wilson, "But to be clear, you can't say for certain what happened that day in Dr. Powell's office, correct?"

"I didn't see it with my own eyes, but I've never known Jason Powell to be anything but a professional, inspiring mentor. As for the complainant, she's sweet, but she can be dramatic, and sort of hypersensitive. She has a tendency to blow things out of proportion, so . . ."

The trail of his thought was the perfect moment for Susanna to thank Wilson for his time and cut to a commercial.

The message was clear: Don't believe a word she says.

*

An hour after Susanna's interview with Wilson, my cell phone rang. It was from the 631 area code, Suffolk County. I hated that area code.

"Hello?"

"Is this Angela?"

"Who's calling?"

"This is Steve Hendricks."

His first name sounded weird. Years ago, when he was part of my regular vocabulary, we called him "Hendricks" or "the Detective." I didn't say anything.

"I . . . I saw the news about your husband. I don't know how I can help. But if I can—"

I hung up, then hit "Block this Caller" for good measure.

*

When Jason and I were in bed that night, I asked him if Olivia had questioned his intern, Wilson, about whether he had ever mentioned those boxer shorts to Rachel.

"She decided it was better not to reveal that detail, since it's not public yet."

"But shouldn't we find that out?" As things stood, that photograph of her kissing Wilson had been used to make her look promiscuous and not for any other reason.

"I think Olivia preferred Wilson's statement as it was, especially that part about my being hot."

"*Sort of* hot," I corrected. "I don't understand why she wouldn't have at least asked him about it in private."

"Because that would be giving him information he doesn't currently have."

"Would that be so bad? I mean, Rachel could have seen something. You said you were tucking your shirt in when she walked in."

"But the police don't know that. She made it sound like I was flashing her or something."

"But maybe she did see more than you thought?"

He rested the book he was reading on his chest and looked at me directly. "I'm just glad this looks like it's over. Aren't you?"

"Of course I am."

"Okay, then." He kissed me and kept reading. As I closed my eyes, I wondered where Rachel Sutton was and how she was feeling.

# 17

Corrine was waiting at the counter for her lunch when ADA Brian King's number appeared on her cell. "Duncan," she said.

"So did you watch it?"

He had called her yesterday to see if she'd seen a kid named Wilson Stewart on *New Day*. Apparently he was one of Jason Powell's interns and had had a fling with Rachel Sutton. Corrine had informed him that she had an actual job that kept her from watching morning television, but she'd find it online when she had time.

Now that she had watched it, she told King that she didn't think it changed anything. "You said from the start the case was impossible, plus it's a misdemeanor at best. Kerry's case is the one that matters now, right?"

The media winds had shifted in Jason Powell's direction in the last two days, but Kerry Lynch would prove harder to discredit. She was the vice president of marketing for Oasis Inc., one of Powell's clients. According to Kerry, Powell was flirtatious during the course of their work together. When he walked her back to her hotel room after a business dinner six weeks ago, he made an advance. When she rejected him, he suddenly grabbed her, threw her down on the bed, and bound her wrists together with his belt.

For King, it wasn't enough. "I said Rachel's case was impossible to prove, on its own. I want to put these two charges together and argue that it's part of a pattern."

"And you can still do that."

Kerry may not have called the police immediately, but she did take photographs of the red marks on her wrists. She also had the presence of mind to hold on to the DNA, placing the skirt and panties she'd been wearing during the attack in a plastic hotel laundry bag. She had handed Corrine the bag as if it contained hazardous materials. "His—well, you'll see. It's on there. I was so sick afterward I started to throw it away, but I didn't want the maids to see. This bag has been stuffed in the corner of my closet ever since. Maybe some part of me knew I should hang on to it."

On the other end of the line, King was still venting about yesterday's *New Day* interview. "I'll bet you a thousand dollars that Powell gets that kid whatever hedge-fund job he wants when he graduates."

Behind the counter, a guy with arms the size of milk gallons called out Corrine's name and handed her a takeout bag, already beginning to spot with grease.

"Where are you?" King asked.

"Getting lunch."

"Where?"

"Lechonera La Isla."

"I don't even know what you just said."

"Best chicharrón in the city."

"Okay, you're making up words now."

"I like how you own your whiteness, King. It suits you." At the register, she fished twelve dollars from her purse, enough to cover lunch and a healthy tip for the jar. She continued the conversation outside as she began the short walk back to the precinct. "Do you have a subpoena yet for the hotel?" Powell had attacked Kerry after walking her back to her room at the W. Surveillance video wouldn't show the actual assault, but the footage might at least place Powell inside a hotel room with the complainant.

"Yeah, I sent it over to their general counsel this morning. I'll e-mail you the contact info so you can follow up. I also subpoenaed his cell phone records."

"Sounds good. And, oh, the preliminary screening of the clothes Kerry gave me confirmed the presence of semen. We need a warrant to swab Powell." A quick oral swab would give them the DNA they needed for a comparison.

"I don't know. The case is weak. She didn't report it until six weeks later," King said.

Corrine did her best to keep her voice calm as she tried to explain the flaw in his logic. "The whole reason you leaked Rachel's complaint in the first place was to see if other victims—ones who never came forward—might contact us. You were looking for a pattern. Bill Cosby. Trump. That gym teacher last year in Queens. Men who do this once, do it often. But now, after that worked and led us to Kerry, you're holding it against her that she didn't come forward earlier?"

"I want the case to be better."

"Most rape survivors don't call the police. And Kerry has a good explanation. She knew how important Powell's work was for her company. And she didn't think anyone would believe her given his squeaky-clean image."

"You don't need to give me the Sex Offenses 101 lecture, Duncan, but I'm the one who has to convince a jury. And it doesn't matter how the real world works—in court, jurors don't like victims who wait almost two months to call the police. Not to mention, she met with Powell in person—at her house—the same day she accused him of rape."

According to Kerry, Jason had insisted on meeting with her alone after Rachel's complaint against him hit the news. Kerry agreed to meet him at her home because she did not want her coworkers to overhear whatever he had to say. He offered her $100,000 to sign a nondisclosure agreement regarding the attack at the hotel. She told him that she wanted to think about it, but went to SVU instead.

"I'm not asking you to go to trial yet. We just need the DNA swab."

"Except judges aren't immune to media attention. They'll want to know his side of the story."

"He already lawyered up."

"That was about Rachel, not Kerry."

"Well, if he invoked about a misdemeanor, he's going to invoke on a rape charge."

"We won't know until we ask. At the very least, the judge will see we did some legwork before asking for a swab. Maybe you can word your questions as if they're related to Rachel. By now, he probably thinks he's in the clear on that."

"But he invoked as to Rachel," Corrine argued. "I'm only allowed to speak to him because there's a new allegation."

"Let me do the lawyering, okay? You're not required to notify him of the new charge. Tell him Kerry Lynch's name came up in your investigation, something low-key like that. See how he responds."

"Now you're telling me how to do my job?"

"Fair enough. Enjoy your chimichangas or whatever."

"Enjoy your turkey sandwich on whole grain."

"Please tell me that was a lucky guess."

"Uh-huh," she said, smiling, as she hung up.

# 18

As each hour passed, I could almost feel the rest of the world caring less and less about Jason and whatever it was that intern may have said about him.

Jason's attorney hadn't gotten an official assurance that he wouldn't be charged criminally, but she said that wasn't unusual. You either got charged or you didn't.

Rachel had stopped coming to work, as one would expect, but it had been three days since the news broke, and she hadn't filed a formal complaint with the university or done anything else to pursue the matter. The three remaining interns—including Wilson Stewart—told Zack that they assumed Rachel was embarrassed that her complaint had spiraled so out of control. The dean had not asked for any further meetings with Jason after their initial conversation about the police report. Jason hadn't lost any clients. He had even managed to record an episode of his podcast without mentioning the scandal.

By the time I finished cleaning up after dinner, it actually felt like the incident might be in our rearview mirror.

In retrospect, I must have felt like we were safely back into our normal life, because I believed Jason when he told me that I had no reason to worry when the police knocked on our door that night.

It was three knocks, actually. The sound of the brass gargoyle against wood is full and aggressive, not to be ignored.

I was doing my nighttime ritual early that night, right after dinner. It seemed to gain an extra step with each additional year of my life as a woman—cleanser, toner, moisturizer, eye cream, neck serum, flossing, and brushing. I froze on instinct.

I imagined the hand holding the knocker. Wondered who the hand belonged to. Wondered if they were alone.

And then I heard Jason letting someone in. Did he even pause to ask who it was? Did he look through the peephole to see whether the fish-eyed face on the other side of the distorting lens appeared to be male or female?

It was an argument we'd had before. That was back when he was still suggesting that I "talk to someone" about these lingering anxieties. I've told him it has nothing to do with the past. It's rational for me to be more afraid than he is.

What is it like to live without fear? Jason has tried to help me be more like him, unafraid, comforted by statistics showing that the odds of "people like us" becoming crime victims were at an all-time low. I try to help him understand that being like him is a luxury. Fear isn't rational, it's primal. And if he wanted to talk about statistics, he needed to look at *two* factors: the odds of something going wrong, yes; but also the severity of the harm should it in fact occur. In the real world, Jason might be the one who opened the door to a stranger, but I—statistically, I, as the only woman in the house—would be the one who truly suffered.

So when he let some person into our home, I stood on the landing, toothbrush still in hand, mouth full of foam, and listened with all my might. I couldn't make out the words, but the voice was female. Kneeling down, I saw two dark, fleshy calves. She was wearing black flats and a knee-length navy skirt. I walked to our bedroom window and looked down to the street.

A generic light-colored sedan was blocking our driveway. I knew immediately it was a police car.

"Jason?" I called out. "Is everything okay?" I thought about Spencer in his room and hoped that he had his Beats headphones blasting, as usual.

Jason walked halfway up the stairs to speak to me. Unlike the house I grew up in, in this home we do not yell from room to room—one of the Mom Rules.

"What's going on?" I asked.

"I guess there was an incident down the street."

He must ha-ve noticed me flinch at the word *incident*, because he quickly clarified: "A fight of some sort. They're canvassing the neighborhood for witnesses. I told them we stayed in for dinner and hadn't seen anything. They're gone now."

He brushed my hair from the back of my neck and gave me a soft kiss. I smelled his soap and Pert shampoo. I actually believed his explanation.

But later that night, once we were in bed, I had that feeling in the pit of my stomach again. I couldn't sleep. I wrapped Jason's hand in mine and took a deep breath.

He could tell I was anxious. He told me everything was fine. He asked me if I wanted to play the alphabet game. "We can do vacation," he offered. He knows it's my favorite.

I found myself smiling and started with A: *Anguilla.* He added *beach*. I followed with *colada.* The last word I remembered that night was *iguana*. I fell asleep with my mind in the Caribbean.

But by the time I woke up the next morning, I realized what should have been obvious all along: police don't block a family's driveway with an unmarked car on a fishing expedition for witnesses to a random assault.

*

After Spencer left for school, I walked down to the pay phone at the corner of Eighth Street and University, called the Sixth Precinct, and said I was wondering whether they'd identified the culprits involved in the assault on our block the previous night. "I'm a mom. I want to make sure my kids are safe," I added for good measure. When they asked for my address, I gave them the apartment building two doors down from our carriage house.

"You said this was last night?" the woman asked.

"Yes, all the neighbors were talking about it. The police were going door to door a little before eight, looking for witnesses."

"Nope, I'm not seeing anything in your area last night. Sounds like someone on your block started a rumor. People will do anything for attention these days."

I replaced the phone in its cradle, knowing for the first time in my marriage that Jason had lied to me, right to my face, as if it were nothing.

# 19

The young woman at the concierge desk was race-ambiguous, with close-cropped bleached hair, deep-set eyes, and light brown skin. The black collared shirt of her uniform was buttoned all the way up, but Corrine could see the curve of a tattoo peeking from the side of her neck. Corrine gave a quick flash of her badge and said she was there to see the head of security.

She noticed an older couple at the reception counter next to her exchange a nervous look. "Nothing to worry about," she assured them. "Welcome to New York."

The hotel in question was the W in midtown. Kerry Lynch's company was based in Nassau County on Long Island, but she frequently stayed in the city overnight when she came in for meetings. In response to a subpoena, the hotel's general counsel had asked the security department to pull surveillance videos from the night Kerry said she was attacked by Jason Powell.

Corrine was a big fan of surveillance cameras, but she could do without the private security guards who tended to come as part of the package. She was anticipating the inevitable questions. How long had she been on the job? What did she do before she was a cop? She told herself that it was the usual banter between wannabe cops and the real thing. But part of her always felt like she was being quizzed for another reason, as if it were her obligation to prove that this black woman deserved to have a detective's badge and gun instead of the polyester uniform of an unarmed security guard.

She heard a booming voice behind her. "I think I recognize that Duncan Donut." Her last name always had provided a convenient nickname for a police officer.

Corrine turned to see a familiar face, slightly rounder and older than the last time she'd seen it. Shane Fletcher had been her sergeant when she first moved into the detective squad. "Well, oh my goodness. We are seriously dragging down the coolness factor in this lobby right here."

"Tell me about it. The concierges tease me because they'd never seen a man wear pleated slacks before."

"Hate to break it to you, but they probably make fun of you for using the word *slacks*, too. What are you doing working at a snazzy hotel?"

"Turns out retirement is boring as a bag of rocks. The wife's the one who figured out a hotel gig comes with major travel perks. Went to Vieques last month, heading to Indonesia in August." Fletcher pulled a folded sheet of paper from his suit pocket. "I almost called you when I saw your name on the subpoena. Figured I'd surprise you instead. You ready to watch some movies?"

*

The surveillance video was slightly better quality than average, but not the best, meaning that the two figures they were tracking were somewhere between gray blobs and a blurry home movie.

Fletcher had already explained the process he'd used to narrow down the footage. He started by looking for people going in or out of the room registered to Kerry Lynch on April 10, the night in question. Once he had eyes on Kerry, he looked for any other appearances between check-in and checkout by her or anyone else she was seen with. Usually Corrine wouldn't trust a private security guard to select which clips she needed to see, but Fletcher was a good cop.

As it turned out, the only person Kerry was filmed with was a man Corrine recognized as Jason Powell. According to Fletcher, Kerry checked in alone shortly after 4:30 p.m., left alone shortly after 7:15, and then returned with Jason at 10:12 p.m. "And go," he announced, hitting the play button.

The two figures moved through the lobby, both in business attire—open collar and a sports coat for him; blouse, blazer, and knee-length skirt for her. After a shift in the camera perspective, they rode the elevator together side by respectable distance by side. After another skip, they were in the hallway of the eleventh floor.

Nothing unusual yet, but Corrine flashed Fletcher a thumbs-up. He had gone above and beyond the call of duty, editing the footage into one smooth scene.

He nudged her, indicating that something good was about to happen.

As Kerry fished what Corrine assumed to be a hotel key from her purse, Jason Powell placed the palm of his hand against her lower back and then followed her into the room as the door opened.

Without prompting, Fletcher hit pause.

"That was her back, right?" he asked. "Not her butt?"

"That's what I saw."

Fletcher raised his eyebrows. The gesture, combined with walking up to her hotel room for a private conversation, seemed more intimate than professional, but the moment moved quickly. It may have been a friendly after-you gesture.

"So we're at ten fourteen when they go inside," Fletcher said.

"Nothing more until this at ten thirty-six."

Twenty-two minutes later. The light changed on the left side of the video. It was the door opening. Jason stepped out, walking backward. The sports coat was gone. He was still speaking to someone inside the hotel room. Kerry appeared in profile, barely past the threshold of the door, handing him his jacket. No, insisting that he take it. She seemed to be telling him to leave.

"Pause?" Corrine asked. Kerry was still dressed, but her blazer was off. So were the heels she'd been wearing when they entered. Corrine nodded for Fletcher to hit play again.

Jason was continuing to talk, and Kerry was still pushing the jacket toward him, finally tossing it toward him and shutting the door. Jason knocked on the door, paused, then knocked again. He hesitated and then looked side to side, as if he were checking to make sure no one else was in the hallway.

He ran his fingers through his hair and walked quickly to the elevator, pulling his jacket on as he moved. He pressed the button repeatedly, shifting his weight impatiently.

Once in the elevator car alone, he rested against the wall, leaning his head back.

"Look, he's talking to himself," Fletcher whispered. "Did you see it? His lips were moving."

The quality of the footage from the elevator was better than in the lobby and hallway. More light. Closer perspective. Probably better equipment.

Fletcher skipped the footage back, and they both watched Jason's lips move again. "I watched it a couple times but stopped to make sure I had enough time to get all the clips lined up. Best I got is, 'Whoop dee doo.'"

Corrine chuckled. "Only men in pleated slacks say 'Whoop dee doo.'"

After several additional viewings, she had a theory. After two more, she was sure.

She spoke the words aloud, in sync with the silent movie. *What did I do?*

Fletcher rewound, and this time they said it aloud together. Jason was saying "What did I do?"

"Guilt?" Corrine said. "Or panic?"

"Yeah, but about what?" Fletcher asked. "I know it was the guest's name on the subpoena, but I recognize the man. That intern's complaint is not the only one?"

Corrine shook her head. Fletcher was the last person who'd speak out of turn about a case.

He volunteered his first impression. "His hand on her back as they went in the room? She didn't come forward until now? He'll say it was consensual. He'll say the tiff at the door was because he didn't stay overnight. And 'What did I do?' He was mad at himself for cheating on the wife."

"Except that's not what he said when I asked him." When Corrine went to Powell's house the night before and asked about Kerry Lynch, he'd immediately said that she worked for one of his consulting clients. She asked him directly whether he'd had sexual contact with Kerry, and he denied it, accusing the NYPD of going on a "witch hunt" based on Rachel's accusation.

"So now all you need is the DNA swab," Fletcher said. "Not a bad case. Not a slam-dunk, mind you, but I've seen worse."

Corrine had the footage on a thumb drive on her keychain when she called King from the car. The conversation was quick. Now that they had the video surveillance, plus Powell's denial of a relationship, he was ready to proceed, but AT&T had just confirmed they'd be sending Powell's call log tomorrow. It was one more step to show a judge that they were being thorough. Once they had the AT&T phone records in hand, he'd ask for a warrant to collect a sample of Jason Powell's DNA. With a positive match, they'd have enough for charges.

Corrine was halfway back to Harlem when her cell rang.

"Duncan," she said.

"It's Kerry Lynch."

"Hi, Kerry. I was about to call you," Corrine lied. One of her few complaints about sex cases was that victims tended to think of the case as "theirs," as if they were private plaintiffs who employed the police and prosecutors.

"Please don't be mad. I should have called earlier."

"Mad about what? Is everything okay?"

"Yeah, I guess. But Jason called me. Did you go to his house last night and ask him about me?"

Part of not reporting to victims as if they were her boss meant that Corrine did not inform Kerry of every step in the investigation. "I needed to get a statement," she said.

"Well, he called me about it this morning."

Corrine thought about the call logs that were supposed to be on their way to her from the cell phone company. Hopefully they'd be recent enough to capture whatever call Kerry was talking about. "What did he say?"

"That he'd kill me if I told anyone what happened at the hotel that night. Please help me. He's not the man he pretends to be."

# 20

When I got to FSS's offices, Zack said Jason was out for a run. "Did he know you were coming in?" he asked.

I wanted to tell him it was none of his business, that I could pop into my husband's office unannounced whenever I felt like it. And, no, I hadn't called ahead. I was sick of Jason trying to protect me from the truth. I needed to ask him face-to-face why he had lied to me about the police coming to our house the night before. Instead, I said, "Oh, I had to return something at Barney's, so I figured I'd surprise him. I'll wait in his office."

Two young men tried not to stare as I passed them in the hall. Interns. I recognized one as Wilson Stewart. I knew they'd be talking about me the second I was out of earshot.

*

I didn't get up from my chair when he walked in. His T-shirt had a V-shaped ring of sweat down to his navel. He was thinner than usual. Why hadn't I noticed that earlier?

He was still out of breath. "Hey you. Zack said you were here." He gave me a quick kiss on the cheek. "Sorry, I'm gross. It's still May, and it feels like the middle of summer. Don't tell me global warming's a hoax."

"Can you close the door?"

He did as I asked and then turned to face me. "Okay."

I had expected him to start explaining the second he saw me. He had to know why I was here.

"Just tell me the truth, Jason."

"Babe, what are you—"

"Don't insult me. There was no assault on our block last night."

"You *checked*?"

"No. You don't get to do that, Jason. You don't get to lie to your wife and then complain that I was smart enough to figure it out."

"Jesus, can I at least take a shower first?"

He flinched when the porcelain pencil cup that had been in front of me on the desk—the one that said "World's Best Dad"—hit the wall two feet to his left. "Damn it, Angela. You on my ass is the last thing I need right now."

"Why were the police really there, Jason? It's about Rachel, isn't it?" I thought again about those interns in the hallway. Did they know more than I did about what had happened between my husband and that girl in this office? "If you don't tell me what you're hiding, right now, I swear to God, I am picking up Spencer from school and taking him to my mother's house. Stop lying to me."

Jason looked defeated as he walked to his bathroom and grabbed a small white towel. He dropped into the adjacent chair and placed his head in the towel, his elbows propped on his knees.

"They asked me if I knew a woman named Kerry Lynch."

I was glad he wasn't looking up at me. I have a terrible poker face. I didn't want him to know that I was already familiar with the name.

"Why?"

He shook his head back and forth. "It was the same detective who called me about Rachel when I was in Philly. She said a new witness name had come up. She asked if I knew her. I explained that Kerry's the head of marketing for Oasis, that water company I told you about. I asked why she was asking. She said she wanted to know the nature of our relationship."

"So what did you say?"

He shrugged. "That I know her from my consulting work."

I shook my head. "Didn't you have a meeting with her a few days ago?"

He stared at me blankly. "How did you know that?"

"You told me, remember?"

"I didn't say her name."

"It doesn't matter, Jason. You told me about the meeting when we were talking about that company. When the police came to the house, what *exactly* did they ask you?"

"They said Kerry's name had come up as a potential witness. They asked if I knew her, and asked *how* I knew her." He paused, and I knew there had to be more to the story. "And they asked whether there was any kind of sexual relationship between us."

"*And?*"

"I told you: she works for a client. That's all, I swear."

"Why didn't you refuse to answer, like you did when the detective called you the first time?"

"I should have. But it's a lot easier to talk tough on the phone than when a cop's standing in the foyer making it sound like a straightforward question. I really didn't see the harm in answering. Rachel met Kerry once at FSS. I figured that's why they asked me about her—like maybe Rachel mentioned Kerry as a potential witness or something."

"So why did you lie to me?"

"I didn't want you to worry. Nothing happened with me and Rachel. I was certain that whatever they were looking into with

Kerry would all be sorted out before long."

"But what if it's not about Rachel, Jason? What if this woman, Kerry, is making accusations too?"

He shook his head. "She wouldn't."

"Rachel did," I snapped. "Why wouldn't this woman?"

I saw a glimpse of concern cross his face.

"I called her this morning and asked her."

"What? Jason, that's crazy. You should have called your lawyer."

"We work together. I talk to her regularly. I asked her if the police had contacted her."

"And?"

"She said no, and then had to run into a meeting. The call was probably less than a minute."

"She could be lying, Jason." Just from watching TV, I couldn't imagine the police coming to our house to ask about a relationship with this woman unless they'd spoken to her first. "You said there's a problem at the company—the kickbacks or whatever. Could it be related to that?"

"Maybe." His gaze drifted into the distance, seeing the possibility for the first time. "Remember how I told you that I'd been trying to get one of the employees to help me prove my suspicions?"

I nodded.

"That was Kerry. When I told her my concerns, I could tell she knew more than she was letting on. She finally admitted that she had found internal documents that could prove their wrongdoing, but she was too scared to give me the evidence. I was trying to convince her to give them to me." His voice trailed off.

"Why is that your job, Jason? Couldn't you have called the police or something?"

"More like the FBI or State Department. But my investors would be fucked, and so would my reputation. I'd go from being Mr. Socially Responsible to a Supporter of Warlords. But if I had actual proof, not merely insinuation, if I were a whistleblower, I'd be protected. And I could probably recoup my investors' funds, too."

"And that's why you met with Kerry this week?"

"I've been trying to convince her for weeks. I told her she'd be protected if she helped me expose Oasis. But then Rachel's ridiculous complaint hit the news. My guess is that Kerry changed her mind and told her bosses what I was up to instead. I could be completely screwed."

A few minutes ago, he had been convinced this was nothing to worry about. Now my husband was panicking.

"What is it?" I asked.

"The last time I met with her. She was supposed to give me documents. She wanted to meet somewhere private."

I felt my eyes widen.

"I went to her house in Port Washington. Fuck, no one else was there. She can make up whatever she wants, and I can't prove a thing."

*

When I got home, Spencer was lying on the sofa, looking at something on his phone. He tucked it under his side when I walked through the door. Stepping toward him, I could see that he'd turned off the screen.

"So what was that?"

I remembered a few boys eagerly passing around a magazine when I was a couple of years older than Spencer, scanning the school hallways to make sure no teachers were watching before covertly handling the transfer. Into the next backpack the magazine went. Trisha and I concocted a plan to get a glimpse at what we were missing. While Teddy Dunnigan was working on his homework at lunch, Trisha undid an extra button on her blouse and leaned over to ask if he knew the math assignment for sixth hour. While he ogled her, I slipped my hand into the open backpack on the floor behind him and made off with our bounty.

By that time, I had seen plenty of R-rated movies and a couple of *Playboys*. I had even let Bill McIlroy cop a feel under my shirt. But I hadn't seen—or heard of, or even imagined—the kinds of things depicted in the photographs in that magazine.

Those pictures would be tame compared to the videos that were now prevalent online. I had read articles about the damage that pornography does, especially to kids, boys in particular. We supposedly had filters to keep Spencer from looking at that stuff, but I had no idea how well they worked, especially for a kid as smart as my son.

"Nothing," he said, a little too quickly.

"Spencer . . . ." I started to reach for his phone, but he snatched it first.

"Not cool, kid."

He relented and handed over his device.

His browser was open to a blog called *The Pink Spot*. I had never heard of it.

The photo at the top of the post was the one making the rounds—Rachel's blurred face nuzzling up to Wilson Stewart. Someone had marked the photo with a red no-smoking insignia.

I skimmed the post quickly enough to gather that the author was complaining about the "victimization" of the "brave woman" who had stepped forward to question Jason Powell's "white male privilege." I hadn't had a chance yet to check that day's Internet activity.

"Now it's a race thing?" I asked, immediately feeling guilty for speaking to Spencer about this. I was supposed to be protecting him. "It's just one blogger."

"Look at the comments," he said, not meeting my eyes.

There were twenty-four so far, not many compared to a mainstream website, but more than a few. I finally found the one Spencer was talking about.

> His wife grew up four blocks from me. Thinks she's hot sh*t. Always goes to the fanciest restaurants when she visits to make sure we know she "made it." Truth is, she ran away in high school for 3 years and came home after she got knocked up. Only thing she has going for her is this guy. If he's guilty, I say, KARMA BABY!

I recognized the name of the commenter, Deb Kunitz, as a girl two years behind me in school.

Another commenter had a follow-up question: I would have assumed his wife was a fellow academic or maybe in politics. Does this add another layer to the story? Maybe he can't handle an intellectual equal?

A second reply followed: Sounds like an interesting angle. Please DM me on Facebook if you're willing to give me specifics. I realized that the reply had come from the author of the original blog post. She had asked Deb for a "direct message," a private e-mail, looking for the details of my background, which apparently might provide "another layer" to Jason's "story."

"*The Pink Spot?*" I said aloud.

"It's like a snarky chick website. Fake feminism, if you ask me."

How did my kid know all this?

"It's fine, Spencer." It would take access to police reports to figure out exactly where I had been for those three years, and even those wouldn't contain all the facts. "Don't worry about it, okay?"

I could tell he was thinking about saying more, but then he flashed a toothy grin over the back of the sofa. "Hey, Mom. Can you explain to me why it's called *The Pink Spot*? Because I don't understand."

"You're trying to put me in the grave, aren't you?"

"Don't kill me, but you totally sounded like Grandma right then." He was back on his screen again, looking at something that had nothing to do with me.

# 21

Kerry Lynch answered the door in her work clothes, but she was holding a nearly empty wineglass, a small, fluffy white dog circling her bare feet.

"Cute little girl," Corrine said.

"Boy, actually, but yeah, he's a sweetie. Aren't you, Snowball? I spoil him like crazy to make up for the fact I'm never home. Sorry you have a shitty mommy, baby."

Kerry had sounded so shaken when she called that Corrine drove all the way out to Port Washington to take her report. In truth, she could also use the overtime.

When Corrine was standing in Powell's foyer the previous evening, she'd seen the family photographs adorning the walls—Powell with his wife and a boy who went from missing two front teeth to a tall, lanky tween. Now that she was seeing Kerry Lynch in person again, Corrine realized that Kerry looked nothing like Powell's wife superficially. Kerry was thin and pale with blade-straight, shoulder-length dark hair. Angela was curvier, with long, dark blond waves. But both women had strong, angular features, almost mannish if they hadn't been so naturally beautiful. "Patrician" is what Corrine thought people might call the look.

Corrine followed as Kerry went to the kitchen and grabbed an open bottle of wine from the counter. She offered Corrine a glass, which she declined, and then headed back to the living room and gave herself a generous refill. The entire house was meticulous.

"Even after what Jason did to me, I heard a side of him on the phone this morning that terrified me. I think I made a mistake going to you."

"I know this won't be much comfort, but I have never had an offender follow through on verbal threats to a witness. If they mean to do you harm, they don't announce their plans in advance."

"You're right. That was definitely not comforting," Kerry said with a sad smile. She patted the spot next to her on the sofa, and Snowball eagerly jumped up.

Corrine wasn't about to tell Kerry that the road ahead of her would be easy. She would be on trial as much as Jason Powell. At least the case against him was beginning to shape up. She told Kerry about the surveillance video she had gotten from the W Hotel and the call records they'd requested, which should corroborate the fact that he'd phoned her again that morning. "ADA King will apply for a warrant for a DNA swab from Jason tomorrow."

"He hasn't done that yet? I assumed it was off at the lab already."

"He wanted to fill out the investigation a bit more first."

"I gave you pictures and physical evidence. You've got that other woman's story, too. What more do you need?"

"I know it's frustrating, but lawyers like to go in a certain order."

"Well, I can tell you right now, that DNA is going to be a match. Jason's going to say it was consensual. And it will be my word against his."

"Actually, we already got a statement from him. He denied any kind of sexual relationship."

Kerry shook her head angrily and took another huge sip

of wine. Corrine had seen this reaction before. Victims fully expected the perpetrators to depict them as willing participants. They braced themselves to be blamed. But for him to deny the encounter altogether was even more demeaning. If it never happened, it means absolutely nothing.

"Trust me, Kerry, that's actually good news. When the DNA matches, we'll have him trapped in a lie. Plus we have photos of the marks on your wrists. And the footage from the hotel is helpful. It's clear you were making him leave your room."

"But I didn't call the police. I didn't come forward until Rachel complained. And I continued to work with him in the meantime. I even met with him this week—here, in my house—alone." She pulled her dog onto her lap. "He can say whatever he wants. Then how will I prove he's lying?"

"If anything," Corrine said, "the fact that he met you at your house conflicts with his story that nothing unusual ever occurred between the two of you."

Corrine was putting the best light on this particular fact. She happened to know that ADA King was troubled by Kerry's decision to meet Jason at her home instead of in a public place.

"So when will he get charged?" Kerry asked.

"My guess is that King will want you to go before a grand jury once the DNA results are back. Please hang in there, okay?"

Kerry nodded. Corrine had done her job for now, keeping the complainant on board.

"There's something else you should know," Kerry said. "Because it's going to come out, I know it."

A different detective would have told her that it really wasn't necessary. Once Jason was charged, anything Kerry said to undermine the pending case would eventually become so-called Brady material—potentially exculpatory evidence that had to be disclosed to the defense.

Corrine said nothing, and Kerry continued. "Three years ago, I had an affair with Tom Fisher, the CEO of Oasis, my company. He was married. His wife read his texts. We got caught. People at work know. They might assume I was at it again—having an affair with a man I met at work. That's part of the reason I didn't say anything when it first happened."

"Did you have an affair with Jason Powell?"

"No. Of course not."

"Then I don't see what a relationship you had with Mr. Fisher three years ago has to do with any of this. Okay?"

Kerry looked relieved. She hugged Corrine at the front door and thanked her before saying good-bye.

# 22

An inch-thick stack of call records arrived for Corrine the following morning. The Powell home had no landline, but AT&T had sent logs for Jason Powell's cell number as well as the other cell phones on the same account. She set aside the two extra logs—presumably for the wife and kid—and focused on Jason's.

The subpoena covered the last two months, about two weeks prior to Kerry's assault, running all the way up until yesterday.

She made a photocopy first and then began highlighting every appearance of Kerry's number. As Kerry had said, they tended to speak two or three times a week, both before and after the incident. Other numbers for Oasis employees appeared on the log, too.

Corrine placed checkmarks next to the two most recent calls from Jason to Kerry. The first was on the day the *Post* had broken the news of Rachel Sutton's complaint. According to Kerry, this was when Jason insisted on seeing her in person before offering to pay her off to sign a nondisclosure agreement. The second appeared yesterday morning, when Kerry claimed Jason had threatened to kill her if she followed through with prosecution.

King had wanted to show a judge they weren't cutting corners. What she saw here was good enough to do the job. She called King and gave him a quick summary. "I'll scan and e-mail the relevant pages to you."

"Sounds good."

"So you're getting the warrant?"

"Let me look at everything once it's all put together."

"Are you kidding me?"

"I'm just being thorough."

"No. Being thorough was getting the phone records, the hotel videos, and a statement from Powell. You have more than enough for probable cause."

"Not your call, Duncan."

"Seriously?"

*

Once Corrine had sent the relevant pages to King, she flipped through the rest of the call records, looking for any patterns that stood out. The most frequent calls by all three members of the Powell family were to one another. Jason's account had the most activity by far, as would be expected, given his work. She assumed that the next busiest, with calls made during school hours, was the wife's. The son's phone was barely used at all. No surprise there. For kids these days, a phone call was as outdated as the telegraph.

She paid special attention to calls made after the news of Rachel's complaint broke. Using Google, she identified two frequent callers as Jason's lawyer, Olivia Randall, and another attorney named Colin Harris. She didn't see anything else that might relate to the case.

She was about to file the records away when her eyes flashed on an incoming call four days ago to what Corrine assumed was the wife's cell. It was a 631 area code, Suffolk County on Long Island—the East End. It was only six seconds long—maybe a wrong number—but something about the phone number seemed familiar.

Corrine looked at the phone on her desk and pictured the pattern of the digits on the dialpad. When she remembered a number, it was usually a combination of both the actual numbers and the shape they made on a phone. That's why this one felt familiar. The 631 area code, plus the next three digits—796—formed a perfect square. Nothing about the next four digits rang a bell.

Now the square-shaped combination of six numbers was burrowed in her brain, and she knew she wouldn't be able to let go of them until she figured out where she'd seen them before. She pulled out her cell phone and scrolled through her recent calls, searching for the 631 area code. Nothing. She knew that iPhones physically retained information for the last thousand calls, but only displayed the most recent hundred. For Corrine, that was only a few days. She began deleting calls from her history to make room for older records. This was the kind of thing her ex used to call her OCD. "Like a dog with a bone," he'd say, shaking his head.

She finally found it five days back: four calls in total. Now she remembered. She needed background information on a rape suspect who'd previously been accused of stalking a woman he met on summer vacation. The calls had been to a detective in the East Hampton Police Department.

She used her computer to look up the general number for the department. Same area code, same prefix, different extension.

She wasn't quite ready to drop the bone yet. She pulled up the driver's license record for Angela Powell, showing a name change six years ago from Angela Mullen. She searched state police records and found a missing persons report from fifteen years ago. She did a check against the date of birth. Angela would have been only sixteen years old. She saw another entry showing the report cleared three years later.

She picked up her phone and dialed the now-memorized square of six numbers, followed by the last four digits of the number from Angela Powell's phone record.

The voice was gruff. Older. "Hendricks."

"This is Detective Corrine Duncan with NYPD Special Victims Unit. I was hoping to talk to you about Angela Powell, aka Angela Mullen."

There was a pause on the other end of the line, followed by a heavy sigh. "I'd like to help her out, but I don't actually know the husband."

He wanted to help *her*, Angela, out, not *you,* a fellow detective. Corrine was certain she hadn't misheard.

"But you know why I'm calling," she said.

"Well, I know her husband was in the news about an intern. You ask me, that case sounds like a big bag of nothing, but of course you know more than what's in the papers. I assume you're calling about Franklin, but I don't think the family wants me talking about it. Her dad made Harbor Grill turn off a Steelers game one time with no explanation. That's how bad they wanted Pittsburgh wiped from the map. Tell you what? If I get her permission, I'll give you a call, all right? Otherwise, police reports are all you're gonna get."

"Fair enough," Corrine said, and hung up.

Googling "Franklin" together with "Pittsburgh" brought up a borough named Franklin, followed by dozens of listings for various businesses. She tried again, adding the names Angela Powell and then Angela Mullen into the search. Nothing.

She tried "Franklin . . . Pittsburgh . . . missing girl." Even before she hit the enter key, the connection was beginning to come to her.

*Holy shit.* She actually said the words out loud when she saw the results.

She checked the dates of Angela Mullen's missing persons report and the date it was cleared. It all fit.

Charles Franklin. She wouldn't have remembered the name off the top of her head, but the case was plastered across the news for a few days when it went down. A neighbor kept hearing a baby from Franklin's house, even though Franklin, a quiet contractor, lived alone for all anyone knew. When the neighbor asked him about it, he told her it was the television, but she had never heard television noise from another house before. Suddenly, the few times she had seen his "nieces" visiting the house took a darker turn, so she called the police to be safe. That phone call set in motion the discovery of a chilling scene inside the house, followed by a three-day manhunt.

The Pittsburgh Police Department sent out one officer—alone—to do a knock-and-talk at the house. He was knocking for a third time and about to give up when the garage door opened, and Franklin's white Lexus SUV reversed from the driveway at high speed and took off down the street.

Inside the house, the police found an upstairs bedroom with an interior brick wall erected just inside the window. From the outside, the neighbors saw curtains and darkness. The occupants inside were barricaded with no light and a padlock on the door. The room contained two twin beds and a crib. From the appearance of dark blond hair on one pillow and dark brown hair on the other, police concluded that at least two people—probably girls—slept there. And, of course, the baby.

An APB went out for both Franklin and the SUV. Three days later, a pair of hikers in Niagara Falls, New York, spotted a man carrying water toward a tent. After the wife heard the sound of a baby crying, she decided that the man resembled the picture she'd seen in a televised Amber Alert that morning as they were leaving the hotel. After checking the details on her phone, she was even more suspicious. She made her husband help her scour the parking areas until she found a white Lexus SUV with Pennsylvania plates, but the tag numbers didn't match the alert. The husband waved down a park ranger. Within minutes, it was confirmed: the plates had been switched, but the vehicle identification number on the dash was Franklin's.

Corrine didn't know all the details of the attempted rescue, but she imagined helicopters and teams of officers in both uniform and plain clothes. What she did know from her quick scan of the news reports was that, when police arrived, Franklin ran toward the tent instead of obeying police commands to stop and raise his hands. He was fatally shot.

Police found a nineteen-year-old woman and her baby inside the tent. The woman said that Franklin had abducted her three years earlier. After she became pregnant about a year after the kidnapping, he abducted a second, younger girl. The woman gave birth to the baby in the locked room upstairs. Then, three days prior to the rescue in Niagara Falls, Franklin suddenly ordered both of the girls to grab the baby and get into the SUV in the garage. As Franklin was backing out of the driveway, the two girls had pounded on the car windows from the back seat when they saw the police officer at the front door, but the doors were locked and they couldn't get out.

Only the nineteen-year-old and the baby survived.

After hearing the news alerts about the search for him and his vehicle too many times on the car radio, Franklin had pulled off I-90 in the dark, stopped near a body of water—presumed to be Lake Erie—shot the younger girl, and dumped her corpse in the water. When Franklin got back into the SUV, he commanded the remaining victim to "look older," or the same would happen to her. The police theorized that he killed the younger victim so they would not fit the description of a man traveling with two girls and a baby; as the older of the two victims, the survivor might be able to pass as his wife. Plus, she was the baby's mother. In short, he kept her and threw the other one away.

What did any of this have to do with Jason Powell? Did his connection to Angela and her son make him a good person? Or was he a predator who recognized something vulnerable in her?

Corrine's thoughts were interrupted by the sound of the phone. She recognized the number on the digital screen as the main switchboard for the district attorney's office.

"Duncan," she answered.

"Hey, it's Brian."

"Hey." It took her a second to connect "Brian" to ADA King.

"Thanks for sending the phone records. And for driving out to Port Washington to talk to Kerry. And for getting a statement from Powell. It's good work."

He sounded different than usual. Quieter. More contemplative. "Yeah, okay."

Silence filled the line. She could tell that he didn't want to hang up.

"Is this about the Martin case?" she asked.

Robert Martin was an Academy Award–winning director who had been accused of raping a twenty-three-year-old production assistant while his crew ignored the sounds of screams from his trailer. After a four-week trial, the jury acquitted on all counts.

He sighed. "And the Santos case. And we may as well throw in Pratt and Isaacson while we're at it."

Santos was the cop acquitted of raping a woman he'd escorted home after her cabdriver complained she was vomiting in the back seat. Pratt was the Columbia Law School student acquitted of raping a fellow student after the annual law review bash.

Isaacson was the hedge-fund guy whose rape case was pleaded down to a misdemeanor after the DA's office had its ass handed to it four days straight in trial.

It had not been a good streak for the high-profile prosecutions of sex offenses in Manhattan.

"This is a winnable case," Corrine said.

"Not good enough. I need a slam dunk."

"No such thing in this line of work."

"I should sell out to the man and defend polluters and Ponzi schemers."

"No, you shouldn't."

"Do you want to go to dinner?"

"I'm going to dinner, King. But not with you."

She could picture him laughing at the other end of the line. "Day-um," he said.

She considered telling him what she had learned about Angela Powell, but she saw no connection between it and the case against her husband. "Talk to you later?"

"Yeah, but hey—I had a reason for calling other than feeling sorry for myself. I got the warrant signed for the DNA swab."

"Really?"

"I realized there were no more excuses for dragging my feet. Go big or go home, right? You'll drop it on him today?"

"Yep. Ready to go now, in fact."

"Sounds good."

As Corrine hung up the phone, her thoughts flashed to Angela Powell, who had once been Angela Mullen, at eighteen years old delivering her baby in a bricked-in room in Pittsburgh, an eight-hour drive from her parents.

She couldn't imagine how that woman was going to feel when this DNA test was a match.

# 23

Heads turned as we passed tables at the 21 Club. I knew we should have gone somewhere low-key downtown, but Susanna had convinced me to meet her in midtown, promising that her "person" would seat us in the back corner. Getting there had required walking through the dining room, accompanied by a woman whose face filled television screens all over America on a daily basis.

"I'm not so sure about this," I muttered after the waiter had taken our orders.

"Please. We walked by one person pending trial for mail fraud and another in the middle of a billion-dollar divorce. I hate to break it to you, but this crowd has more than enough of its own problems to dwell on than your do-gooder husband."

I was thankful that the tables to either side of us were empty. "Except he's not the do-gooder anymore, is he? Now there's apparently another woman, and we have no idea what she may have said."

I had given Susanna the rundown on Kerry Lynch when she called to check on me the previous night, and she'd insisted on taking me out to this lunch.

I didn't hesitate to share everything I knew. She'd been my friend for ten years now. No one other than my parents and Spencer had been a constant in my life for that long.

When she first began treating me as her friend and not just her caterer, I worried that maybe she already knew about me. I thought she might be working an angle to earn my trust. I began testing her, mentioning details about Spencer as a baby, wondering if she'd ask about his father. I even asked her once out of the blue whether she'd ever been to Pittsburgh, and she seemed completely confused by the question. She had no idea that I was anyone other than a young mom from the South Fork who cooked good food and needed a friend.

When I decided to tell Susanna that I was the girl rescued from Charles Franklin, my parents thought I was insane to trust a journalist, of all people. But Susanna was almost like a surrogate mother. After everything she had done for me, I wanted her to really know me.

She cried when I told her and said she was sorry I was carrying that on my own. A couple of times, she asked me if I was sure I wouldn't be happier if I told my story to the world. I could make enough money to move out of my parents' house. I told her the same thing I would later tell Jason: I didn't want my story to be public, and it didn't seem right to make money off it, anyway.

And when I told her I didn't want to write a book, or give an interview, or go to the therapy she offered to pay for, all she asked was to let her know if I ever changed my mind. She never leaked a word. When it came to me, she respected an impenetrable wall between her job and our friendship.

Now, over lunch, she was trying to reassure me that everything was going to be all right. "I know it's verboten to say, but women do lie about these things." She had lowered her voice, even though we weren't within earshot of anyone else.

"You're going to have to give back your sisterhood card if someone hears you, Susanna. You know what they say: there's a special place in hell for women who don't support other women." I had told her about the police coming to the house, asking Jason if he'd ever had sex with a woman named Kerry Lynch. She agreed with me that it sounded like Kerry had leveled a new accusation, and because of the question about sexual relations, it had to be more serious than Rachel's initial claim.

"Look, I get it," Susanna said, tucking her chin-length, perfectly frosted bob behind one ear. "I'm always the one saying that when it's he-said, she-said, I'll pick the woman every time. Because ninety-nine percent of the time, women are telling the truth, and a hundred percent of the time, it's grueling to come forward. Women are blamed, stigmatized, scrutinized, doubted. Even with you . . ."

Her voice trailed off. I suppose that in a weird way, if I had to be a victim, I was one of the lucky ones. I wasn't a drunk college student accusing another drunk college student about a fifteen-minute incident at a frat party. I was a sixteen-year-old girl whose one mistake was to accept a ride home in a Lexus SUV from a man who told me he was a twenty-four-year old realtor from Philadelphia, visiting his grandparents for the week. Once I was in the passenger seat, he held a cloth over my face and repeated as necessary until I woke up naked on a twin bed in a pitch-black room with a pain between my legs because, as much as I had been "acting like trouble," as my father put it, I still hadn't done that. Not yet. I didn't come home for three years, and only when police killed my abductor. Charles Franklin was actually thirty-one when he took me, but what did I know? Grown up was grown up.

So I was about as victim-y as a victim could be. But "even with me," as Susanna said.

My parents, the police, and my therapist all told me to avoid coverage of the case. But they didn't know how I used that laptop some victims' rights group had purchased for me to help catch up with my education. I saw the discussion boards filled with comments from strangers rehashing every fact they could find about the case, including the neighbor's observation that she had seen me outside a few times and once paying for food at the grocery store. She said I looked familiar and asked me where I lived. I told her that I was Charlie's niece, Sandra. *Why didn't she ask for help?* some of the true-crime message boards wanted to know. *Why didn't she tell them who she was?*

I was about as perfect as a victim could be, but even I could not escape blame.

Susanna was still delivering her monologue. "The public's first instinct is to disbelieve the woman, because we don't want to admit these horrible things actually happen. So to counter that instinct, we good feminists take the position that we believe every single woman, every single time. And then the *Rolling Stone* article about the University of Virginia happens, and it hurts us all. So I don't know what this woman's angle is, Angela, but I have to think there is one. Because Jason didn't do whatever she's accusing him of. For once, I'm glad these cases are harder to prove than people think."

Susanna had started out covering a crime beat in Miami after graduating from Florida State. "How so?" I asked.

"Whatever this woman's story is, it's going to boil down to his word against hers, and the prosecution needs proof beyond a reasonable doubt. Even if they have DNA evidence, the DA has to prove it wasn't consensual. What? Why are you looking at me like that?"

We stopped speaking as the waiter arrived with our meals—steak tartare for both of us, the best in the city.

"The way you're talking about it so casually," I said after he had left. "A trial. DNA. Consent. This is my husband. We don't even know for sure what he's accused of."

"Sorry. You know me. I'm blunt. I meant in the abstract. I was trying to make you feel better by breaking down the worst-case scenario. But of course it won't go to trial. It's going to be fine."

"There's no consent to argue, Susanna. Jason told me that nothing happened between him and this Kerry person."

"As long as he didn't say that to the police. I assumed he invoked his rights to a lawyer."

I didn't answer.

She put her fork down, clearly frustrated. "Jesus, someone as smart as Jason should know you never talk to the police. *Ever.*"

"He didn't see the harm. He works with the woman. End of story."

"It doesn't matter. And again, I'm talking in the abstract again, if he—not *Jason*—but if a man in that position said nothing, he could always argue consent if the police matched his DNA. But if they find DNA evidence after the man denied any kind of encounter? He's caught in a lie." Once again, she saw from my expression that she'd gone too far. "But obviously, in this case, it's fine. If Jason says there's no relationship, there's no relationship."

I made a point to ask what was going on with her. I hate it when people monopolize a conversation with their own problems, no matter how big they are. She told me about two stories she was working on. A woman had left her husband for a man she met on the Internet, only to learn that the "other man" was an eighteen-year-old, not the forty-year-old executive he claimed to be. So far, the woman was standing by her new boyfriend, claiming that his deception was no different than shaving a few pounds from the physical description of an online bio. The second story was about the latest methods for obtaining passports, social security numbers, and other official documents based on stolen identities. "People never get tired of following the cat-and-mouse games between white hats and black hats."

Manchester City Library
Burnage Library: 0161 227 3774
Renewals: 0161 254 7777

**Customer ID: **********6756**

**Items that you have issued**

Title: The happy couple
ID: C0000020464923
**Due: 15 November 2023**

Title: The wife
ID: C0000020236053
**Due: 15 November 2023**

Title: Thrown
ID: C0000020388528
**Due: 15 November 2023**

Total items: 3
Account balance: £0.20
25/10/2023 11:59
Issued: 3
Overdue: 0
Hold requests: 0
Ready for collection: 0

www.manchester.gov.uk/libraries

"Maybe your smitten lady can get a fake ID for her teenage boyfriend. While you're at it, save your research for me. If my face lands on a tabloid cover, I'm out of here."

My attempt at humor fell flat.

"You're worried about being discovered," she said. It was a statement, not a question.

I told her about the comment posted on *The Pink Spot* blog. "I knew that girl back home. She'd say anything to put me in my place."

"Please, that website's got like fifty followers."

"Does that really matter? One viral tweet could change everything."

"Trust me. No legitimate media outlet's going to go there without your permission. If I have to call every contact I have in the business, I'll shut it down."

Susanna had just insisted on paying the bill when my cell phone rang. It was Jason. I made my way to the front entrance and hit accept.

"Hey there. I'm about to leave lunch with Susanna."

"The police were here. They had a warrant."

I felt the steak tartare churn in my stomach. "Are you under arrest?"

"No. It was a search warrant."

"Did you call Olivia? What are they searching for?"

"Angela, we need to talk."

# 24

He had been having an affair with her, and the police had arrived at our house to collect a sample of his DNA. The reason he had summoned me home was to break this piece of news to me in person.

Kerry wasn't merely a client contact. He had slept with her during that "lunchtime" meeting at her house last week. I didn't ask for every detail of the relationship, but it obviously wasn't the first time. He warned me to expect a DNA match.

I was the one who insisted that we tell Spencer. I didn't want our son to hear about it from some kid checking his iPhone at school.

When it became clear that the matter wasn't up for debate, Jason wanted to be the one to explain it to him. We finally decided to speak to him together.

We started by assuring him once again that his father was innocent of the allegations against him. Jason began to lay out Kerry's motive for discrediting him, but it was too much detail for Spencer to absorb. He knew we were both in his room, standing above him as he was perched on the edge of his bed, for a reason. Something bad was about to happen. He didn't need excuses. He needed to know that his world was safe.

"The police will have evidence that links your father to this woman," I finally said. "Physical evidence. But what she's saying about him isn't true."

His confused expression was quickly replaced by disgust. "You mean he cheated on you."

Jason reached for Spencer, but he jerked away. "Get out."

Jason blinked, searching for words. My son, however, knew exactly what he wanted to say. "Get *out*! Get out of this house. Get the fuck out of my room!"

I wanted Jason to argue, to stay here until our son found some way to live with the news. Instead, he turned and walked away. I heard footsteps on the stairs. Part of me wanted to follow him, but Spencer needed me.

"He's not going to leave the house, Spencer. He lives here. We all live here together, and that's not changing. At least, not right now."

He asked how I could be so calm. "Why aren't you more pissed off? He cheated on you. He's ruining everything."

I told him that marriages were more complicated than he could understand. I was letting him think that maybe I had known. Maybe I wasn't the duped wife after all. "Obviously, your father and I have some things to talk about. But the number-one issue right now is this woman. She's taking a consensual situation—"

"An affair, Mom. He had an *affair*."

"Okay, an affair. She is taking their affair, and she is using it to accuse your father of a horrible, horrible thing. The most terrible thing one person can do to another. You understand that, right? Cheating on me, lying to us, it's not okay—at all. It's awful. But she was an equal partner in that. She knew your father had a wife and son. And now she is making up a disgusting crime. And she's doing it out of greed. Your father has been trying to expose her company's corruption. And instead of helping him, she saw a chance to make him look bad."

"I can't believe you're defending him. You're the one who follows all your little rules and routines so our life can be 'good and boring.' And now he's blowing it all up, and you're going to pretend that everything's fine?"

"Trust me, Spencer. It's not fine, and this isn't easy for me. But, believe it or not, as much as Jason screwed up, he's actually still the good guy in this situation. This company—"

"You just called him Jason."

I didn't see his point.

"You always call him Dad, or my father."

"He's that, too. Always, Spencer."

"What if I don't want him to be anymore? I'll change my name again. He never even adopted me. You might be married to him, but I'm not."

"Spencer, I am begging you. Please try to be on his side for the time being. If this case goes away, we'll talk about how to move on as a family from there, okay?"

"I'm not on his side, Mom. I'm on your side. You promised when you married him, it would always be you and me, no matter what."

I said that to him right before we got in my parents' car to head to the wedding. I didn't think he remembered. He was still so young.

"And I would never make that promise if I hadn't meant it. But right now, Spencer, Jason's side *is* my side. And our side. If he goes down for this, everything falls apart for all of us. Do you understand that?"

He nodded. He had tears in his eyes, but I could tell that his acceptance of the situation was real, at least for now. I had never given Spencer a reason to doubt my judgment. I was running on earned trust for the time being.

I was about to close his bedroom door, but he had one more question for me. "Did you know about her? That other woman?"

"Not now, Spencer."

*

I wasn't surprised to find the rest of the house empty, or that Jason's phone was turned off when I tried to call him. This is what Jason did when he was upset. He walled himself off.

Colin knocked on the door about an hour later. I knew my entire face looked bee-stung from crying.

"I'd ask if you're okay, but that would be pretty stupid, huh?"

I was already half a bottle of Cab down in the living room. I walked to the kitchen, retrieved a fresh glass, and split the rest of the bottle between the two of us from the sofa.

"He's at your place?" I asked.

He nodded. Again, Jason was predictable. Colin's apartment, across the street from Union Square Park, was where he usually went when he needed some space. He even had a spare key, supposedly in case Colin locked himself out, but I knew he'd used it the few times we'd gotten into horrible fights.

"So did you know?" I didn't need to specify the subject of my question, or was it the object? I always got the two confused.

"About this woman specifically? No."

"But you knew something. You knew there was some*one*."

"I wondered a couple of times. He told me to mind my own business."

"Sounds like a confession to me," I said, taking a big sip from my glass.

"Not necessarily." I let the silence fill the room, hoping—or maybe nervous—that he would say more. "To be honest, I think I was worried he'd accuse me of having selfish reasons to pry."

"Why would that be selfish?" I asked, looking away.

"To hope that maybe there were problems between the two of you."

I swirled the wine in my glass. The night before Jason and I got married, the three of us were drunk on Indian Wells Beach, hours after it was supposed to be closed. Jason stripped down to his boxers and jumped in the water, leaving Colin and me alone by the lifeguard stand. He had told me that he was supposed to go to Susanna's party that night Jason and I first met. "I could've met you first. But I hooked up with a bartender at Nick and Toni's and no-showed at the party. Guess you dodged a bullet and got the good one instead." We had never talked about that moment again.

"He says it started three months ago," I said. "The *affair*." The word felt so old-fashioned.

Colin didn't respond.

"You said you wondered a couple of times," I said. "That doesn't sound like only the last three months. That sounds like more than a couple of times, and for a while."

As he continued to look at me in silence, it felt like confirmation of all my suspicions.

"When's Spencer done with school?" he asked.

"Tomorrow." I had completely forgotten to make a last-day-of-school cake, an annual tradition.

"I know I'm a shitty friend for saying this, but you're too good for this, Angela. Get out of here. Take Spencer out east."

"And live with my mother? Shoot me now."

"Only for a little while. Or I can help you."

Colin had money, but not that kind of money. I shook my head. Colin was Jason's friend more than mine, but he had always looked out for me. I remembered all those doctors he had called after my miscarriages.

"Then throw Jason out. He can stay with me. You don't need

this shit. Let him deal with this on his own. He's the one who fucked some batshit-crazy woman who would pull something like this as revenge."

"He said it was because of the company. That they're paying kickbacks in some third-world country. Something like that could put them in prison."

"Yeah, he told me that too," he said flatly.

"But that's not the revenge you were talking about, was it? Is there something else?"

He didn't say anything, and I imagined all the other reasons that my husband's lover might hate him enough to do this.

I knew it was a mistake, but I went to the kitchen and opened another bottle of wine anyway. When I returned to the living room, I was slurring my words.

"Do you think Jason assaulted her?"

"Are you kidding? Of course not. He's a fucking idiot to cheat on you, but no, he didn't do what that woman's accusing him of."

I was replaying Susanna's words from lunch. *We good feminists take the position that we believe every single woman, every single time.* I couldn't believe it was still the same day.

"Jason told me that this woman"—I didn't want to speak or hear her name ever again—"was supposed to help expose the company."

"She obviously switched sides. The timing makes sense. She went to the police right after Rachel's complaint became public. She probably assumed that Jason was going down—maybe she was even a little jealous of what she perceived as a flirtation with some intern—and so she went to the company, told them that Jason was planning to expose them, and came up with a solution to set him up."

When I had first seen her name in Jason's calendar, I had sort of suspected. But I had pushed my fears aside. Maybe if I had questioned him further, if I had followed him, if I had somehow stopped him from meeting with her that day. Instead, I now had to picture him driving out to her house. Being with her, only hours after kissing me and telling me I smelled good. Giving her the very evidence she needed to frame him. We had cooked lamb chops together that night.

I was hearing Susanna's voice again. *Sometimes women lie, and it hurts us all.* "It's evil what she's doing," I said.

"You've got to assume that a company willing to cut deals with warlords is capable of anything. But a lot of wives would say Jason's getting what he deserves, under the circumstances."

"Maybe I'd feel that way if it weren't for Spencer." I had been anxious about Jason's increasingly public profile, but Spencer was so proud of his father's activism. My son was only thirteen years old, and he was already passionate about saving the planet, income equality, and a host of other issues. He saw Jason's work outside of the university as the stuff of superheroes. "I can't have his father sent to prison for something he didn't do. I don't want Spencer to be the son of a sex offender."

"Oh, Jesus. Angela, I'm so sorry." Colin's voice cracked. Four years ago, when I told Colin not to bother with Spencer's adoption papers after all, Jason had asked my permission to tell Colin why Spencer's biological father wasn't in the picture. I agreed, expanding the very small world of people who knew about my past by one. Colin treated me no differently once he knew. He never even mentioned it to me directly.

"I have to stay with him. At least until this is over," I added. Spencer and I were the only family Jason had. His parents had both passed away by the time we met. The aunt and two cousins he had in Colorado might as well be strangers. "If I left him now, it would look like he was guilty, right?"

"Honestly? Yeah, maybe. But is that really why you're staying?"

"Why else?"

When he finally spoke, I could tell he was choosing each word carefully. "Jason doesn't talk to me about you, just so you know."

"Okay?" The transition was confusing.

"But I asked him, a long time ago, about whether you'd had counseling for, well, you know. Something like this—well, maybe you'd find it helpful now."

"Colin, I appreciate it. Really, I do. But one has nothing to do with the other. I promise."

I could tell he wanted to say something more, but he just nodded. Then he added, "As long as you know that you *can* leave, Angela. You have options. You'd still have Spencer, your mother, Susanna. Even Jason would understand. And, of course, you'd still have me."

When I walked Colin to the door, I had this image of him hugging me good-bye, kissing me on the cheek, and leaning in to see if something else would happen. I felt myself anticipating it, wondering how I would respond, feeling justified to let it go further.

Instead, he handed me his half-full glass and told me to call if there was anything he could do to help. The house felt quiet when he left. I walked to the pantry and pulled out everything I needed to bake my son a proper cake.

*

I was still thinking about Colin's words two hours later as I smoothed the frosting. *You can leave, Angela.*

Even after Charlie kidnapped me, you could still blame me for what happened. I only tried escaping once. After a couple of months, he told me that he wanted to let me leave my room, but only if he could trust me. I promised that I would do whatever he wanted. The idea of being able to walk past that bedroom door felt like freedom. He offered me a deal: When I heard the garage door close in the morning, I could try the bedroom door. If it was open, I could be in the house free while he was gone at work, but only if I promised not to leave. It seemed too good to be true, but I jumped at the agreement. I did it once, like a perfect little victim, noticing that there was no phone in the house and all the shades were drawn. I watched TV with the volume low. I drank soda whenever I was thirsty. I made a peanut butter and strawberry jam sandwich. It felt almost normal except for my vigilance to clean up every stray breadcrumb and to scrub my dishes clean. And then when I heard the garage door open at the end of the day, I put myself back in my room, exactly as instructed. When he came to the room that night, he said I had been "such a good girl." It didn't stop him from climbing on top of me, but at least he didn't hurt me. In the morning, I tried the door after I heard him leave, and felt my heart drop. It was locked, and remained that way for another twenty-four mornings.

Then one morning, it wasn't. I was out again. I was alone. And I thought I finally had my chance. I had been a good girl. I had earned his trust. And now I was going to get out.

I went immediately to the side door, the one I was pretty sure led to the garage. My plan was to make sure he was gone, and then leave through the front. I'd run house to house until I found someone to call the police.

Charlie was hiding in the closet at the end of the hall. He grabbed me the second my hand touched the knob on the door to the garage. And then he really hurt me. I was like a rag doll, the way he threw me, how I almost floated in the air with each punch and kick. I'm not sure how long he left me in the room alone after that, but it was long enough for me to be so hungry, I thought I might just die. I never tried to leave again. I never even let myself dream about it. I just got used to living there with him, earning new privileges.

By the end, we were almost like a family, as twisted as I know that is, now. He brought home a second girl. And I know how awful this is, but I was happy to have her there. I had a friend. No, she was more than a friend. We were like sisters in a sick, twisted fairy tale. She took some of the burden of Charlie's needs from me. And of course there was Spencer.

All of us together made Charlie feel safer, helping create a fantasy that maybe we weren't there involuntarily after all. We even got to walk outside a few times, as long as we took turns, one outside while one stayed home with the baby. We had to say we were sisters—his nieces—and we had to come back, or the other one and Spencer would pay the price.

The few times I went to counseling when I came home, the shrink told me I had to work on not blaming myself—blame for getting in the car, blame for being the kind of girl the police didn't look for, blame for not getting away when I had the chance. There's a name for it—Stockholm syndrome—but I don't think that describes me. I did what I had to, to stay alive, and it worked. I saw Charlie fall to the ground when the police shot him, and like that, it was over. I was fine.

If there's a syndrome that affects me today, it's survivor's guilt. I don't cry for myself. I cry for the girl I shared that tiny room with for nearly two years. She died, and Spencer and I lived.

Colin had wanted to make sure I knew that I could leave. Of course I did. I was no prisoner. Like always, I was doing what made sense, both for me and my kid. I wasn't going back to life on the East End without a fight. I'd deal with Jason once all this was past us.

*

By the time Jason returned the next night, I had already heated up leftovers for dinner alone. He saw the partially eaten last-day-of-school cake wrapped in plastic on the kitchen counter.

"Shit, I forgot. Is he upstairs?"

"No, I told him he could stay over at Kevin's."

"I'm sorry. I figured you guys could use a night without me, and then I spent most of the day at Olivia's office. She was grilling me like I was already on trial. I thought maybe she was padding her bill, but Colin says she's known for getting in the prosecution's head. He seems to think she might be able to convince them not to charge me."

That didn't sound likely to me, but Susanna had said it was harder to get a conviction than most people realized.

"Spencer's history teacher called me today. She said some of the kids go to this camp up near Connecticut. They hike and grow their own organic food. Sounded a little hippie-dippie, but he'd have a couple of friends there."

"Like an away camp? You hate leaving him with a sitter for a long weekend."

"Well, things have changed, haven't they? He'll be away from the city, and there's no Internet there."

"Is that really necessary? If Olivia gets this taken care of—"

"That's a big if. And we don't know how long it will take. I don't want Spencer living like this. His teacher told me it was all the kids were talking about this week."

"The camp?"

"No, Jason. *You*. You were what our son's friends were talking about the last week of school."

"How much is camp?"

"Three weeks, with the option to extend another three."

"How much does it *cost*, Angela?"

"Are you fucking kidding me? After all the money you've

been making—"

"Which goes to his school and to our mortgage and to taxes and to my agent and to running a business. Two clients have already dumped me. And I still have to pay the rent on our offices and paychecks for the staff. Do you know how much I had to give that defense attorney as a retainer?"

Of course I didn't, because he hadn't told me. But now he told me he'd taken $50,000 from our savings account—almost all of it—as a retainer. If the case went to trial, we'd need to open a line of credit against the house. Olivia estimated that it would be $300,000, plus any expert testimony they might need.

"How much is left?" I asked.

"I mean, it depends what you count. I've got almost a million in my retirement account, but I can't touch it without paying massive penalties. And we have the equity in the house."

I knew it had been a mistake to extend ourselves to buy this place. Who owns an actual *house* in Manhattan, let alone in Greenwich Village, let alone a carriage house with the ultimate luxury of a parking garage? We could have bought a nice apartment, with money left over to buy a decent house in East Hampton, instead of renting in the summer. But this place was on the National Register of Historic Whatevers. It was *significant.* It needed us, in Jason's view. We had to *lock it down*, although it meant using his entire book advance as a down payment, with an enormous mortgage to fund the rest.

"How much do we have left in savings now?" I asked.

"About twenty."

I would have guessed three times that. "The camp is only eighty-five hundred; five thousand for three weeks. I never ask for anything, Jason. If you can spend half a million dollars to prove your mistress is a liar, you can throw in a few more bucks to protect our son from the details. He's going."

I expected him to argue, but he simply nodded. "I'm probably not supposed to touch that cake, am I?"

I smiled involuntarily and handed him a plate from the cabinet, knowing that something in our relationship had changed. He needed me to stand by his side through this. He needed me, period.

*

The following morning, the news broke. A woman—unnamed, of course—had accused Jason Powell of rape. The NYPD had taken a DNA sample for comparison. A criminal law professor from Hofstra was quoted as saying, "The DNA will be make-or-break. But, let's face it, with a high-profile suspect like this, why would they ask for a sample if they didn't expect it to match?"

I was in the kitchen an hour later when I heard a knock at the door. I looked through the peephole. The woman was about my age, wearing a white cotton blouse and navy capri pants. Something about her looked familiar. Maybe she was a mom from school, or a neighbor collecting signatures to block that high-rise proposed three blocks down.

When I opened the door, she asked if Jason was home, then asked if I was his wife. I don't remember exactly what I said, but a story posted on the *Daily News*'s website two hours later reported that "a woman who answered the door at Powell's home, which he purchased for $7 million two years ago, said, 'This is all lies,' before retreating inside."

Once it was dark, I went to the front porch with a screwdriver, removed the gargoyle doorknocker by myself, and threw it in the garbage at the corner. As I walked back home, I realized it was the start of Memorial Day weekend, exactly seven years since I first met Jason. This wasn't a future I ever predicted for myself.

# 25

Ginny Mullen locked the front door of the house she had cleaned on Ocean Drive. She usually worked with her friend Lucy, but Lucy's grandson was running a fever and couldn't go to day care, and Lucy's daughter had appointments at the hair salon, and her son-in-law, who was one of the best tree trimmers on the East End, still had his hands full thanks to the storm three weeks ago. So Lucy was the babysitter for the day, and Ginny had cleaned this five-thousand-square-foot home—the biggest house on her list of clients—on her own.

She had returned the key to the hidden outdoor lockbox when the owner, Amanda Hunter, pulled into the round gravel driveway in her black Range Rover. Amanda stepped out wearing a fitted tank top and yoga pants, her arms sinewy and still tanned from last month's trip to St. Barths. She was probably forty years old, but worked hard at the gym and with Botox to look younger.

"Hey there, Ginny. I thought you'd be finished by now."

She would have left three hours before if Lucy had been there to help. "Sorry—I'm working alone today, so it took a little longer."

"No problem. Sorry, I'm a little bit sweaty. Pilates teacher kicked my butt." She didn't look the least bit mussed to Ginny. "Oh shoot, I forgot to leave you money, didn't I?"

It was an ongoing problem with Amanda.

"That's okay," Ginny said. "I always know you'll leave it next time." She didn't complete the rest of the sentence—you'll leave it next time after I text you a reminder.

Amanda was riffling through her purse now, pulling out random bills. "I think I have it. Or most of it."

"Really, it's okay."

Back into the purse went the bills. "I'll write it down so I don't forget. So, are you doing okay? With your son-in-law and this latest news? Oh, stupid me. I shouldn't have said anything. It's just, here he is, like the perfect catch, and now this."

Ginny assured her that Angela was fine and that "things would be sorted out soon," whatever that meant, then made her way to the Honda Pilot she had parked at the far end of the driveway.

"I like your new car, by the way," Amanda called out as Ginny climbed into the front seat. Ginny threw a final wave as she drove away in the car that Jason's money had helped her buy.

*

Back home, she powered on her iPad—yet another gift from Angela, purchased with Jason's money, connected to the WiFi that Angela insisted that she needed but which Ginny rarely used. She typed in "Jason Powell," then added the phrase "latest news," Amanda's words ringing in her ears.

"NYPD Investigating Jason Powell for Rape," screamed the headline. According to the article that followed, law enforcement sources had confirmed that, separate from last week's complaint against Powell by an intern, the police department's special victims unit was pursuing a different woman's complaint that Powell had forcibly assaulted her.

Ginny checked her phone. No calls from Angela. No surprise.

When Angela first started dating Jason, Ginny worried in a way she hadn't since Angela was found and returned home. It was natural for her to distrust a summer visitor from the city, consorting with "a local" to prove he wasn't a complete outsider.

Ginny of course had never blamed Angela for what happened to her, but the truth is that her daughter would have been safe if she hadn't been so obsessed with escaping her own community. Ginny would never forget the first time Danny found out where Angela really was when she broke curfew. In the past, Ginny had covered for her, telling Danny that she'd given Angela permission to stay out late, or had forgotten that Angela had told her about a slumber party. But when a twenty-six-year-old banker crashed his BMW into a stop sign on Cedar Street with two drunk teenage girls in his car, Danny finally saw a different side of his little girl.

The banker tested positive for cocaine. Fortunately, no one drug tested the girls, returning them home to their families. The first thing in the morning, Danny was down at the police station, insisting that the banker be arrested for kidnapping or reckless endangerment or some other crime for running off with his fourteen-year-old daughter. Some poor police officer had to break the news to Danny. The banker had no idea he was partying with minors. The police found Angela's fake ID in her purse. To top it all off, the other girl in the car was fifteen-year-old Trisha Faulkner, whose entire family was rotten to the core. Most of the men had been in and out of prison, and the women were always offering explanations for bruises and worse. Trisha was known for being deeply troubled, acting out with drugs and sex at a shockingly young age. Sensible people kept their distance.

But apparently Angela wasn't being sensible.

Ginny remembered listening from the bedroom door when

Danny went into Angela's room to ask her what she was doing in a car with a grown man.

Angela had broken down in tears, apologizing for her mistake, but then tried to explain what drew her to people like that—summer people. She said that for nine months a year, she looked around and saw nothing to be hopeful about. Everyone she knew worked all day, every day, and nothing ever changed. But once the season started, people showed up who had more than jobs. They had careers and plans and traveled the world—a world she wanted to be part of. She said that people like the BMW driver "made her feel special."

Ginny was prepared to comfort Danny when he joined her alone in the kitchen afterward. She wanted to assure him that he was a good man and a good provider, and that Angela was going through a phase after suddenly blossoming into a beautiful girl who looked older than her fourteen years. She had expected her husband to blame himself for not giving Angela a better life.

Instead, he had slumped into his chair and glared at Angela's door. "I never thought I'd say this, but I'm ashamed of our daughter." He forbade Angela from talking to Trisha Faulkner, which seemed only to draw them closer in the weeks and months that followed.

Ginny knew Angela didn't tell her everything, but she still confided in her enough for Ginny to know that there was something honorable in Angela's devotion to her friend. Angela said Trisha didn't have anyone who cared about her, including her own family, and was counting down the days until she was eighteen so she could leave home. She hinted that something bad was happening to Trisha, but that her mother didn't believe her, and she was afraid to talk to the police. Angela didn't fill in the details, but she seemed to be confirming what many people already wondered about the men in that family.

What Danny and Ginny saw as reckless, Angela seemed to view as a search for better options. These two girls were determined to get out of the East End, and were trying to absorb every bit of knowledge they could from people they thought were better and wiser, simply by virtue of their resources.

The car crash incident wasn't the last of the curfew violations that summer, or for the next two years. They tried grounding her, but short of installing locks on her door, they couldn't keep her from walking out. Ginny would tell herself that at least Angela came home every night. Trisha, meanwhile, would disappear for days or weeks at a time, suddenly turn back up in town, and the trouble with Angela would start again.

And then on July 17 two summers later, when Angela was sixteen years old, she disappeared. Three years after, the police killed the man who'd taken her, and Angela came home with Spencer. She was finally safe. She got her GED. She started working. She had a good business started. And then Jason came along.

Jason wasn't a coked-up banker. He wasn't that monster who offered Angela a ride home from a beach party she was too young to be at. But something about him was grandiose, his "goodness" a bit too on display. Like every part of his life was about cultivating an identity. He couldn't just be normal.

And most importantly to Ginny, he was an outsider, and so when he first appeared in Angela's life, Ginny couldn't help but think about fourteen-year-old Angela, sitting on her bed and telling her father that the lives of the Mullen family weren't good enough for her and that she, in some small way even at that young age, saw her looks as a way to achieve something better.

Despite Ginny's worries, though, Jason had turned out to be a far better man than she ever expected. He wasn't simply toying with a beautiful local beneath his station. He actually followed through. He married Angela. He was raising Spencer. And though Ginny knew that Angela would have preferred that Jason never leave the walls of the ivory tower, Ginny also suspected that he would have already declared a run for office if it hadn't been for Angela's misgivings.

But this new allegation was far worse than the initial one. The last time Ginny spoke to Angela, Jason had been thrilled with the "good news" that the intern was getting trashed in the media. Ginny could hear the mixed feelings in Angela's voice over the phone. If it were any other case, Ginny would be the one writing a letter to the *East Hampton Star* to deplore the blaming of the victim. Angela's whole life revolved around Jason, so of course she was choosing his side. But Ginny believed that some part of Angela actually felt for that intern. She of all people knew what it was like for people to believe you can't really be a victim if you're "that kind of girl."

Her thoughts were interrupted by a knock at the door. She peered through the pebbled arch of glass in the wood to see a blurry figure. The logic behind the design of this door had escaped her for the past thirty-three years, but she didn't care enough about it to change it.

Once she opened the door, she recognized her visitor as Detective Steven Hendricks. His gray beard was a little bushier than the last time she'd seen him, and his hairline had receded a tad farther, but he still had those damn glasses hanging from a cord around his neck. Danny always said the man was trying to look "cerebral."

She didn't invite him in.

"Please hear me out."

He had called her twice in the last week. She had deleted both messages.

She stepped aside so he could enter. The house suddenly felt smaller and in even more need of the TLC that Angela kept offering to pay for. Ginny immediately remembered the way Hendricks had scanned their home fifteen years earlier, when Angela first went missing. She could feel him judging them, like he already knew the full story from the look of their house and a two-year-old police report from a single-car accident with Trisha Faulkner and their daughter in the car.

"What do you know about the accusations against your son-in-law?" Hendricks asked.

"Not sure why that's your business." Other than passing him a couple times at the grocery store, Ginny's last contact with Hendricks had been a note he'd written almost a decade ago, stuck in their screen door. He said that the biggest mistake he had ever made as a police officer was not trying harder to find their daughter. The note had ended with, "All I can say is that I'm sorry." Ginny had never shown the note to Danny. Danny was dealing with enough guilt of his own. She always wondered if it contributed to the stroke that killed him five years ago.

"Even an old guy like me can reach out when necessary."

"Reach out to who? Jason? Doubt he's in a mood to talk to police right now."

"No, I meant to the NYPD. Let them know there's another side to the story—assuming there is, of course. Police get a gut feel on a case and fill in the blanks from there. If they think Jason looks wrong for this, I can present his version. Be his advocate, so to speak."

Ginny resisted the urge to remind him that he had formed a gut instinct about Angela when she first disappeared and then filled in the blanks as he saw fit. The car crash. A stop on the beach for a minor in possession of alcohol. The friendship with Trisha, who ran away the way other girls changed lipsticks.

Ginny had made so many visits to the police station that the staff started heading for the bathroom when they saw her walking toward the entrance.

When Trisha left town for good shortly after her eighteenth birthday, it seemed to validate Hendricks's version of the facts: Angela had run away for a life somewhere away from Springs, and then her fucked-up BFF Trisha followed suit as soon as she was legal.

"Why are you offering?" Ginny asked.

"You know why. When I got that phone call from Pittsburgh PD, saying that one of the girls in that house was Angela—well, I felt my heart stop. I still can't sleep some nights, knowing what she was going through, and the way I ignored all your worries. I know Danny died without ever forgiving me—"

"He blamed that animal who took her. And he blamed the Faulkner family for getting her involved in trouble. He didn't blame you," she said. Everything she said was true. She didn't add that Danny also blamed himself. "Anyone ever hear from Trisha again?"

Ginny had spent three years playing a bizarre game of whack-a-mole, chasing down every oddball rumor that popped up as to Angela's whereabouts. *She joined a cult of aspiring yoga fiends.* Ginny found the cult, but no sign of her daughter. *She met a rich, older man and moved to a state where it was legal to get married without parental consent.* Turned out, there was no such state. When Trisha disappeared, the word in town was that she had gone down to Rincón to join her friend Angela. Ginny had spent half their savings account on flying a private investigator all the way down to Puerto Rico. Nothing.

"Not that I know of."

"I like to think that maybe as much as she was a bad influence on Angela, Angela was a good influence on her. She always told Angela all she wanted to do was get away from her family as soon as she was eighteen, so maybe she's got a nice life."

"And I thought Angela had a nice life too, once I heard she got married and moved to the city. It gave me some peace about my role in all of what happened. But now this. I mean, let's say hypothetically that the NYPD reaches out to me about Angela. What do you want me to say? I know you're touchy about her privacy, but I could vouch for her husband, say he's a good man."

"I don't know, Steve. I'm not sure how Angela's going to react to that."

"Ask her, okay? It helps to have a cop in your corner, even if it's a dumb guy like me."

*

Ginny was surprised when Angela picked up on the second ring.

"Hi, Mom."

Normally, her daughter tried to hide her annoyance at being disrupted. Ginny didn't take it personally. She knew that Angela hated the slightest bit of surprise. Her routine made her feel safe.

But on this day her daughter actually sounded happy to hear from her.

"Are you okay, Gellie?"

"Trying to be."

Her thirty-one-year-old daughter, already mother to a thirteen-year-old, sounded so tired.

Ginny told Angela about the visit from Steve Hendricks and his offer to act as a kind of advocate for Jason to the NYPD.

"I can't believe you let that guy in the house."

"I think he really does blame himself for not finding you sooner."

"*Finding* me? He couldn't bother to *look* for me. Why are you defending him?"

Angela knew that not only Hendricks, but most of the town, had assumed that she ran away when she went missing. She had also learned how many people had come to pity Ginny for insisting that someone had kidnapped her daughter. But to this day, Angela had no idea that Danny had essentially given the town permission to feel that way. He was convinced Angela had left them. He even apologized to Hendricks for Ginny's "pestering."

"I'm not defending him," Ginny said. "But he's offering to help, and maybe you need it. I'm simply relaying the message."

"Too little, too late," Angela said. "He tried calling me last week, and I hung up on him. Felt kind of good, actually."

"You're right," Ginny said, deciding to drop the matter for now. "Fuck that guy. I learned that from your son, by the way. Kid cusses worse than I do."

# 26

Memo
To: Powell File
From: Olivia Randall
Re: Client Interview Notes
Date: May 26

Long interview and mock cross of Client yesterday. Full audio saved digitally. Highlights and takeaways:

- Client says Lynch was initiator. Kissed him after walking him to car after dinner (Morton's) on Long Island. Stopped, said she had too much wine and "why are the good ones always married." First sexual encounter was two weeks later at her house after she asked him over for a drink after end-of-day meeting at company (eight months ago).

- Three months ago, Client became aware of irregularities at business (Oasis Inc.). Unexplained payments not aligned with work performed on-site. He disclosed concerns to Lynch. She hinted that company engaged in kickbacks and doctored financial statements to cover up. She led him to believe she was looking for proof internally, but he never saw evidence.

- Lynch began asking Client to leave wife about four months ago. He never promised, but didn't say no either. Said he stayed for son (no formal adoption; therefore, Client has no parental rights if divorces wife). Says he felt "trapped." Didn't want to lose Lynch. Didn't want to leave family. Plus stress of needing her to help prove concerns against company so he could extract himself professionally with clean hands.

- No e-mails, texts, phone messages to confirm ongoing affair. Per him, Lynch was caught in yearlong affair with CEO of Oasis (Tom Fisher). Fisher's wife was suspicious and read texts. Lynch was humiliated. Almost fired except she threatened to sue. Still on outs with company. Per Client, Lynch paranoid that company was looking for dirt on her, would fire her if they knew of affair with consultant—that's why no texts, etc.

- He told no one of affair. Colleague Zack Hawkins noticed Lynch would be in Client's office with him alone, once tried to walk in and found door locked.

- Client was defensive, arrogant on cross. Try to keep him off stand unless substantial improvement in future mocks.

- Denies grabbing Rachel Sutton (see above re defensiveness). Doesn't recall exact words but said something like she "needed to live a little before she locked that down." He was changing clothes at time. Admitted it was "possible" he "prolonged the process to get a rise" out of Rachel, whom he found "cloying" and "immature."

- Other women may come forward. Prior infidelities during marriage (out-of-town hookups, Tinder one-night stands, etc.), but per Client, Lynch was only ongoing affair. "I thought I loved her. I can't believe she's doing this to me."

- Client believes it's possible Lynch getting financial benefit from Oasis/Fisher in exchange for undermining him. But also thinks she is angry at him for feet-dragging on leaving the wife.

# 27

*Four Days Later*

I almost took a U-turn on the Saw Mill Parkway—literally, as in the middle of the highway. Listening to Spencer singing along to my playlist of early-aughts hip-hop—LL Cool J, Ludacris, Mary J. Blige—I realized how much I was going to miss him. There was a break in the metal barrier in the middle of the highway, those spots where the police wait for speed traps. I eyed it, thinking how easy it would be to just go back home.

But then I remembered how hard I had worked that morning to keep him busy—*eat your breakfast, don't forget the sunscreen, how many pairs of underwear did you pack?*—in the hope that he wouldn't have time to go online and see any possible breaking news about Jason's case.

Olivia had called the night before to report that the moment Jason had warned me to expect was official. She had a source in the crime lab. The DNA on that woman's clothing matched Jason's. Of course it did. He had admitted to sleeping with her only days before the swab was taken. Every day felt like a new hammer dropped, but the pounding wasn't going to stop. The DNA results would hit the news. Jason would be arrested. He would be charged. There would be a trial, then a result, one way or the other.

So I kept driving, hoping that somehow our world would feel normal again by the time camp was over.

*

Jason was on the phone in the kitchen when I made it back. He told whoever it was to hold on for a second and then walked over and hugged me. I let myself be held, knowing I should hate him more, but missing our son. Jason had wanted to come with us. I told him that I wanted Spencer to myself for the morning, but the truth was that Spencer didn't want Jason to go. He knew it was his father's fault he was being sent away.

Jason went back to his call, and I walked upstairs to our bedroom and closed the door. I looked at the Lisa Unger novel lying open on my nightstand. Susanna had given me one of her books more than a year ago, swearing I would love it. I never got around to reading it until I needed something to distract me from my actual life. Now I was on my third one.

But instead of picking up the book, the way I should have, I reached for my laptop. I pulled up the log-in page to NYU's e-mail system and typed in Jason's e-mail address, followed by his password. He didn't know I had it, or at least I didn't think so. I only knew it because he had been the one to get cable installed after we moved into the carriage house. I had called him at work to ask the password to upgrade our Internet speed after Spencer complained that we were living "like cavemen."

GRETCHEN83

Even then, I must have already been jealous, because I had immediately asked him who Gretchen was. Turns out, it was his grandmother. And 83 was August 3, our wedding anniversary. Now I typed that number to finalize my invasion into his privacy. I had already read every message between him and that woman. Between him and anyone at Oasis. I searched for messages from Rachel, but found nothing. I opened random messages simply because they were to or from another woman. Since he'd confessed to the affair, snooping on my husband's e-mails had become part of my daily ritual.

I heard footsteps on the stairs and quickly marked the open message—from someone named Melanie Upton, who apparently was the senior associate director of human resources at NYU, sending her number to Jason so they could discuss his question about his retirement account directly—as unread. I was closing my laptop when Jason walked in.

"So that was Olivia. She met with the DA who's handling the case."

I prepared myself for the blow. "Are they going to let you turn yourself in, or do I have to keep sitting here day in and day out, wondering when they're going to barge in with handcuffs?"

"You think you're the one in limbo? How do you think I feel, Angela? My colleagues and students are calling me a rapist. Meanwhile, I keep showing up at school so the university doesn't have an excuse to stop paying me and revoke my tenure. Zack is going to have to cover the podcast for now so we don't lose advertisers, but that's a temporary fix. Clients are calling, asking what's going on. I'm numb. And I'm terrified."

I didn't bother reminding him that NYU had asked him to take a leave of absence—with pay—for the sake of reducing the "disruption" on campus. Jason's response had been to threaten to sue if they made any changes to his status when he hadn't even been charged with a crime, let alone convicted. He continued to insist that the only way to show he was innocent was to pretend as if everything were normal. Who was I to argue? I had spent the last twelve years putting one foot in front of another to prove that what happened in the past didn't matter.

"Well, forgive me that I no longer have the luxury of doing what I do every day, which is to take care of our son and this family. Instead, I had to hide Spencer away at some bullshit hippie camp for rich kids, just so he wouldn't be on the Internet reading the details of your secret life outside this house. So don't say this isn't about me. Now, are you going to tell me what the DA said or not?"

"Olivia laid out Kerry's motive to lie." I hated hearing that woman's name come out of his mouth. "She said the ADA looked pretty overwhelmed when she started getting into the details of the problems at Oasis. My guess is the guy can't find the countries we're talking about on a map. She told us not to get our hopes up, though."

"Oh, I don't think I need that warning."

He was tentative as he sat on the bed next to me, as if he were seeking permission. "You can bail if you want. I haven't asked you to stay."

I shook my head.

"And I really am sorry about Spencer going to camp."

"I know." I could feel myself starting to cry.

"You're scared for yourself, too, aren't you?"

I nodded. Everything was falling apart. Ever since his agent told him that his book was going to be #1 on the bestseller list, I had this terrible feeling that nothing would be the same again. All I wanted was to be Angela Powell, wife and mother, with my rules and routines and rituals. Good and boring. If I could have one wish, I would erase the entire world's knowledge of my existence before I reappeared in East Hampton with Spencer.

"Every time the phone rings, I'm convinced it's going to be someone asking me about him." My shoulders were shaking between sobs. I didn't need to tell Jason that the "him" was Charlie.

I let him hold my hand. "That's not going to happen. And, even if it did, would that be so bad? I hate to say it, but this could wind up being a blessing in disguise—for you, obviously, not me. If it all came out, you'd be free. That cloud over your whole life would be gone."

If this were the first time we'd had this conversation, it might have felt like he really did want what was best for me. But Jason had always known about Susanna's open invitation to help me "go public," as she called it, and had never questioned my rejection of it until he himself became a public figure. He talked about the cloud over my life, but it had become a cloud over his too. And maybe the freedom he cared about now was his and not mine.

When I didn't respond, he knew to pivot the conversation again. "Oh, and Olivia wanted to talk to you. I told her you'd give her a call when you have a chance. I mean, if that's okay?"

I nodded. "Yeah, I'll call her in a bit. I just want to chill out for a while after that drive."

"No problem. I was about to order some wine from Astor Place. Any requests?"

I shook my head. As far as I was concerned, there were only two kinds: red and white, and I'd drink either with anything.

"By the way, did you call the dealer yet?" I asked.

"Jesus, Angela, seriously?"

"What? That wobble in the front end's still there, and it's still under warranty." The last time he drove it, he said he could barely tell what I was talking about. I should have known that he wouldn't make the service appointment.

"Excuse me for not keeping up with your to-do lists during all this."

"You want your wife and son to get in a car accident because you're too busy dealing with your mistress to make a phone call?" I knew I was being a bitch, but one of the rules when we bought that car was that he'd be the one to oversee the maintenance. One of our other splurges when Jason started making outside money was to upgrade our wagon from the Subaru to an Audi. The only improvement I cared about was the built-in GPS and satellite radio. I had no interest in taking care of a fancy German car with all the other bells and whistles.

His voice softened. "Fine, I'll call the dealer."

"And can you ask them to install the GPS update while they're at it?"

I was almost daring him to say something. How many times had he told me to use my phone like everyone else? Both he and Spencer teased me mercilessly for my airplane-mode-in-the-car rule. *It's called airplane mode, not car mode, Mom!* I didn't care what everyone else did. I'd read an article two years earlier about people who crashed when their phones rang unexpectedly. I wasn't going to risk Spencer's life because I couldn't go offline for a little while. I knew the two of them cheated by silencing their phones instead, but the rule stood.

Once again he pretended to defer to me. "No problem," he said. "And please let me know once you've talked to Olivia. I appreciate your doing that."

He was about to leave the room when I stopped him. "You didn't tell her, did you? About me?" I had seen what she'd done to Rachel to help her client.

There was no hesitation in his reply: "Of course not."

I didn't believe him.

# 28

Brian King was wrestling a dumpling between chopsticks when Corrine knocked on his open office door.

"You can use a fork, you know. Chinese people will forgive you."

"Seems wrong somehow. I once stopped seeing a woman because she ordered a banana daiquiri at a wine bar."

"Good riddance to her. I've got something for you." She dropped the lab results on his desk. The DNA on Kerry Lynch's skirt and panties was Powell's. "We were expecting it, but now it's official."

"Hate to break it to you, but I already got the heads-up. Is it bad that I was kind of hoping it would be a bust?"

He nudged the takeout container in her direction, and she plucked a dumpling with her fingers.

"I know you've got a losing streak right now—"

"The *office* has a losing streak," he corrected.

"Fine, whatever. But this case is winnable."

"Except he's got one of the best defense attorneys in the city. Not surprisingly, she called me within half an hour of my getting the results, asking for a meeting. She's got a way of nabbing inside information. I think half of law enforcement is secretly in love with her."

"If she were a man, you'd admire his vast network of contacts."

"If she were a man, I wouldn't have asked her out two years

ago, only to get shut down. She was in here this morning giving me a preview of what we're looking at if we go to trial. They're claiming consent, and not just the one time. According to Powell, he and Kerry have been having an affair since last October."

"Bullshit. Why didn't he say something the first time I asked about her?"

"Because you showed up at his house while his wife and kid were within earshot. And he didn't think it was relevant. They'll argue you misled him into thinking you were still investigating Rachel Sutton's complaint, so he didn't see the harm of lying about a completely consensual extramarital dalliance."

"We did mislead him. That's what you told me to do."

"Yeah, well, maybe we were being a little too cute. I wouldn't be surprised if a judge suppressed his statement altogether."

Corrine reminded him of the footage from the hotel elevator. "He said, 'What did I do?' It's basically a confession."

"You don't understand how Olivia Randall operates. It's scorched earth. She'll hire experts to say that lipreading isn't scientifically reliable. And if she loses that, she'll get a linguistics professor to testify he said something else. Every single piece of evidence will be a battle. And even if the evidence comes in, she'll say he was so anguished about having cheated on his beloved wife that he was racked with guilt when he left her room." He re-created the moment, placing his hands on his head. "'What did I do?' And my boss has made it damn clear that I have to win this case."

"Well, I think I have something that potentially helps."

When she first ran Powell for priors, the only entries she found were an incident when Powell witnessed a domestic violence assault in Washington Square Park and a report from a fender-bender. After Kerry came forward, Corrine ordered copies of the reports to make sure she wasn't missing anything.

The assault incident was from eight years ago and, if

anything, made Powell seem like a hero. He saw a man push his girlfriend to the ground and continue to try to grab her arm as the two of them walked away together. He followed the couple, asking the woman if she needed help. The man took a swing at Powell, who responded by punching the man in the face and breaking his nose. A bystander called 911, making it clear that Powell had acted in self-defense.

At first glance, the report from the car accident, five years later, was a snoozer. A taxi pulled away with a fare and sideswiped Powell's Subaru in full view of a patrol officer. According to the report, Powell planned to seek repair of his car through his own insurance and did not want the incident reported. Corrine suspected that the taxi driver had mouthed off to the officer, because he had insisted on writing up the accident and forwarding the report to the city's taxi and limousine commission. It was the kind of thing that happened hundreds of times a month in this city, except that on that specific day, Jason Powell had a passenger in his car, a twenty-four-year-old white female named Lana Sullivan.

So curiosity kicked in again, and Corrine ran Lana Sullivan for hits. Three years ago, if the patrol officer had run her for warrants, he would have come up empty-handed. But that was three years ago.

"Way too much information," King said. "Get to the punch line: Who's Lana Sullivan?"

"Two prostitution convictions since she took that little car ride with Powell, plus an outstanding warrant—at least as of this morning—for an FTA from misdemeanor court six months ago."

"You picked her up on the warrant?"

"Gave her a chance to clear it and get a new arraignment ticket if she had a chat with me." She'd fail to appear for that one, too, but that wasn't Corrine's problem. "She confirmed that Powell was her john that night."

"You know how many dicks she's seen since then? She was telling you what you wanted to hear."

Corrine was shaking her head. "She'd never been arrested at that point. A cop made her show ID. She was scared, so the incident was clear in her mind. She said Powell spent more time making excuses for employing her services than actually using them. He was talking about how the wife didn't let him touch her anymore, but he loved her too much to leave."

King looked unimpressed. "His entire defense is that he's a married man who sleeps around on his wife. Proving that he went to a hooker three years ago doesn't really change anything."

"No, but it might make a difference to the wife. Right now, she probably believes him. If she starts to see another side of him—"

"The side that bitches about her to random hookers—"

"Maybe she's got something to say to us." New York's version of the spousal privilege was narrow compared to other states. The government could force a spouse to take the stand, and only private communications between spouses were protected, not other forms of evidence, such as observations through sight or smell. In short, there was a lot of wiggle room as long as they could convince Angela Powell to cooperate.

"All right, you're not pissing me off after all," King said. "That was good work."

Corrine wondered if she should tell King what she knew about the wife's background, but wasn't sure she could trust him. He was under pressure to win. She could imagine him threatening to use the information at trial to get her to testify against her husband. For Corrine, using her husband's infidelity as a chip was fair game; using Angela's own victimization was crossing the line.

"You still look miserable," Corrine said. "Do you ever not look miserable?"

He faked a large, cheesy smile. "I'm ecstatic. Honestly:

What's your read on Kerry?"

Corrine shrugged. "You want the real answer?"

"No. I asked you a question so you'd make up a bunch of bullshit."

"You know how it is. The stories never line up. No one's version is ever a hundred percent accurate. The hard part is figuring out which parts are wrong, and more importantly, *why* they're wrong. Bad guys out-and-out lie because they're trying to protect their asses. But victims? That's trickier. Some of them almost apologize for the bad guys as they're reporting the facts, because they're full of guilt, blaming themselves. Or they mitigate the awfulness of what happened to them, because the full weight of it would kill them if they stopped to absorb it. Or they say they didn't drink, or didn't flirt, or didn't unhook their own bra, because they're afraid that to admit the truth would be giving him permission for everything that happened after."

"You should give lessons on this stuff, Duncan. That was heavy. So what about Kerry? Which camp is she in?"

"I assume you have a reason for asking. What's scaring you about her?"

King paused to throw the takeout container in the garbage can beneath his desk. "I think Olivia Randall got under my skin. This trial's going to be a cluster. Randall says Kerry's lying because Powell was about to expose her company for falsifying some kind of financial records to cover up kickbacks to bad guys in where-the-fuck-a-stan-istan. The whole thing made my head hurt. Did Kerry mention any of this to you?"

Corrine shook her head. "No, but there's something else. It could be related, I guess. An affair with the CEO."

"You knew that?"

"I didn't think it was either material or exculpatory." Those were the magic buzzwords for Brady material, the evidence that King would have been required to turn over to Powell's defense team.

"Well, his attorney says it gives Kerry a motive under the circumstances to help the company malign Jason Powell. She was on the outs at work because of the affair. According to Powell, Kerry told him that the only reason she wasn't fired was because she threatened to sue them for discrimination. She was super paranoid about the company monitoring her e-mails and company cell phone, so that's supposedly why there are no texts or messages to back up his claim of a relationship with her."

Corrine reminded him that the absence of an affair would also explain the absence of romantic correspondence between them.

"I know, but I've got to admit, it makes me more than a little nervous that Powell knew she was cheating with the boss. If they were purely business, how would he know the details of an affair she had three years ago?"

"He had other contacts at the company. Kerry told me everyone at work knew. Grist for the rumor mill."

"Except Powell knew the wife's name—Mary Beth, by the way. He knows they have three kids, and that Mary Beth was so pissed off when she found the texts that she told their oldest daughter what Dad had been up to. And he claims to know that the daughter showed up at Kerry's house, calling her a slut from the front yard. You think those are the kinds of details an outside consultant overhears at a meeting? Sounds to me like bedtime chatter, swapping tales about the exes."

"So let me talk to Kerry," Corrine said. "See what her version is."

"I already tried, and that's an even bigger problem. She got defensive, accusing me of blaming the victim. And she refused to talk to me at all about her company. She claimed it was proprietary business information, and that sharing it could get her fired."

"By the very company Powell claims she's colluding with." Corrine could already picture Powell's defense in the courtroom.

"Exactly." King wasn't done listing his concerns about Kerry's motivations. "Oh, and don't let me forget this part: Did you know Kerry hired a lawyer?"

"She may need one if she thinks the company's looking to fire her."

"Except she didn't hire an employment lawyer. She said she hired someone to protect her 'victim's rights.'" He placed air quotes around the words with both hands. "She wouldn't give me the lawyer's name, but she definitely doesn't want to answer any hard questions—the kinds she'll face on cross. And if Olivia Randall finds out our victim's hired a lawyer already, she's going to claim that the real motive for this case is money in a civil suit."

"So where does that leave us?"

"It leaves *me* with a case my boss wants me to take to trial. I tried telling him I have a bad feeling, but all he knows is that we've got a rich celebrity accused by two different women in a week. If we don't charge him, he'll be accused of favoritism. When I told him Olivia Randall was here trying to get the case dumped, he told me I could offer him seven years. Seven years? You can kill someone in this city and get seven years. He's going to make me try the case, and Olivia Randall's going to make it feel like getting stabbed in the eye every single day for a month straight."

"So are we going to arrest him on a warrant, or let him turn himself in?"

"Oh, there's no doubt he's getting a perp walk. I've got the affidavit for the arrest warrant ready to go, just like I promised the boss. You ready to pick this guy up? If we're lucky, you might bump into the wife and have a little chat with her about the hooker. She may be a total doormat, but no woman wants to know she's been swapping bodily fluids with a pro."

# 29

I should have known that nothing good was going to come of my phone call to Olivia Randall when she began with her attempt at small talk. "So Jason told me you drove Spencer to camp this morning?" I heard a pause midsentence and pictured her checking her notes to confirm my son's name.

"Yeah, up in Westchester, outside South Salem. Almost Connecticut, really."

"That's great that he gets to go to camp. Gives you a break, right?"

I was glad we weren't speaking in person, so she couldn't see my glare.

"Jason said you wanted to speak to me?"

She thanked me for calling and explained again why she had kept me out of her meetings with Jason and Colin. I assured her it wasn't necessary to repeat the reasons.

"So my understanding is that Jason has told you that our defense is that the contact between him and the complainant was consensual."

"Uh-huh."

"Did he also tell you that he doesn't have any texts or e-mails to prove they had a relationship?"

"No." He hadn't told me that, but it explained why I hadn't been able to find any, despite all my attempts.

"Obviously it would be helpful if a third party could corroborate his version."

"If anyone could, it would have been Colin. He already told me that he suspected, but didn't really know anything."

"I wasn't talking about Colin. I was talking about you. Jason indicated that you may have been aware that there was someone else."

"You're asking me to lie for him. Just say it."

"No, I'm explaining how you might be in a position to help, if you wanted to. I understand that this isn't easy. To be clear, Jason has no idea I'm talking to you about this, and it has been a real challenge to get him to open up to me about your marriage, although I'm sure you can see how it will be relevant to his case."

I closed my eyes. I could feel all of the doors ripping open around me, and there was no way I could pull them shut. Every new word she spoke made me feel dizzy.

"He says that intimacy—or physical intimacy, at least—has not been a regular part of your marriage, and not at all for three years."

"Are you kidding me?"

"Please, hear me out. We have a good argument for consent, and all we really need is reasonable doubt. But it's hard to paint Jason as the good guy when his defense is that he was leading a secret life, cheating on his wife. If that part of your relationship was over, if you knew—if even part of you knew . . . Some couples have unspoken understandings. Maybe the two of you even had a good reason for separating that aspect of intimacy from your marriage."

She knew. She fucking knew. It wasn't going to be enough for me to smile and stand by Jason's side and make sure the whole world knew that I believed he was innocent. She needed *me* to be the reason he cheated. I would be the screwed-up wife who was too frigid to keep a young, attractive man happy in the bedroom. He would seem heroic for loving me in the first place and then staying with me despite all my damage.

I cut to the chase. "You think the DA will back off if he knows I'm the girl who spent three years getting tortured by Charles Franklin."

"I'll be honest, Angela. This is not exactly my favorite part of the job. But, yes, your background gives a different dimension to your marriage and therefore to Jason's interactions with this woman."

So I was right. Jason had told her about me, unless, of course, Olivia had found out on her own, which seemed plausible. "I didn't know about Kerry," I said. "At least, not specifically about her. And definitely not about a three-month *relationship*."

"So three months is longer than you suspected?"

Of course. Why did she sound confused? Had it been longer? "Jason told me it was three months."

"Okay, but you're saying that you did suspect outside encounters of some kind, but without, let's say, an emotional affair. Is that a fair representation?"

If this was what it felt like to have someone who was supposedly on our side question me, I could not imagine what it would be like to get cross-examined by the lawyer trying to put my husband behind bars.

"I need to think about this. I don't want to talk any more right now."

"That's fine. I totally understand. But, Angela, please remember: this woman is trying to destroy your husband, which means she's destroying your family. That's going to have consequences for both you and Spencer." At least this time she didn't hesitate on my son's name. "Helping Jason helps the two of you, too."

I heard Jason calling out my own name from downstairs. "Hold on," I yelled, breaking one of my own house rules. "I'm talking to Olivia."

"Angela!"

Jason was screaming loud enough for people outside to hear. I asked Olivia to hold on and walked from the bedroom to the top of the stairs. I saw Jason being placed in handcuffs in the threshold of our open front door.

For more than a week, I had been expecting this moment, imagining it about to turn the corner at any second. But Jason hadn't. His expression was panicked, and his eyes looked up at me, pleading.

"Olivia, they're here," I said into the phone. "The police. They're arresting Jason. He didn't do this. Please, you have to help him."

# III

# PEOPLE
# v.
# JASON POWELL

# 30

What does it mean to know something?

I remember Mr. Gardner, my ninth-grade teacher, asking us that question. He was widely regarded as the school's smartest, most challenging teacher, which meant that most of us had no idea what he was talking about most of the time.

It was supposed to be a lesson about the importance of choosing words carefully. He began by asking us how many facts we thought we knew to a certainty. A long list grew on the chalkboard: the price of a Snickers bar in the vending machine, the name of our PE teacher, our birthdays. Then he said, "Okay, so what if I told you that the penalty for being wrong about one of these facts was having to spend the entire summer in school? Now how many things do you know?"

We immediately second-guessed our so-called knowledge. Maybe prices were being changed at the machine as we spoke. Maybe Ms. Callaway got married, changed her name, and never told the students. And maybe the hospital was wrong about whether we were born a little before midnight or a little after.

"And if the penalty for an error was losing a limb?" Mr. Gardner asked.

The lesson: we don't really *know* anything. Not really.

To know something, he argued, was not the same as to be certain beyond all doubt. And to believe something was definitely not the same as to know it.

With that as a backdrop, I'd say the first time I *knew* Jason cheated was almost exactly two years ago. We had taken a rental in the Hamptons for six full weeks. The cost of renting a small cottage, half a mile from the ocean, was twice what my mother made in a year. That was the bizarro economy of the South Fork these days.

It was a splurge, but Jason assured me we could afford it. He had launched the consulting company and had extra money coming in, on top of the book money we had sunk into the house. We only had one car, of course—the Subaru, before Jason decided we should get the Audi—but that wasn't a problem. Most days, the three of us were together. To the extent we needed supplementary transportation, the rental house came with bikes. And I could always call my mom in a pinch.

That particular day, I had gone to Susanna's to help prepare for a dinner party. Jason said he had a meeting at a potential client's house in Bridgehampton, so Spencer tagged along with Mom on a housecleaning. I was riding my bike home from Susanna's when I thought I spotted our car parallel-parked on Montauk Highway, in the overflow parking area for Cyril's. It was postbeach cocktail hour, the time when people popped in for late lunch lobster rolls, predinner raw oysters, and a lot of frozen blender drinks.

I was stopped on my bike—one foot on the gravel, one on a paused pedal—next to my own car, watching my husband talk to a woman I'd never seen before. He was drinking beer from a pint glass, looking exactly like himself, but the woman was more easily readable. She was flirting. She flipped her long hair a lot, licked her glossy lips, maintained good eye contact. She could have given instructions in a magazine. When I saw her touch Jason's knee, part of me wanted to storm into the crowd, announce my presence, and ask Jason to introduce me to his friend.

I didn't. I pedaled back to our rented cottage and waited for him to come home. When he finally arrived almost three hours later, he immediately took a shower. I picked up his shirt, dropped so casually on the floor, and held it to my face. It smelled like the beach. That night, when he crawled into bed with me and held my hand, I fiddled with his ring. His tan line was faded.

Was it enough proof that I was willing to spend the rest of summer in school, or lose a limb? No, but all the signs were there. We hadn't touched each other—not that way—for more than a year. More hours away from home, with vague explanations for his whereabouts. That girl at Cyril's. He'd clearly taken off his ring. At that point, I "knew," to the extent that word has meaning. And yet I didn't say a thing. What Jason's attorney had called an "unspoken understanding" had been set into motion.

At the time, that's not how I thought of it. Even as I leaned on the borrowed bicycle in the gravel parking lot, watching him flirt with a stranger, I almost felt closer to him. It was part of the bargain that was now our life together. We were supposed to have a normal marriage, but one half of the couple—me—wasn't normal, so neither were we.

But I had lived with far more dangerous secrets, and so we went on.

# 31

Corrine immediately spotted two news vans when she pulled up in front of the special victims unit. A group of people clustered on either side of the walkway leading into the building.

Her original plan had been to fingerprint Powell at the Sixth Precinct, less than a mile from his address, then transport him to Central Booking on Centre Street. King disrupted that plan by instructing her to go to SVU instead. It wasn't the usual process, and it meant a round-trip drive to Harlem and back.

Now that she counted at least four cameras, she realized King had given SVU as the location for the perp walk. She actually felt bad for Powell as she marched him, still in handcuffs, through the gauntlet. He had no way to hide his face. She could feel him jerking away from each flash of a camera. Once they were inside and she unlocked the cuffs, the only thing he said was, "I have a thirteen-year-old son."

He stared straight ahead as she took his prints, followed by his mug shot.

The press was gone by the time she walked him out a mere thirty minutes later, having gotten what they came for. As she transported him to Central Booking, he remained silent. He didn't even ask to have the radio turned on, the way some people do, or ask where he was going next. His lawyer would have been pleased.

Once she was done with the paperwork at Central Booking, her plan was to head back to Powell's place. The wife would be home, glued to her phone. The lawyer was probably busy trying to get a head start on cutting him loose. If Corrine was lucky, she'd catch the wife alone.

She was three blocks away when she realized she wanted to know more about Angela Powell before knocking on her door. She pulled over and brought up the number she had saved for Detective Steven Hendricks in East Hampton.

*

"I just booked Jason Powell for rape."

Hendricks spoke like an old, experienced cop, his tone completely unfazed. "So how bad was it?"

These days, you weren't supposed to distinguish. Rape was rape.

"The victim had him up to her hotel room after dinner, but there's evidence of injury, and he denied all contact with her and we have DNA." Corrine believed you had to share some amount of information with other cops if you expected their cooperation. She was giving Hendricks enough to know that there were shades of a date-rape dynamic to the case, but more than a complete he-said, she-said.

"He's arguing consent?"

"Basically," she confirmed.

"Is there any way to keep the wife out of it? Angela's had a rough time of it, and this guy was supposed to be her happily-ever-after."

"My impression is that she's managed to keep her identity fairly private." She didn't tell Hendricks that she never would have known who Angela was had it not been for his phone number in her call records.

"Her parents made sure of it. I went with them to Niagara Falls when they got the phone call. I was the last person they wanted to deal with at the time, but they at least knew me. Angela was practically catatonic. They couldn't get her to hand the baby to anyone until she saw her mother."

"You didn't have a good relationship with the family?"

"The short version is, I could have tried harder. I thought she was a runaway."

"And that's why you've been trying to help her now."

"Pretty much. So how can I help her?"

"Convince her to jump off a sinking ship. The DA is determined to get a conviction. She could leave now, take half his money, and find a new happily-ever-after."

"I'd be the last person able to convince her."

"So who has her ear?"

"Her best friend is Susanna Coleman, but—"

"I'm not going through a journalist."

"Of course not. Which is why I was going to say the person she'd really listen to is her mother, Ginny. Her dad, Danny, died a few years back, but Ginny was always the one who looked out for Angela. I thought she was going to clock the doctor who wanted to examine Angela and the baby after they were rescued. The way she saw it, Franklin and the other kidnapping victim were dead. If the police wanted to keep investigating, that was their business, but she took her daughter and grandson home and told the Pittsburgh police to pound sand."

"Where'd the other girl come from?"

"Franklin picked her up in Cleveland. That sicko made the girls use fake names. I think Angela was called Michelle. She called the other girl Sarah. They didn't find the body for two weeks and never identified her, last I heard."

Corrine realized that part of her had been hoping Hendricks

would be close enough to the family to persuade Angela to start looking out for herself instead of her husband. It was still worth a try. "The husband will be arraigned tomorrow. I'm about to approach the wife now to see what she knows. What if you gave her a call first?"

"I think she'd hang up and take it out on you for having any association with me."

"Wow, she dislikes you that much?"

He paused on the other end of the line. "The only time that family let me do one thing for them was to help them get a birth certificate for Spencer—that's the son. I found a doctor willing to look at the police reports and say it was a home birth in Albany, father unknown, so Franklin's name wouldn't be anywhere near the baby's. They did thank me, but it wasn't enough to earn their forgiveness."

Corrine wondered which cases would continue to haunt her, years from now. She considered telling Hendricks not to kick himself, that every cop inevitably makes a wrong call. But she had no idea whether Hendricks was a good cop. Maybe he deserved to be blamed for what Angela went through.

She thanked him again for the information and started the car engine.

He offered her one more piece of advice. "If I had to guess, she's in denial. She built an entirely new life for herself and probably wants to think it's all going to be okay. If it starts looking dire, go to the mom. Ginny Mullen. Angela may think she's part of some other world now, but when push comes to shove, she trusts her mother more than anyone."

Eight minutes later, Corrine stood at Angela Powell's door.

# 32

I checked my phone again for updates. Nothing.

Have you heard anything? I sent the text to Colin and watched the ellipsis on the screen as he typed his response. How could a text message take so long?

They transported him to SVU in Harlem instead of the 6th Precinct. By the time Olivia got there, they were taking him back downtown for processing.

So what does that mean? I hit enter.

Dots, followed by That he won't get in front of a court until tomorrow. Sorry—at a client dinner and can't leave. Will call you ASAP. So sorry, A! Hang in there.

Two hours later, I was still alone. The house was so quiet, I was starting to regret turning down my mother's offer to come into the city for the night. I didn't want her to hear about Jason's arrest on the news, the way she'd heard everything else so far, but I should have known it wouldn't be a quick phone call. Of course she immediately asked about Spencer, so I had to tell her that I had sent him to camp, which led to an argument about why I hadn't sent him to her instead, or at least told her that her grandchild was going to be gone for weeks. Now, I would have happily continued that conversation, simply to have another person in the room with me.

I jerked when I heard a dull thump at the door. That hideous knocker was gone, so whoever was on our porch was intent on letting me know they were here.

I walked gingerly to the front door so I could check the peephole in silence.

I recognized the woman standing there as the detective who had read Jason his rights while a uniformed officer had placed him in handcuffs.

"Call our lawyer," I yelled through the door.

"You really want to talk about this through your door? There's people walking by on the street."

I unlocked the bolts and opened the door. If I had met this woman in a different context, my immediate reaction to her might have been a positive one. She had a heart-shaped face that seemed to rest in a natural smile. She had dark brown freckles and her only makeup was a little blush and some pink lip gloss. She stood with her feet a comfortable distance apart, making no effort to hide the extra pounds straining against the buttons of the crisp blue shirt beneath her blazer.

But tonight, she was the woman who had arrested my husband and then made sure to drag him around the city long enough that he couldn't make it home for the night. In her left hand was some kind of document.

"I don't have anything to say to you," I said, "and I'd appreciate it if you didn't yell implied threats for my neighbors to hear. If you're here with papers, you should go through Olivia Randall."

She held up her free hand. "I know you've got no reason to

trust me, but I'm actually here to help you, Angela. I'm Corrine. Corrine Duncan." She extended the same hand for a shake, but I didn't accept it.

"I never told you to call me by my first name."

"Mrs. Powell. It's Powell now, right? Not Mullen?"

I felt my knees give way beneath me.

The detective moved backward until she was one step down on our stoop. "The last thing I want is for you to be collateral damage because of something your husband's done."

"He didn't do anything." In the nearly twelve years since I came home, not a day had passed that I hadn't feared exposure, but I realized now that my worries had faded over time. Now they were raging in a way I hadn't felt since I first ventured outside my parents' house after going back to Springs.

"Obviously there's another side to that story," the detective said. "The district attorney's office agreed to charges. The judge signed an arrest warrant. Your husband looked me straight in the eye and told me he never touched the complainant in this case, and yet we have DNA evidence proving otherwise. I'm assuming he lied to you, too."

"I have spousal privilege," I said. "I don't have to talk to you."

"So you have a lawyer?"

"I told you before: Olivia Randall. I'm going to call her right now," I said, turning to retrieve my phone from the coffee table in the living room.

"She's your husband's lawyer, Mrs. Powell, not yours. And she'll do anything to win a case, including use you and anyone else in a position to help or hurt her client. I don't know what Randall told you, but the DA can subpoena you. A few of your private conversations might be protected, but other matters are fair game. What time did he come home? Did you notice anything unusual about his appearance or clothing? Things like that."

"I'm not going to help you railroad my husband. You should be investigating that woman and her company."

"The woman has a name—Kerry Lynch—and she's afraid right now. She's afraid of her name being printed. She's afraid of being blamed for what happened. She's afraid that her life's never going back to normal again. Does that sound familiar? It's natural to want to protect your husband, but open your mind for one second and just imagine that she's telling the truth. If that's the case, do you really want to help Olivia Randall victimize her a second time? This case isn't going away. No plea bargains. No probation deal. This is actually happening, Mrs. Powell. Will your husband still have a job pending trial? If he gets convicted, are you and your son going to visit him in prison? These aren't things Olivia Randall will help you with. She's looking out for Jason, not you."

"You're trying to scare me."

"I want you to ask yourself why you're so damn sure Jason's innocent. If it's based on evidence, then fine, stick with him, and we'll see which side wins at trial. But if it's only because you think you know him—"

The detective handed me the papers she was holding. It was marked as an incident report, dated that morning, documenting an interview with a woman named Lana Sullivan. She was a prostitute who claimed that Jason had picked her up three years earlier when she was walking the streets in Murray Hill. I flipped the page to find an explicit description of the sex acts she performed upon him inside our car when it was pulled to the side of the road near the playground by the UN. Whoever drafted the report should have been a professional writer. I could visualize every moment.

I handed the report back to the detective. I didn't want a copy in my home.

"I left out the part where your husband basically blamed you for the fact that he was hiring a prostitute."

I couldn't look away from her gaze.

"He told her that his wife had 'problems,' and that's why he needed to go elsewhere. I know about what happened when you were younger. I can't imagine what you went through."

No, you can't, I thought. "That was a long time ago. It has nothing to do with Jason."

"Unless it does. There's a pattern forming here, Angela. Your husband likes to have power over women."

What was she insinuating? That Jason had chosen me *because* of my past? That Jason was now targeting other women because I was no longer available to him? That I was only defending Jason because I had been trained to be subservient? All of the above? I knew I should throw her off my property, but the look in her eyes stopped me. There was something about the way she spoke to me, as if she was genuinely trying to protect me. Could empathy be faked this well?

I forced myself to break from her eye contact. "We're done here, Detective. I need to find my husband."

She nodded, but reached into her blazer pocket and handed me a business card. "I promise I'll keep asking myself every day, What if Jason's innocent? But please, like I said, just imagine for one second that he's not. Call me if you ever want to talk."

As I picked up the phone to call Olivia Randall, I tucked Detective Corrine Duncan's card inside my purse. I didn't want Jason to find it if he ever managed to get home.

# 33

I went to the arraignment the next morning. I wore the closest thing I had to a suit—a gray dress I had purchased for Jason's book launch, topped by a black blazer—thinking it would be like a trial. But the whole thing took less than ten minutes once Jason's name was finally called.

Jason was charged with one count of rape, and one count of attempted offensive physical touching for whatever happened in his office with Rachel Sutton. The one surprise was the date of the alleged incident with Kerry Lynch. It wasn't the week before, when he drove to her house in Long Island. It was supposedly on April 10, nearly two months earlier. I found myself wondering how she had chosen which of the many times she had fucked my husband to use for her false allegation.

His bail was set at $100,000. I watched helplessly as deputies placed him back in handcuffs and escorted him out of the courtroom. I had panicked, but Olivia explained that his bail only required $10,000 cash. Once I covered it, we were down to a four-digit balance, more than I ever had in savings before I met Jason, but still, I was worried.

By the time Jason got back to our place, it was after midnight. I was sitting on the sofa, flipping channels aimlessly, when I heard a key in the door.

I rushed to the door and gave him a hug. "I had no idea where you were." He smelled dank, and his eyes were bloodshot.

"I was wondering where *you* were," he said.

"What? I've been sitting here, waiting."

"My battery was dead, and I couldn't find a cab. I finally gave some guy forty bucks cash to order an Uber from the detention center."

We spent a few minutes blaming the police, corrections officials, and Olivia for the mix-up before he asked if Spencer had called.

I felt a tug in my chest. I had forced Colin to tell me what Jason would have been subjected to over the last twenty-four hours. He tried to gloss over the specifics, but I now knew that my husband, among other things, had to "squat and spread" for a full-body search to prepare for a jail cell. It was one glaring degradation among the smaller ones of handcuffs, transport, fingerprinting, photographing, churning him through the system like a widget in a factory. But despite all of that, Jason had remembered that tonight was supposed to be Spencer's first phone call.

The rule of thumb for Spencer's camp was that the kids could call home every two days to check in. "He called. He sounded great. Happy."

"Did you tell him anything?"

I shook my head. "That was the whole point of sending him there, right? And I spoke specifically to the camp counselor to make sure she hadn't heard a single whisper about it among the kids. It sounds like they run a really tight ship. No gadgets, no computers. I told him that you had something on campus tonight."

I didn't mention that Spencer hadn't asked about him.

"I'm sorry I doubted you about the camp. You made the right call. The thought of him seeing me . . ."

He looked exhausted.

"Are you okay, Jason?"

Without saying anything, he pulled me into his arms. I felt him shaking but by the time he released his grip, there was no sign of tears. "I'm so tired. I need a shower—"

"Of course."

As I heard the water run, I put on a black cotton tank top and a pair of black bikini panties. I brushed my teeth, climbed into bed, and dimmed my nightstand light to its lowest setting.

I could feel the steam from our bathroom when he walked out ten minutes later, a bath towel wrapped around his waist as he roughly dried his hair with a hand towel. "Damn, that felt good. Um, do you want me to go to Spencer's room or something?"

"No, I want you here." I folded the covers down on his side of the bed.

He dropped both towels to the floor and climbed in, rolling away from me, so I was facing his back. "Thank you for being there. Olivia thinks it helped with the bail."

I moved closer to him, draping my top arm across his waist. "We should talk about this, Jason. I'm still here for you."

He didn't move, and he didn't speak. I placed one hand on his stomach. When he didn't respond, I moved my palm down two inches. He sat up. "What are you doing, Angela?"

"I'm—I'm trying to be your wife."

"You *are* my wife."

"I'm trying to be close to you."

"Now? After I spent a day in jail? When I was sure I'd come home and find you gone?"

"I'm not going anywhere, Jason."

He jumped out of bed, picked up the bath towel from the floor, and wrapped it around his waist. He still looked so tired. "No. No, this is not how this is happening, Angela. Three years ago, you made it pretty damn clear you were through with this part of our marriage. And it took me getting accused of—" He couldn't bring himself to say the word. "No, I'm not doing this."

"Is this my fault?" I asked quietly, before realizing the words were coming out of my mouth. "I mean, I knew—or suspected, at least—that you weren't always at the office. You didn't always have a faculty meeting. You could go out with Zack. Flirt at a bar. Maybe more. I figured it was part of a deal, because of me, because it was a fair trade."

He was looking at the door, like he'd rather be back in whatever cell he slept in the previous night.

"I didn't know we were that far apart, Jason. The police were here. They told me about the woman who was in the car when you had that fender-bender in the Subaru. I saw the date. It was a couple of months after that night, when we were still in the old apartment. I'm not sure what's worse: the hooker or Kerry—you were never supposed to care about them."

"The police talked to you?"

"That prostitute remembered everything she did with you."

He was starting to cry. "Try to remember that you know me," he continued. "You're finding out every horrible thing I've done during our entire marriage, all at once. And I know it's terrible, but I'm still me. I'm still *in*—a hundred percent with you—if you are. I don't expect you to believe me, but that was the only time that happened. With a person like that, I mean. After that night—that fucking awful night that changed everything—I didn't know how to approach you that way again. I'd hold you, walk in while you were showering, all the old ways we used to get started. And you were . . . just . . . gone. And I missed you. And I felt so guilty for what I did to you, about how I must have made you feel that night. But I was angry, too. How many times had I suggested therapy? You could go alone, or with me, or with your mother. But you didn't. And I could see that you were still scarred. Of course you were. I've pretended to understand the decision your parents made, but—I'm sorry, Angela—it's totally whacko."

"I don't like to dwell on it. I thought you understood."

"I tried to, I really did. But before I knew it, we had that terrible night, and we were . . . broken. That's how fast it felt to me. Like we were perfect, and together, and then someone dropped us to the floor and we shattered like glass. And then I'm coming back from a meeting in Long Island and see this woman, and I just know why she's on the street. And, I swear, Angela, in my mind I justified it. I didn't want to cheat. I didn't want to connect emotionally to any other woman but you. It seemed like a way to do something empty and meaningless, without really crossing that line. The next thing I know, a taxi's sideswiping the car with this stranger in the passenger seat. I should have insisted right then and there that you and I make it right. That we fix the break. But instead, I kept making bad choices."

I remembered him, after that night, trying to convince me to go to therapy. It was the last time we ever spoke about the possibility until all this happened. But at the time, I didn't think it was my problem, or even his. It was just something that happened. It was us. We'd deal with it.

And then, about a year later, I rode by Cyril's and saw him flirting with that girl, and he came home with a filled-in tan line on his ring finger and the need to take a shower.

So I knew. He crossed that line, and I crossed it with him. That's how we dealt with it.

We both thought we had our secret, and we'd go on. But now the dangers of an "unspoken understanding" were clear. There had been no understanding at all. We had no meeting of the minds.

*I didn't want to connect emotionally to any other woman but you.* That's how he had felt when he picked up that hooker, but that's not how he felt after he met Kerry.

"So it *is* my fault," I said, trying to maintain my composure. "I'm the reason this is happening."

"Of course not. I'm just trying to explain what went on in my head, from my perspective."

"You had an affair, Jason. You cheated. It was more than three months, wasn't it?" He said nothing. "Please stop lying. I wish you would trust me that the worst part of this has been the lying."

Now, he didn't bother to hide the tears. He just shook his head.

"How long?"

"Longer than three months, okay?"

"The date they listed in court was in April, not that day you met her at her house. Was she planning this for two months?"

"I have no idea. Olivia thinks she picked a previous date so she could claim she only came forward after reading the news about Rachel. It might seem hard to believe that I'd do something even worse right after someone else filed a complaint."

"So were you with her that night? At the hotel?"

"Jesus, Angela, I don't know, okay? I didn't keep a log of every time I saw her. Right now, I'm worn out."

I imagined him going through his calendar, trying to reconstruct all of the nights he had lied to me to find time for her. Well, I had already beat him to it, studied all the possibilities. That night, he said a client was freaking out about quarterly financial reports. Now I had so many suspicions. The weekend he was supposed to be at Stanford. The trip to London last month. How much of it was bullshit?

"Did you love her?"

He closed his eyes, and I could feel his shame across the room. He slept in Spencer's bed that night.

*

When I woke up the next morning, he was already gone. So was his phone. So were his earbuds and running shoes.

When he got home an hour later, he was covered in sweat and had a yellow mailing envelope in his hand. "We need to call Olivia. I got served with papers. Kerry and Rachel are suing me."

# 34

The lawyer who sued Jason was even more famous than he was. Her name was Janice Martinez, and according to Wikipedia, she graduated from University of Michigan Law School, started out as a prosecutor in Brooklyn, and then opened a private practice specializing in "seeking justice for crime victims in civil court." *Glamour* had featured her as a "Fighter for Feminism" four years earlier. Airbrushed photos of her in Escada dresses and Louboutin heels accompanied summaries of her best-known sexual harassment and assault lawsuits.

She was the kind of lawyer who was known more for her work in front of a camera than in court, and she was milking her case against Jason for every bit of attention. Two hours after the process server stopped Jason on the sidewalk, Martinez held a press conference, which was carried live by the major cable news stations. She stood at a lectern at the head of a conference room filled with reporters and cameras, flanked by Rachel Sutton and Kerry Lynch.

Martinez explained that Kerry had come forward with her case only after seeing Rachel demonized on social media. "This is an example of women standing up for other women. Only because Rachel braved the storm did Kerry step into the light. We believe there may be other victims out there. I want them to know we are here for them. There is power in numbers."

The most serious claims were related to Kerry: battery and false imprisonment, which Olivia said was holding someone against their will, no matter how short the amount of time. Rachel was suing for intentional infliction of emotional distress.

I clicked off the television, thinking that I had more cause for emotional distress than either of these women.

I remembered that detective telling me that Olivia Randall was Jason's lawyer, not mine. It seemed like everyone had a lawyer looking out for them except for me.

I found the detective's business card, zipped in the smallest side pocket of my purse. She had written her cell number in cute, round digits along the bottom, followed by "24/7!"

I made a call, but not to Detective Duncan.

Susanna picked up immediately, in a hushed voice. "Hey."

"Did you see it?"

There was a pause, followed by, "I was there. I just walked out of the room. Angela, I'm so sorry. Janice Martinez doesn't take a case unless she expects major media attention and a huge payout."

# 35

Ginny was using the hose of a Dyson vacuum to suck up Cheerios beneath the Colemans' sofa cushions when Lucy walked into the den, a mop in one hand, her cell phone in the other. "Sorry, Gin, but Kayla texted from the salon. Your son-in-law's in the news again."

Ginny powered off the vacuum. "I know. He's out on bail. I tried getting Angela to come out here, but she's determined to be the good wife, standing by her man." She'd been sworn to secrecy by Angela about the actual facts of the case, but made a point to add, "It's more complicated than the news makes it sound. He's innocent."

"Okay, but turn on the TV. Kayla said there's some kind of press conference."

*

Ginny caught the tail end of it on the television in the Colemans' kitchen, enough to know that these women wanted Jason's head on a stick—and they wanted money.

She went to the driveway to call Angela out of Lucy's earshot. Angela answered with a depressed, "Hey."

"You need to let Jason deal with this on his own, Angela."

"Jesus, Mom, he's my husband. If someone had accused Dad of something horrible, would you have up and left him?"

"Your dad didn't cheat on me with some crazy woman who tried to ruin his life when she didn't get what she wanted."

Her daughter was so tough and so smart, but was also remarkably trusting, at least of the people to whom she was closest. Where most people might have a sliding spectrum of trust, Angela was all or nothing. She avoided strangers, assuming the worst about them. But she was loyal to a fault to the few people in her inner circle: Spencer, Ginny, Jason, Susanna, Colin. Ginny could murder someone, and Angela's response would be, "Well, they must have had it coming."

So, Angela being Angela, of course she didn't believe that Jason had actually victimized this woman. Ginny felt a sour taste in her mouth, just thinking about it. The way she saw it, where there's smoke, there's fire. Two accusations from two women? He was probably guilty of something.

But Jason was playing Angela like a fiddle. He had her so worried about protecting him that she was glossing over the fact that he wouldn't be in this boat if he hadn't cheated on her.

She was not going to let her daughter go down with the ship.

"He might be innocent of this charge—"

"Not 'might,' Mom."

"But he's not innocent. The man had an affair."

"He doesn't deserve to go to prison for that."

"No, but you also don't deserve to be miserable—or broke—because of what he did. I saw that lawyer on TV. Do you know who she is? She makes a living suing celebrities for their penis problems."

"Oh my God—"

"Wake up, Angela. Have you asked yourself what would make this woman lie?"

"I told you—"

"You told me what he told you, and I'm not buying it. No woman makes this up to help some company out of trouble. If she's lying—and that's a big *if*—it's because she's hurt. He made her feel bad enough that she thinks this is fair payback."

"I don't know what you're trying to say, Mom."

"I'm saying that maybe he made her *feel* victimized, even if it's not how the law sees it. He probably told her he loved her. Made her think he'd leave you to be with her. That she was going to be the one standing next to him when he ran for mayor. That she'd get to live in that fancy house. She's a woman scorned, Angela. He cheated on you—for months. He doesn't deserve your loyalty."

"Mom, please, stop."

Ginny could tell that her daughter was seconds away from hanging up on her. When she spoke again, her voice was softer. "Please, all I'm asking is that you talk to a lawyer. If these ladies take him to the bank, you'll lose everything too. At least try to protect what's yours and Spencer's, okay?"

Angela didn't argue, and she didn't hang up. Ginny hoped it was a sign that her point had been made.

"How's my grandson?" she asked.

She could hear a sad sigh on the other end of the line. "He sounded good when he called last night. They ride horses and do archery. He learned how to navigate his way out of the woods with a compass and to hang garbage from a tree so the bears don't come."

Ginny could tell how much her daughter missed Spencer. How long did she think she could protect him from the truth?

"And to think, he could have stayed with his grandmother for free instead of being dropped in the middle of the Hunger Games. My offer stands for you to come out here. Or I'll even go there."

Angela declined, as Ginny knew she would, but when she said "Thank you," she sounded like she meant it.

As Ginny was flipping radio channels on the drive home, a DJ was rating Angela and the two women who were suing Jason on a scale from 1 to 10. Apparently Angela would be an 8 or even a 9, except she seemed the type who would "just lie there like she was doing you a favor."

Her hands were still shaking on the steering wheel when she pulled into her driveway.

# 36

Jason was charged the day after he was arrested. He was sued the day after he was charged. And the day after he was sued, he was notified by the university that he was suspended from teaching immediately.

An hour before the last class of the semester, the dean appeared in his office, accompanied by the university's in-house counsel. His students were being notified by e-mail that class was canceled. Their final papers would be graded by another professor on a pass/fail basis. His interns did not need to finish their final week at FSS to earn their academic credit. He was prohibited from supervising or communicating with any students in his capacity as a professor until the cases against him were closed and the university had completed its own review.

Jason called me with the news as he was boxing up files on campus to move to the FSS offices.

"Are they still paying you?" I asked. I felt petty asking about money when his career was falling apart, but he was the one who had told me that we were on thin financial ice.

"I'll get my salary through the summer, but it's obvious they're going after my tenure. Olivia's going to find me an employment lawyer, but told me to stay away from campus for the time being."

"What did Olivia say about the lawsuit?"

"Not much. I'm supposed to meet with her at noon to talk about it. Colin said he'd go with me."

I pictured her logging more hours on her bill. I thought about that e-mail I had seen in Jason's account from the Department of Human Resources. He had had a question about his retirement account. Was he dipping into it?

"We can always sell the house," I offered.

"Jesus, Angela, where did that come from?"

"Well, with the legal fees, and the lawsuit—"

"We're not losing our home, do you hear me? I'm the one who fucked this up. I'm the one who's going to fix it, okay?"

"Okay, fine." I knew I didn't sound either okay or fine.

"I need someone to still have faith in me." I could hear his voice crack. I hated the idea of him crying alone in his office, wondering if he'd ever be welcomed back into it again.

"I still have faith in you," I told him. I just wasn't sure that faith was going to be enough.

*

Susanna called me from my stoop a little after two o'clock. She knew I was ignoring knocks at the front door.

She didn't bother sitting down. She took one look at me and went directly into the kitchen and opened the refrigerator. "There's no food in here," she declared. "No wonder you're skin and bones. Are you eating anything?"

I gave her a quick hug. "Did we switch roles when I wasn't looking? I'm usually the food pusher, and you're the one starving."

"That's because I'm the one still working on television next to a bunch of thirty-year-olds whose journalism credentials are a list of beauty pageants. You, my dear, are supposed to have a kitchen full of food."

"Spencer's at camp, that's all. Trust me, I'm eating. Your story today was really good, by the way—like a how-to manual for a juicy episode of *The Americans*." Susanna was beloved for her somewhat cynical but always cheerful morning banter, but I knew that this morning's segment about fake IDs had been the result of nearly a year of research. "So what will happen to the employees who played along? If you ask me, they deserve medals of honor."

"The one story I can't stop thinking about is Lucia's. If she hadn't gotten fake passports for her and her kids, her husband would have killed her when she tried to leave. And the passport clerk who handled the paperwork only did it because his sister couldn't afford chemo. So, yes, if you can set aside the mafiosos in the middle, you could say it's a win/win scenario."

I continued to press her for details about the ins and outs of her research for the story until she finally cut me off. "Okay, that's enough with the change of subject, missy. You're trying to avoid talking about the fact that you're not taking care of yourself."

"I'm fine."

She followed me into the living room and sat next to me on the sofa. "You don't sound fine." She was staring at me, and I could feel her reading my thoughts. I wanted to hide. "Are you thinking about leaving Jason?" she asked. "Because no one would blame you under the circumstances."

I shook my head.

"There's something else bothering you," she said, "more than what you've told me so far."

I hadn't seen her in person since we had lunch at the 21 Club before Jason was forced to tell me about his affair with Kerry, but I had given her the bare-bones version of developments since then. It wasn't the same as telling her what was really on my mind.

"Jason's lawyer wants to use my background as part of his defense."

Her eyes widened in disbelief.

"I know Jason's innocent," I said, trying not to cry, "and I want to help him, but it's not fair that I should have to pay the price for what he did."

"So then don't," she said, releasing me from her embrace. "Tell that lawyer it's off-limits."

"I'm not sure I trust her. She'll find a way to use it. She'll leak it to the press. Or just blurt it out in court before we can stop her."

"Tell Jason that if she utters one word about you, you'll leave him. Trust me: if she's trying to make him sympathetic, the image of you standing up in court and walking out will backfire."

"Except it *is* relevant, Susanna."

I could tell from her expression that she didn't see the connection.

"Jason and I don't—we haven't, you know, for years. And it's because of me. Olivia says it will make his affair more understandable if people knew that I wasn't . . . available to him in that sense."

"No," Susanna said, shaking her head adamantly. "No way. If he had an affair with this woman, then that's his defense. He'll get acquitted. And that's all he gets. He doesn't get to blame his infidelity on you, Angela. Please, I know you're determined to stand by him, but you don't owe him this."

"Except maybe I do. It's my fault. I've said all these years that the past is the past. That I started over again. That I'm fine. That I'm 'good and boring.' Except obviously I wasn't."

She placed an arm around me. When she spoke, she sounded less determined. "Why didn't you tell me all this, sweetie? I thought you guys were so perfect."

"We are. Or we were. I thought we were. We just didn't—" I rotated my hand as a substitute for the actual words.

"I'm sorry to pry, but why not? I mean, I remember when you first got married and stayed at my place while the guesthouse was being remodeled. I could hear you through the walls."

I placed my hands over my face. "So embarrassing."

"It wasn't *that* bad. But I'm serious, did something change? Or were you never really able to enjoy that with him? Was that . . . not real?"

I could tell that the latter explanation made her feel sad for me, as if I had missed something important in my life. The answer to all of her questions, I suspected, was yes. It was . . . complicated. I have no way of knowing what I would have been like if I had never gotten into Charles Franklin's car. But I did know that when I read magazines like *Cosmo* or *Elle*, or overheard women gossiping about sex at the parties I catered, I didn't feel like I was as comfortable with sex—or as happy about it, or as eager for it—as I was supposed to be. It's not as if I hated it, or even disliked it. I enjoyed the closeness of it, and had learned to appreciate the physical pleasure that came with it. I just didn't *need* it or necessarily want it, other than as an indication that my marriage was normal—that *I* was normal.

I saw no reason to explain all of that to Susanna right now, because her first question was the one that really mattered. Yes, something had changed in my relationship with Jason.

I decided to tell her. If I was going to tell anyone, it should be Susanna. "The last time we were together was three years ago, and I freaked out."

"What do you mean? Like a flashback?"

I was surprised that she used that precise word. I had only spoken to her once about my flashbacks, and only for the purpose of explaining why I had no interest in writing a book, doing an interview, or going to therapy. *Other than the rare flashback . . .*

"I don't know," I said. "Sort of. But it was bad. I cried, and we fought, and—" I was surprised at how upset I was getting, remembering what had happened that night.

"Sex with your husband shouldn't make you cry. If you were having a hard time, because of what you went through, he should have understood. And sometimes people simply aren't in the mood. It doesn't have to be a whole thing."

"He—I don't think he knew."

"He didn't know what?"

"That I didn't want to—" I was shaking my head, beginning to cry.

"Angela, please, it's me. Just tell me. If Jason did something to you that you didn't want him to do—"

I heard the front door open, followed by the sound of voices. Jason was back from his meeting with Olivia, and Colin was with him. I wiped my face with the back of my sleeve and put on a smile.

Jason paused to give me a quick kiss on the head and to say hello to Susanna, and then headed upstairs. He closed the door of his den.

I asked Colin how the meeting with Olivia went.

"She actually said the civil lawsuit was good news."

"Someone might try explaining that to Jason," Susanna said. "I've got to be honest: he looks worse than I even expected."

Colin glanced up the stairs to make sure that Jason was out of earshot. "Honestly, I think part of him was still in denial. He really thought this was going to go away. Today was a wake-up call. The university's going after him, plus three major clients called FSS today and pulled out."

I found myself wondering whether Jason had planned to tell me about the clients.

“None of that sounds like good news,” Susanna said.

“Olivia thinks it might be,” Colin explained. “The civil case makes Kerry look greedy, which plays into what Jason’s been saying all along. Olivia says she can use it to call into question Kerry’s motive.” I hated hearing that woman’s name used in my house. “Plus, a civil suit means we can use civil discovery.”

He must have realized that I hadn’t followed his last point.

“Civil cases have different rules for getting access to evidence. In a criminal trial, prosecutors sit tight on most information. But now that Kerry has sued, Olivia can demand access to the evidence because it’s relevant to the civil suit. Most importantly, Olivia can depose Kerry, meaning she can question her without a jury sitting there.”

I noticed that he was only talking about Kerry, as if Rachel didn’t even matter.

“So does that mean Martinez can depose Angela?” Susanna asked. I hadn’t thought of the possibility.

“I suppose, but I can’t imagine why she would.” Susanna gave my hand a brief squeeze as Colin tried to strike a lighter tone. “Trust me: She was going to sue him eventually, so it’s better that she did it in time to screw up the criminal case. Now, I’m going to drag Jason out of his office so I can make the two of you eat something.”

As Colin walked up the stairs, Susanna placed her hand on my forearm and jumped right back into our previous conversation. “You need to tell me what happened between you.”

I shook my head. For three years, I had blamed myself for breaking what I hoped was only a small part of our marriage. Now I didn’t know what to think. What I did know was that I still wasn’t ready to talk about it.

*

We ate lunch at Lupa in silence. While the waiter was running Susanna's credit card—she insisted—Jason got a text message from Olivia Randall. She was filing a motion for access to all evidence held by the NYPD and the district attorney's office. She also wanted to suspend the criminal case against him while the civil suit was pending.

"So what does that mean?" Jason asked, looking to Colin.

"Do it," Colin said. "You hit pause on the criminal charges to deal with the civil case first. If you reach a financial agreement, the criminal charges might go away."

Susanna shot me a concerned look. Colin was already talking about a settlement. I heard Jason's phone *bloop* as he hit the send key.

"I told you that lawsuit might be a blessing in disguise," Colin said as we walked out of the restaurant.

Nothing about this felt blessed.

Spencer called that night from camp. Jason was home, but Spencer refused to talk to him. I wanted to tell him how much his father needed to hear his voice, but the whole point of sending him away had been to protect him from what was happening at home.

"How long do you plan to freeze him out?" I asked.

"However long he was cheating on you. How does that sound?"

He had only been gone four days, and it felt like I hadn't seen him for months. I tried to tell myself it was worth it. At least in his mind, his father's only crime was an affair. But camp wouldn't last forever.

# 37

"What do you know about Mozambique?"

Thanks to all their calls on the Jason Powell case, Corrine immediately recognized the number as ADA Brian King's. "You're kidding me, right? I'm African American, not East African."

"That's not what I meant. And you at least knew it was in East Africa, so you know more than I do."

"Why the geography quiz?" she asked.

"I was reading up on Kerry Lynch's employer."

Corrine knew that Powell's attorney was threatening to turn the trial into an indictment of Kerry's employer for some kind of kickback scheme.

"Is it bad?" Corrine asked.

"I have no idea. I just wasted an hour educating myself on private water companies that serve developing countries. Getting clean water into those areas of the world can literally save lives, but it also involves doing business with some sketchy regimes."

"Sketchy regimes? Is that an official State Department designation?"

"What am I, the Council on Foreign Relations? This stuff's way over my head. Apparently a bunch of companies have stopped doing business in parts of the world that are most in need of water. Oasis, on the other hand, continues to land privatization contracts, making them darlings among Jason Powell's crowd."

"But maybe raising questions about how they're able to venture where others won't?"

"Well, that's what Olivia Randall says, and it doesn't help that Kerry had an affair with the CEO. And meanwhile, Kerry won't talk to me about it. I called Oasis's in-house counsel with some general questions, and they basically told me to piss up a rope. This trial's going to be a shit show—if it even goes."

King had already been nervous about the complicated arguments Olivia Randall was promising to raise at trial, and that was before Kerry surprised them yesterday by filing a civil suit in the highest-profile manner imaginable. Corrine respected Janice Martinez's work on behalf of crime victims, but she also knew that the woman's priority was not obtaining a criminal conviction and sentence. She believed in punishment through the pocketbook. Now she was insisting that all communications with Kerry go through her, and was refusing to let Kerry answer any questions about her employer or her affair with Tom Fisher, insisting that those topics were irrelevant.

"I also read up on Powell himself."

"Sounds like you did a lot of reading today."

"I found an article he wrote for *Huffington Post* a year ago about the kinds of good works private companies are doing around the world—water purification systems like Oasis, low-cost solar lighting for third-world regions, a nutritional supplement that could cut infant mortality rates by a third in mothers without proper nutrition. The jury's going to want to give him a medal."

"Except they know by now that a man can be solid on his politics and a predator behind closed doors."

Corrine considered once again whether she should tell King

what she had learned about Angela Powell's past. If he was worried about the jury seeing Jason Powell as a saint, it certainly wouldn't help matters if they learned that he had married the woman who survived Charles Franklin's horrific abuse and raised the son she had borne as a result. Corrine was actually surprised that Powell's own lawyer hadn't lobbed the information into the public yet. But if she had to guess, Angela was the one blocking that move. That detective in East Hampton had made it clear how hard the family had worked to keep the past in the past.

Having now spoken to the woman face-to-face, Corrine had no doubt that Powell's wife had spent years developing a carefully crafted persona. She hadn't flinched when Corrine told her about the prostitute. Standing quietly by her husband was one thing, but Corrine couldn't imagine Angela jumping into a spotlight for him.

Corrine decided to keep the information to herself for now.

"Unless he's not a predator," King was saying. "If he was having an affair with Kerry and had suspicions about Oasis, it would make sense that he'd go to her to see what she knew. But maybe he made a mistake trusting her."

She quickly ran through the logic of Powell's defense. If Kerry believed that Powell was going to bring down Oasis, her own livelihood was on the line, too. She could have told her bosses—including the one she once had an affair with—that Jason was a problem, and then used their relationship to fabricate a sexual assault claim on the heels of Rachel's initial complaint against him.

"You should have gone to law school, Duncan. That was a magna cum laude summary right there."

"I hate to break it to you, but I make more money than you with OT, and can retire in five years with a pension. You can keep your JD."

"You sure you won't go out with me?"

"Stop asking. It's getting sad. If I didn't know better, I'd say you're starting to believe Powell."

"Don't quote me on this, but I don't know what to think at this point. It bothers me that Powell knew so much about Kerry's relationship with her boss. It makes me think he's telling the truth about the affair."

"You do know a woman can be raped by someone she's had consensual sex with before, don't you?"

"You don't need to fem-splain sex offenses to me."

"Please don't try to make that a word."

"Look, I get it: I've prosecuted plenty of date rapes. Marital cases, too. But Kerry's denying any kind of relationship with Powell. It comes down to her credibility."

"If she had come in saying she'd had an on-and-off affair with some consultant at work, and one night he forced himself on her, what would you have done when she reported it weeks later?"

He didn't respond.

"I mean, hypothetically, if she did have something going with Powell, does that really matter?"

"I take it back. You shouldn't have just gone to law school. You should have taught it, Socratic method and all."

"The point is, Kerry might have lied about some things, but not the ones that matter. Maybe she thought we wouldn't believe her unless it looked less like date rape and more like 'rape-rape.'" She used her free hand to make air quotes.

"That's not going to fly with a jury," King said. "And if I even hint to Janice Martinez that I'm questioning Kerry's account, she'll make me look like a misogynist Neanderthal with the press."

"So you put on your case, and let Powell do the same. Let the chips fall as they may. Isn't that what juries are for?"

"That's not how it works, and you know it."

It seemed to Corrine as if that's exactly how it worked—or at least, should work. King seemed to think that it was his job—and his alone—to decide who should be punished and by how much.

"Anyway, I don't know why I brought all this up. I was calling to tell you I got a subpoena from Olivia Randall, demanding access to our evidence because it relates to the civil case. Plus, she wants to suspend our prosecution until the lawsuit is resolved."

The implication was clear. If they settled the civil suit, a joint request to dismiss the criminal case would be part of the package. "So what are you going to do?"

"What can I do? I'll turn over what we have. As far as the timing goes, maybe you're right. Let the chips fall. If the case goes away, it's on Janice Martinez."

As Corrine hung up, she could feel the case slipping away. Whatever was going to happen now would happen. Her work was done.

# 38

*Three Days Later*

What do you wear to court for your husband's rape case?

I stood in my walk-in closet, remembering how absurdly fantastical it had felt when Jason and I first viewed the carriage house with our realtor—Julia, Juliette, Julianna, whatever her name was. The closet was nearly as big as my bedroom at Mom's house, and it was in Manhattan, where everything was supposed to be smaller.

Now, two years after we'd moved in, the closet was still less than half full. I never was a clothes person. What did I really need? Jeans and T-shirts, some sweaters, a few dresses for special occasions. I opted for my go-to navy Trina Turk jersey dress, with three-quarter sleeves, A-line cut, and above-knee hem—originally purchased for Dad's funeral.

I made a point to blow-dry my hair perfectly—the attachment aiming down on a big, round brush. I was careful with my makeup, using the expensive brushes pushed on me by the Sephora salesgirl instead of my fingers. I checked the mirror before I left the bedroom. Not bad.

Jason was waiting for me at the bottom of the stairs. If you didn't know the context, you might have guessed it was our anniversary or some other special occasion. Sometimes I forgot how merely looking at him used to make me feel.

"Olivia still doesn't know whether she'll be there?"

Jason shook his head and popped a Nicorette from his pocket into his mouth.

*There* was the courthouse. *She* was Kerry Lynch.

We held hands as we walked out the door, a driver waiting for us outside. *Please don't let her be there.*

*

When we entered the courtroom, I spotted Janice Martinez at the front of the spectators' rows, conferring with a male lawyer on the other side of the bar. I assumed he was the prosecutor. A quick scan revealed neither Kerry Lynch nor Rachel Sutton. When Martinez sat alone in the first row as the judge finally took the bench, I allowed myself a sigh of relief. Coming there with Jason had been hard enough. I did not think I was strong enough to be in the same room with that woman.

Twenty minutes and two cases later, I flinched when I heard the courtroom door open. I snuck a quick glance over my shoulder, steeling myself for Kerry's entrance. The late arrival was Susanna. She had promised to do her best to make it after *New Day* aired, but her schedule was notoriously unpredictable.

She gave me a light pat on the knee and slid a few inches down the bench. The courtroom was full of reporters.

It felt as if all eyes were on me as the bailiff called Jason's case and the judge asked Olivia about the pending motion.

"Your Honor, our motion seeks two objectives—one that I believe is uncontroversial, one that may require explanation. In the interests of efficiency—"

"You decided we should err on the side of discussion. Oh joy. Please tell me."

According to Olivia, the judge, Betty Jenner, was far more

defense-oriented than she appeared. In her spare time, she apparently loved wine, art, and the theater. In the courtroom, she enjoyed unleashing her dry wit to keep lawyers on their toes.

I followed along while Olivia recited the dates of Jason's arraignment and the filing of the civil suit. "I have filed several demands for discovery, including subpoenas to ADA King for access to any evidence pertaining to the lawsuit filed by Ms. Martinez." Olivia also listed a host of reasons to set over Jason's criminal case while the lawsuit was pending.

The few times I'd seen Olivia in person, she seemed so normal. Better than normal, really. Sexy, confident, a little bit mean. I even wondered if she and Colin had something going on. Now, in court, she seemed completely different. My mind wandered, thinking about how most people spent their whole lives playing a character. Not me, or at least I didn't think so.

The judge was asking the prosecutor, Brian King, his position on Olivia's request for evidence.

"Your Honor, the subpoena was served only three days ago."

"So I gather you haven't turned anything over yet." She did not sound happy with the response.

"Some of the evidence is digital, and to be honest, we were caught off guard by this civil suit."

The judge offered a wry smile, appearing to appreciate the backhanded comment. "So what you're telling me is that the discovery is forthcoming? Do we have a date?"

"Imminent, Your Honor."

"Oh, imminent. How exciting. Should I set my Apple Watch?"

"End of business today."

"Five o'clock. Excellent. Now, I'm assuming that was the easy part. What are we doing about two cases pending about the same subject matter?"

"They're not the same," the prosecutor said. As he defended the difference between a private civil suit and a criminal prosecution brought by the state, I remembered a lawyer explaining the same thing to me when my parents filed a lawsuit on my behalf against the estate of Charles Franklin. He was dead, so we couldn't send him to prison, but I still had a civil suit to pursue. It turned out that a Pittsburgh contractor could afford a house and a Lexus and only have a total net worth of about a hundred and fifty grand, but it allowed my parents to hold on to their house until I started pitching in, too.

The prosecutor concluded his remarks by suggesting that both cases could proceed separately and simultaneously.

"And what do your complainants desire, Mr. King?"

"You'd have to ask Ms. Martinez, Your Honor."

The judge's eyes widened. "You haven't consulted with your own victims?"

"Our communications are going through Ms. Martinez, who, when notified of the defendant's motion, decided to appear today personally."

"Well, how courteous, and I'm sure not at all related to the number of reporters here."

A few chuckles broke out in the courtroom. How could anyone find this humorous? My husband's future was at stake.

Maybe I was biased, but Janice Martinez's voice struck me as nasal and screechy. "Judge, I represent two women in the pending civil case against Jason Powell. As I already explained to both Ms. Randall and ADA King, my clients aren't officially taking a position on the current motion. However, I would like to note that having two cases pending at once would likely lead to delays in both."

"That sounds to me like a position, Ms. Martinez."

"Simply an observation."

"Uh-huh. You don't have a preference to resolve the criminal case first?" The judge was tapping her fingers on her bench, appearing to make a point that was lost on me.

"No, Your Honor."

The judge nodded, as if some suspicion had been confirmed.

The prosecutor must have understood the unspoken exchange of information, because he jumped in to stop whatever was about to happen. "This move is a blatant attempt by the defendant to use the civil case to buy his way out of the criminal justice system. Once the parties reach a financial settlement, Ms. Randall will argue that it affects the validity of our criminal case."

Both Olivia and Martinez interjected. Olivia called the prosecutor "paranoid." Martinez said the argument was "offensive."

The judge wasn't happy, either. "I'd be careful, Counselor. If I didn't know better, it sounds like you're accusing your own victims of being open to the idea of selling their testimony, and I'm sure you didn't mean to suggest such a thing. Now, in the interests of judicial economy—"

The prosecutor was already shaking his head, hands on hips. Something in my gut told me he was the one who was right.

"You have something to say, Mr. King?" the judge asked. "If not, I'm tolling this prosecution for thirty days. Unless there's some problem, I expect not to hear from any of you until then. Ms. Randall, Ms. Martinez—it sounds like the two of you should talk."

*

Outside the courtroom, Olivia asked if she could borrow Jason alone. As they made their way to the far end of the hallway, a man I recognized from the courtroom started to follow them, but Olivia turned around and barked, "Get near me while I'm talking to a client, and I'll never talk to the *Post* again." The chastened reporter dashed to the elevator in time to catch the closing doors.

Once Susanna and I were alone, I asked her if she understood the judge's decision.

"It sounded to me like those women are willing to take money instead of going forward with the criminal case."

"Isn't that bribery?"

"It's a fine line. You can't pay a witness for silence, but if the parties reach a settlement, the DA might drop the charges. At the very least, any judge would read between the lines and be lenient in sentencing."

"I guess that's good news overall, right?" I couldn't believe that paying off my husband's mistress and intern passed for good news these days.

"Well, I'm afraid I have bad news."

She led me to a nearby bench to sit down. "Wilson Stewart, that intern who hooked up with Rachel, called me. That's why I was late."

I felt a knot tightening in my stomach.

"He wanted me to know that he exaggerated what he said."

"How so?"

"He said he made her sound flakier and more histrionic than she really is. He also said Jason's lawyer made it clear that Jason was impressed with his work and was looking forward to helping him land in a good job, but that he couldn't do that if he was brought down by a false claim."

"Honestly? I don't put anything past that woman. I'm just glad she's on our side, not theirs."

"To be clear, Wilson still says he has no idea what really happened and has never seen Jason be anything but professional."

"Uh-huh," I said vacantly.

"So did you know Olivia had dangled a job recommendation

in front of him before I agreed to have him on the show?"

I said nothing. What does it really mean to "know" anything?

"Angela, you let me put a man on television to lie."

"I didn't think he was lying. Olivia was the one who set it all up—"

"And you just said she would do anything to win. Yet you allowed her to pull me into it."

"I'm sorry, Susanna. I don't know what else I can say. Please don't be mad at me right now. I don't think I can get through this without you."

She shook her head. "I'm not *mad* at you. I'm just really caught off guard by this. Maybe there's more to what happened with that girl in his office, in which case—"

"There's not, Susanna. Jason's no saint, but he's not some sex maniac."

"You said the other night that something happened between you. Something bad, and that's when the two of you stopped . . ." She didn't need to finish the sentence.

I didn't understand the transition from my point to hers until I let it sink in. "No. Oh God no. It was nothing like that, I swear."

"Then what was it?"

"I told you. I just freaked out. And then I think he was scared to be with me after that."

"That's not how it sounded when you were talking about it. You said something bad happened, and that you cried. You said you 'didn't think he knew that you didn't want to,' and then you clammed up. You were making excuses for him for *something*, Angela. What did he do to you?"

I heard Olivia cough and turned to see her heading toward us, Jason right behind her. Susanna reached into her bag and pulled out a thin stack of stapled papers, folded in half, and tucked them in my purse discreetly. "I printed something out for you. Promise me you'll read the entire thing and think about it with an open mind. I hope I'm wrong, but please, promise me."

"Fine. Of course."

She gave me a hug after walking us to our waiting car. I turned my head as I spotted a photographer in the distance. She told me again that she didn't need a ride anywhere and waved as we pulled from the curb.

While Jason checked his e-mail on his phone, I snuck a peek inside my purse, parting the fold in the papers to read the headline of the article Susanna had printed for me: "Why Women Don't Always Know When They've Been Raped."

I snapped my purse shut at the sound of Jason's voice. "King wasn't kidding about imminent."

"Huh?" I was still trying to process the words I had just read.

"Olivia texted me. She already got a zip file from the DA with their discovery. He must have hit the send key right after the hearing."

"Oh."

"She's going to send me a summary with any questions she has."

"Sounds good." More hours billed. Good for her, bad for us.

"Thanks again for coming with me. I know it's not easy."

"It's fine." He reached over to hold my hand, but I pretended not to notice.

I listened as he worked out plans to take our car to the dealer the next morning. I resisted the urge to tell him that six days had passed since I had reminded him we needed a service. The world didn't stop turning because of his legal problems.

"You don't need it this week?" he whispered.

I shook my head. Where was I going to go?

"I'll get a loaner just in case."

I could tell from his expression that he was proud of himself for his own thoughtfulness.

# 39

From: Olivia Randall
To: Jason.Powell@nyu.edu
Re: Discovery from NYPD/DA
Date: June 6

Good morning, Jason. I went through the zip file ADA King sent me yesterday. Most is what we expected: statements from Rachel, Kerry, Zack, Wilson, and you; DNA testing; footage from W Hotel on the night of the alleged incident. There are a couple of surprises, however:

1. In the hotel surveillance footage, you and Kerry appear to be arguing as you leave her room. You continue to look upset once you are in the elevator alone. They will depict it as her ejecting you from her room, and you appearing nervous/scared/regretful afterward. They will argue that this proves that your sexual encounter that night was not consensual.

2. In Kerry's statement (attached), she claims that when she rejected your advances, you grabbed her, threw her to the bed, and bound her wrists with your leather belt. Contained in discovery were photographs that purport to be injuries of Kerry's wrists. What I see in the images (also attached) appears

consistent with very tight binding (no broken skin, but visible bruising).

3. A police report from a car accident three years ago. Your passenger was Lana Sullivan, whom police interviewed last week. She claims you hired her for prostitution that night.

We should meet to discuss further, but in the meantime, give some thought to the following questions:

1. Do you recall an argument with Kerry that night at the W? Why you might have appeared upset?

2. As we discussed, the DNA on the clothing she gave to NYPD cannot be linked to a specific date. The items are described as a black skirt and black underwear (no further details), turned over in a plastic bag marked with a W Hotel insignia. (She is wearing a black skirt in the W Hotel surveillance video.) It's easy to imagine that she might have had a spare laundry bag from a hotel chain she uses regularly. Do you recall if Kerry was wearing a black skirt and underwear the last time you saw her? I would like to argue that the DNA was from an encounter you had with her after Rachel Sutton's complaint became public.

3. Photos of injuries. I can argue that these aren't authenticated; there's no way to establish that the injuries are of her, or could be self-inflicted. But we should discuss whether you have an alternative explanation.

4. Regarding the prostitution report: any judge would likely suppress this as irrelevant and prejudicial, but I have concerns this could get leaked. You've been reluctant to disclose details of

other extramarital activities to me, but the fact that they tracked down a prostitute from three years ago means they are searching for a pattern of misconduct. Janice Martinez will do the same. We should discuss what that narrative will look like if it all goes public. On that note: any movement regarding Angela's position on this point? I know she's concerned about protecting her background, but there would be no need to mention Pittsburgh, etc., although that would of course be ideal.

A sit-down interview with a friendly outlet—maybe her friend Susanna—would be very well-timed. All she'd need to say is that whatever understanding the two of you had is a private matter and that she has full confidence in your innocence. She did not seem receptive when I broached the subject. I know you're not willing to ask directly. I plan to discuss with Colin.

# 40

When Colin called and offered to bring lunch, I was expecting takeout Chinese or deli sandwiches. Instead, he arrived with a shopping bag with the logo of Gotham Bar & Grill.

He began unpacking carefully stacked containers from the bag. "I know how cooped up you've been. I figured I could at least bring the best of the city to you." My trip to the courthouse with Jason the previous day had been a rare excursion from the house.

"You're not working today?" He was wearing a fitted plaid shirt and jeans instead of his usual Big Law suit.

"A closing got postponed. Figured I deserved a day off."

Opening the containers, I spotted all of my favorite dishes: tuna tartare, seafood salad, mushroom risotto, sliced duck breast, a pork chop. "Is a small army joining us?"

"I wanted you to have some choices, and I figured you and Jason could use the leftovers."

I started to get plates from the cupboard, but he stopped me. "Go have a seat." I sat at the kitchen table while he pulled dishes, silverware, and glasses from the cupboards. A stranger watching us would have assumed he lived here. The finishing touch was the final item waiting in the bag: a bottle of Sancerre, wrapped in a chiller sack.

"You are an angel," I said as he took a seat next to me.

I was three bites in when he told me I looked happy. "I can't remember the last time I saw you smile."

"Shows how much I like my food." I was surprised at how content I felt, even though I knew it was fleeting. Jason was gone for the day—his first full workday since his arrest. He was suspended from the university and had lost several clients, but had scheduled back-to-back meetings with the few remaining ones who had agreed to meet with him. Against my advice, he was also planning on recording an episode of his podcast, his first appearance on the program since I'd first heard of Kerry Lynch. He insisted that it had to be done. Zack had been carrying on without him, but the Equalonomics brand was Jason's. He seemed oblivious to the increasing numbers of one-star reviews being posted on iTunes of the podcast: "Politically correct sex offender. Irony much?" "Boycott the asshats still advertising on this program." "Will he be able to pod from prison?" "Of course this sanctimonious libtard is a rapist. Totally predictable."

There was a reason I hadn't been leaving the house for meals, or anything else, for that matter. And until this day, Jason had been home too. Only a few weeks ago, that would have been enough to make me happier than any kind of extravagance, but the past two weeks had felt stifling and heavy. This house had become joyless.

I reached for the duck and slid another slice onto my plate. It was only then that I realized Colin didn't look quite as happy as I felt in that moment.

I put my fork down and shook my head. "I'm so stupid."

"What—"

"It's no coincidence you called the first day Jason's out of the house, here in your casual clothes with this amazing meal. Did he send you here? What news does he want you to break? What is it now?"

He reached over and placed a calming hand on my wrist. "Angela, I promise. Jason doesn't even know I'm here." He removed his hand and held it up in a scout's honor for emphasis.

I believed him. "I'm so sorry. I'm just— I'm constantly on edge, like everyone's watching me. Talking about me. Judging. I can't keep living like this."

"I totally understand."

When I continued eating, the food didn't taste as good. I took another sip of my wine.

"You do know me so well, though," Colin said. I waited for him to explain. "I promise that I was coming here anyway, with food already ordered, and wine already chilled. But that look you saw on my face just now—I was trying to muster up the courage to talk to you about something. Susanna called me while I was on my way to Gotham."

"And?"

"She wanted to know the implications to you and Spencer of this lawsuit against Jason. Is something going on?"

"Of course something's going on. That woman's trying to take us for every dime she can get. I'm sure Susanna's just worried about me, but I'm not stupid. We could end up broke. I've already thought about that. I can go back to catering. Spencer can go to public school. The good thing about growing up poor is that you already know what it's like."

The thought of returning to the East End was intolerable. We could go somewhere else and start over. Scottsdale or Tampa. One of those places that normal people go to.

"It wasn't merely a general sense of worry, Angela. Susanna specifically asked me whether you could protect yourself by filing for divorce before any kind of judgment is entered."

I sighed. "The thought never crossed my mind. I'll talk to her. Don't worry about it."

"But that's why I came over. It never crossed my mind, either, and I realized I owe you an apology for that. When this all came down, I told you—as your friend—that you didn't have to stay. And you told me you wanted to, at least to get Jason through this. But I didn't talk to you about that decision as a lawyer. And since then, all I've been trying to do is help Jason."

"Me too."

"Just hear me out so I can live with myself. If you filed for divorce now, there's a good chance that you could take your part of the assets and shield them from a judgment. You could get the house—"

"I could never afford to carry it—"

"That's not the point. You'd have the equity. Half of his pension, half the liquid assets. It's possible they'd argue that your settlement with Jason was a sham to try to protect assets, but given the nature of the allegations against him, it would look completely legitimate. And if you and Jason get back together down the road, well, then, so be it. A court's not going to stop you from getting remarried. Or, who knows? Maybe you'd want to be on your own by then."

"Does Jason know you're telling me this?"

"No, and at this point, I honestly don't give a fuck if I'm violating professional ethics. I figured I'd tell you the options, and if you want me to talk to him about it, I'm happy to. If not, I'll never bring it up again. Not to defend much of what Jason has done, but he really is trying to protect you."

"It doesn't always feel that way."

"I probably shouldn't tell you this, but since I'm an open book today, Olivia Randall called me yesterday. She wanted me to see if you'd do some kind of public interview, basically saying you and Jason had an open marriage." Before I began to respond, he had a rebuttal prepared. "I told her you would never agree to that, and as your friend, I would never suggest it. Importantly, she said that Jason refused to ask you, too."

"That woman's a pit bull."

"Well, she's Jason's pit bull."

"She's really good, huh?"

"Yeah. That's why I recommended her. Up there with the very best."

"Plus, she's a woman," I said.

"Well, yes. It doesn't hurt to have a woman speaking up for you on this type of a case."

"She's pretty, too." I blurted what I had been wondering since I first met her: "Are you guys a thing?"

"We went out a few times. It was a while ago. Olivia's not—a relationship person. Why did you ask?" His eyes were filled with a blend of fear and hope. I remembered the way a certain look from Jason used to be able to stir something overwhelming in me. I felt a yearning for something I never thought I would miss.

I shrugged, but held his gaze. "I was just wondering. It seemed to make sense, the two of you, together."

"No, of the women I've let slip by, she's not the one who makes sense for me."

The one. The one he wished he had met at Susanna's party the night she met his best friend instead.

"That thing you said about splitting things up, what do you think I should do?"

He sighed heavily. "Please, don't ask me that. I'll do anything else for you, but not that. He's still my friend."

"And I'm still his wife."

He looked up at the ceiling. "Fuck, I hate this."

I leaned toward him, pausing to see if he'd stop me. He didn't. I kissed him, gently at first, and then so urgently, I was on my feet, leaning into him.

"Angela, wait—"

"You said anything. You'd do anything."

He drew in his breath.

"This is what I need right now," I whispered. "I need this."

The first time was clumsy and frenzied, almost violent, the edges of the cold kitchen tile scraping against my back. When it was over, he rolled me on top of him and held me in his arms. I didn't speak because I didn't want him to leave. I remained perfectly still while he held me, stroked my hair, tickled the small of my back, whatever he wanted. When I felt him respond beneath me, I slid lower, not worrying about whether those flashbacks that came and went beyond my control would suddenly return. I took him by the hand and led him upstairs, opting for Spencer's room only because I didn't want Colin to see reminders of Jason and stop what we had started.

I didn't care that I was in my son's bed, or with Jason's best friend. For the next two hours, I wasn't a mother, and I wasn't a wife. I was with this man who knew me and wanted me and had made me want him, at least for this day. We did everything I wanted, at the pace I set, and when we were finally done, I asked him to leave and to never mention it again.

When he was gone, I ate the food he had brought until I couldn't take another bite, then went upstairs to my room to reread, once again, the printout that Susanna had given me at the courthouse.

# 41

I was freshly showered and getting ready to leave a voice mail for Susanna when she picked up. "Oh thank God, I was starting to think you were never going to speak to me again."

"That would never happen." I hadn't talked to her since we were at the courthouse yesterday.

"I was giving myself one more day before I was going to call you."

"But you did call Colin," I said.

"He told you?"

"Of course he did. You asked him whether I should get a divorce."

"Honey, please don't be mad at me. I am seriously worried about you. What you said to me the other day about Jason—that's not normal in a marriage. You've got me looking at this whole thing in a different light."

"You think he's guilty."

"No, I didn't say that." The way she said it made it clear that she didn't *not* say it either. "Hear me out. I don't think it's for me, or even you, to decide whether he did this or not. He has the courts for that. My main priority is to look out for my best friend and her son."

I could feel the phone start to shake in my hand. This didn't feel real.

"Look, when Kerry first came forward, I assumed she'd be some kook and a DNA test would clear the whole thing up. Then when the DNA came back, I thought, well, so he's an asshole who cheated on my friend, but he's not a criminal. I was standing right next to you in the bunker, ready to defend him, because he's our Jason. But I'm stepping back now, Angela. He's not the good guy here. Whether he's guilty or not, he's a liar. And a cheater. He hired a fucking prostitute, for Christ's sake, and that's only the one time you know about. And then whatever happened between the two of you—it sounds like he let you think all these years it was somehow your fault. And I don't think it was. If he was doing something you didn't want him to do, that is never your fault."

"You don't need to tell me what rape is."

"I'm sorry, but I think that's exactly what I need to do."

The article she gave me was supposedly an explanation for why some women don't realize when they've experienced an assault that would legally constitute rape. According to the author, women are taught to fear strangers who lurk in alleys and behind bushes, emerging from the shadows with a gun or a knife to attack us when we least expect it. We're also taught that victims of the crime are damaged, broken like Humpty Dumpty, never to be put back together again.

In reality, most women are attacked by someone they know—the essay said about 80 percent. Only about 11 percent of cases involve a weapon.

The author suggested that women underreport sexual assault because they aren't sure it's a crime when their case doesn't fit the armed-stranger stereotype. They tell themselves it was a drunken date gone bad, that he must not have heard them say no, that it was somehow their fault. She posited that "cognitive dissonance" was at work: for their own psychological survival, women would rather excuse what happened to them than to label themselves with the ultimate stigma—rape victim. Some went so far as to apologize to their assailants for even momentarily suggesting that the "r-word" might apply.

Susanna was trying to tell me I was one of those women. "You went through something unimaginably horrible as a teenager, Angela. I'm not equating anything that may have happened with Jason to that. But isn't it possible that you convinced yourself it was normal because at least it wasn't what you suffered through before?"

"Don't even compare them."

"I'm not. Jason is not that Franklin monster. But that doesn't mean Jason is good, or loving. You obviously experienced something traumatic with him. I know how much you love him. And then you told me that something happened between you, and for three years you've been allowing yourself to live in this constructed world, trying to pretend like you're okay, the way you always have."

"I really did think we were okay. I don't understand why this is happening."

"Please, trust me. I've spoken to so many survivors about this, women who spent years feeling alone and self-conscious, and then they tell the story of what happened to them, and it's like the sky opens up. What happened that night with Jason? I promise, you can tell me."

I was regretting ever mentioning this to her. I could tell she was never going to leave me alone until I gave her some explanation. "We were—you know. And everything was good. Really good, better than usual. And then I told him that he could tie me up."

Susanna was silent on the other end of the line. I was glad I was telling her this over the phone. I felt my face burning.

"I had read one of those magazine articles about how to spice things up in the bedroom and got it into my head that I needed to make an effort. He was pretty into it when I was the one to bring it up. He took a belt and he wrapped it around my wrists. When he buckled it to the headboard, it's like a switch flipped. I freaked out, and had a flashback, but it was too late. I couldn't move my arms. I was just . . . there. When it was over, he realized I was upset and felt guilty about it. I think it made him afraid to touch me again."

"What do you mean, it was too late?"

"I mean, I had already told him I wanted to do it."

"But when you freaked out, what happened?"

I closed my eyes, not wanting to answer her question.

"Angela, what happened?"

"I was trying to pull my arms free and telling him to stop, but he kept going. He didn't realize until after, when I was crying. And then we never really talked about it. It was this thing we couldn't get past."

I could feel Susanna thinking through the phone line. "Okay, this is what we're doing," she announced. "You're packing a bag and coming over here right now. And I'm hiring a separate lawyer for you."

"I'm fine—"

"Damn it—" I had to hold the phone away from my ear. I could not remember ever hearing her raise her voice, let alone to me. "Stop saying you're fine. You may think you're fine, but your situation is not."

"Nothing's changed."

"Of course it has. Angela, don't you see it? What you described to me? That is rape."

The word felt like a punch.

"You're his wife, and you were struggling and crying and

saying no, and he—that is a crime. And if he did that to you, he could have done it to Kerry Lynch, too. And that bullshit story he told you about changing his clothes in front of his intern— No. You have to get out of that house before this all comes crashing down. I'm not going to let you stand by his side while he loses everything. You have to leave right now. When I called Colin earlier, he said that Jason's lawyer already e-mailed him the discovery she got from the DA. You were in court yesterday. She was stalling the criminal case in the hopes of buying that woman off—the prosecutor himself said so. They could settle that case at any second. You have to protect yourself—and Spencer."

I was still reeling from her initial response. I was replaying that whole night in my head, looking at my bed as if I were an outsider, picturing myself with my wrists above my head, my face turned away from him. That wouldn't have been a signal to him that something was wrong. I often turned my head. It was my way of dealing with the flashbacks. I'd close my eyes and wait for them to stop. I never told him, so I couldn't fault him for that. But that night was different. I was struggling—thrashing—trying to get free. I said his name. I said stop and I said no, but he was in some other place, like I wasn't there, until it was over.

And while I was picturing myself, naked and crying with my arms bound while my husband processed what had happened between us, Susanna was talking about civil settlements and assets and timing and filing dates.

I didn't like Susanna's use of the same word to describe that night with Jason and the three years of Charles Franklin's torture. They were different. But what happened with Jason definitely wasn't the same as what I'd just experienced with Colin. That's why I had needed him today—to remember what it was like to share that act with someone who loved me. Maybe it was using him, and maybe someday I would apologize, but for now, it was something special, only for me. I would add it to my box of secrets.

I thought about what my mother said, right after Rachel Sutton came forward. Misunderstandings don't happen when a situation is black and white. They only happen when there are shades of gray, when there could be two different versions of the same damn thing.

I was seeing two versions of what happened that night with Jason—the one I believed for the past three years, and the one I was seeing now.

"I'm sorry, Susanna, I can't do this right now. It's too much." It was taking everything for me not to scream.

"Can I come over? Please?"

"No. But thank you," I offered quickly. "I know you're looking out for me. I promise I'll call you tomorrow."

I needed to think. And I needed to read. I reached for my laptop and logged into Jason's e-mail account. Susanna said Olivia had sent the case evidence. I wanted to see it for myself.

*

My laptop was still open, in front of me on the bed, when Jason got home.

He was emptying the contents of his pockets onto the tray on his nightstand. "Hey, I just talked to Olivia. Good news! That plaintiff's attorney is open to settling. The idea of paying anyone a dime makes me sick to my stomach, but this might finally be going away. I can always do consulting work for another shop, but we may need to sell the house. I don't have an exact number yet. I swear, I'll make it up—"

He didn't seem to notice that I was glaring at him as he

ran on about various settlement numbers, each of them more than my parents ever made in their best decade, combined. He seemed to have forgotten that I told him that I'd stand by him through this because I believed he was innocent and knew he needed me. He thought I would celebrate the "good news" of paying off his former mistress—or maybe victim, or both—as if he'd never cheated on me, as if there was no possibility that I was leaving.

"Get out."

"Angela—"

"Get out. Get OUT!" I was slamming the laptop up and down on the comforter, seconds away from hurling it at him. I jumped from the bed and charged at him, pushing him out of the door to the staircase. "I swear to God, get out of this house. Now. Or so help me, I will call the DA myself and tell them whatever they want to hear."

He turned when he reached the bottom of the staircase, one hand on the front-door knob. He looked confused and hurt. He was waiting for me to change my mind.

"Go. I just need some time. This is all too much."

His gaze dropped to the floor. "I don't understand. What happened—"

"Seriously, I can't look at you right now. You need to leave."

When he was gone, I locked the door, knowing that his keys were still on the nightstand. I had the house to myself again, and it felt good.

*

When Spencer called that evening, he told me about his new friend, Isaac, who used to be named Isabelle. Spencer said some of the noncity kids were freaked out until it turned out Isaac was basically better at everything than they were. I was about to say good-bye when he surprised me by asking to say hi to Dad.

"Aw, sweetie, I'm so sorry. I forgot an avocado from the market and asked him to run over to Citarella." I immediately regretted the specificity of the lie, but Spencer didn't seem to suspect anything.

"All right. Um, I guess, could you tell him that I did want to say hi?"

"Absolutely. He's going to be so upset to miss you."

"Whatever." He was putting on a tough front, but I could tell that his self-titled "ice age" against his father was starting to thaw.

I had no idea how I was going to tell him the truth, if I ever figured out what that was.

I had just hung up when my cell phone rang again. The screen read "Colin Home." I was about to decline the call until I realized how much I wanted to hear his voice.

"Hey."

"We need to talk—" The voice wasn't Colin's. Of course, Jason had gone to his best friend's apartment.

"I said I needed some time. An hour isn't time."

"Angela—"

"Don't call me. I will call you when I'm ready. If you call me before then, I'll know you don't respect what I want."

I thought about the way Colin looked at me only hours earlier, when I told him as he left that I didn't want him ever to mention what happened between us unless I brought it up first. It was a look of acceptance. He understood that I knew things about myself that he did not. I had just made a similar request of Jason.

I turned my phone off, then reached over to his nightstand and turned his off for good measure.

# 42

Corrine pounded on the Powells' front door again. What kind of people don't have a bell or a knocker for a house this size? She made herself comfortable on the stoop steps and pulled the rubber band from the *New York Times* sitting on the welcome mat. It was nearly three o'clock. Someone would show up eventually.

She had skimmed the front-page headlines when she heard locks tumbling behind her. Rising from the steps, she turned to find Angela Powell in checkered pajama pants and a Stanford sweatshirt.

"Sorry, I assumed you'd be up."

"Migraine."

"Oh, the worst. Apple cider vinegar with honey. It does the trick for me. I did try to call first."

Angela didn't bother to mask her disinterest. "So when I didn't answer, you just came over instead of contacting our lawyer?"

"I told you before, Olivia Randall's not your lawyer. She's Jason's."

"Well, in case you haven't heard, the criminal case is on pause."

Angela started to close the door, but Corrine extended her arm. "That's the litigation, Mrs. Powell. Police can still investigate cases. Especially new cases."

Angela inched the door open farther, but still didn't allow Corrine to enter.

"Is your husband home?"

"No. He's working to keep his clients despite being falsely accused of a heinous crime."

"And was he working last night?"

"He was here."

"You were with him?"

"How else would I know unless I was with him?" Angela sounded proud, as if she had outwitted an adversary. "Our friend brought over a huge bag of food for the day. Thanks to you people, we can't even show our faces around New York City these days."

"What friend?"

"Colin Harris. He brought takeout from Gotham. Call the restaurant. There was enough for lunch and dinner. What's this about?"

"Kerry Lynch is missing."

For the first time since she opened the door, Angela paused, allowing the words to register as she formulated her comeback. "Maybe she realized that she was about to be exposed as a liar framing an innocent man to cover up for a company that does business with warlords."

"That's a harsh allegation about a missing woman."

"Forgive me if I don't feel sorry for her."

"Was Mr. Harris also here with you last night?"

"No, just us. We couldn't fall asleep and watched *La La Land* in bed."

"On TV?"

"We streamed it."

"Where's your son?"

"Camp. Upstate. He called last night," she added. "My cell

phone around seven thirty. You can verify that, too."

Corrine nodded. She'd get the phone records and make sure the information lined up. "And he spoke to both of you?"

"Yes, of course. Now, if we're done, I'd start looking more carefully at Ms. Lynch if I were you."

"You mean, *for* Ms. Lynch."

"No, I mean *at* her. Because I guarantee that whatever she's pulling right now, it has something to do with the scam she's running with her employer." Angela stepped aside and gestured for Corrine to come in. "Feel free to take a look. I assure you, she's not here."

Corrine pursed her lips and nodded, realizing that she wasn't going to get the response she'd been hoping for. "I know you don't believe me, Angela, but I'm on your side. How well do you really know your husband?"

"I know he's innocent."

Corrine might have pressed harder if she hadn't known about this woman's past. "At some point, you're no longer a bystander. You become an enabler. And after that, I can no longer help you. Don't let Jason take you and your boy down with him."

# 43

The second the door closed, I began shaking. I calmed myself by forcing myself to think through every task I needed to complete, in a very precise order.

Once the Impala was gone, I turned on my cell phone and waited for it to power up. I checked my voice mail. The only message besides the detective's was from Susanna, asking if I was mad at her. Jason had respected my request to give me some space.

My first call was to Olivia Randall. I left a message telling her that the police had come to the house asking about Jason's whereabouts the previous night, and that I'd explained that he'd been with me all night. My next call was to Colin.

"Hey, you." His voice was gentle.

There was so much I wanted to say, but all I could think about was the fact that I had just lied to a detective. "Where are you?"

"A closing in midtown." He sounded alarmed. "Are you all right?"

"Was Jason at your apartment last night?"

"Yeah. He said you had a fight. A really bad one." He lowered his voice further. "At first, I was worried he came to me because of what happened with us yesterday. But he said he wanted to crash for the night. What's going on?"

"Kerry Lynch is missing."

"What? Since when?"

"I don't know, but a detective was just here asking me where Jason was last night, and she also said Kerry was missing."

"Since last night is hardly missing."

"I was going to say he was at your apartment," I said, "and then I realized how bad that would look. I was so done with him last night, but when she started asking me questions with that accusing tone, my instincts kicked in. I've gotten so used to jumping to his defense, I did it on autopilot. Should I call her and tell her the truth? I have her number."

He paused, clearly weighing the options. "No. It's fine. Whether he was with me or with you is irrelevant. Changing your story now will only look worse, and they could wind up targeting you for not coming clean in the first place."

"But what if they find out I lied?"

"They won't. The only way that would happen is if Jason was somewhere other than my place, and he wasn't. So your story's fine."

"Okay, but Jason really was there with you, right? Every minute?" I pressed a palm against my eyes, wondering if I was getting an actual migraine.

"Yes. Of course. Don't worry about it. Given Kerry's history, she probably hooked up with a guy and will turn up later tonight."

As I hung up, I realized that just as I had grown accustomed to covering for Jason, Colin could be doing the same, especially after what happened between us the day before. Colin was hardly ever home. Had he really stayed at the apartment all night with Jason?

And I thought about Spencer. I had managed to drag him into my lie. If I called him now, they'd say I told him to back up the false alibi.

I tried to imagine what Spencer would do if the police contacted him. If I had to guess, he would tell them he wasn't saying a word without his mom. It was the way I raised him. I was his person. On the other hand, if he didn't see the harm—and he wouldn't, because I had sent him up to that camp so he'd be oblivious about what was happening here—he'd repeat my stupid story about sending Jason out for an avocado. And then what?

I was trying to decide what to do when my phone rang. A 914 area code, Westchester. Spencer's camp counselor. I steadied my voice. "Hi, Kate. Is everything all right?"

"Spencer's fine, but I wanted to let you know that he's been in the infirmary—he managed to get into some poison ivy."

"Can I talk to him?"

"Yep, I'm sure he'd like that."

"Hey, kiddo. You doing okay?"

"I want to cut my left arm off, but I'll probably live. It itches like hell."

"They gave you something?"

"Some stinky lotion and a Benadryl, but she won't give me the hard stuff!" He was yelling to make sure Kate heard the last part.

"Good. Hey, Spencer, I need to ask you something, okay? If anyone—anyone at all—asks you about when you called last night, I need you to tell them that you spoke to both me and Dad, okay?"

"Mom, what's wrong?"

"I just need you to do that for me, okay?" I tried to keep my voice from cracking. I was asking the most honest person I knew to lie.

"Yeah, okay."

Spencer would do whatever I requested, in part because I never abused the privilege. I saw how other moms barked orders at their kids. I never told Spencer to do anything blindly without explanation, not even to talk to his own father when he was angry at him.

I hung up, ashamed that my son's loyalty had provided a solution to my problem, but relieved. There had to be a reason for the timing, right? I saw it as a sign that the gods were trying to help.

My final phone call was to Jason's office. He had told me he had back-to-back client meetings, trying to save some business. He wouldn't have canceled them.

"Fair Share Strategies, this is Zack." Jason had forwarded his direct line to Zack's extension.

"Hey, Zack. It's Angela."

"Ah, yes. Jason's in a meeting, but he told me to interrupt him if you called."

The brief hold felt like an eternity. I had let these allegations from other women get into my head. When I saw Jason yesterday, I had convinced myself that he was guilty of victimizing not only them, but me. I had even wondered if he had ever really loved me. Now I knew how wrong I had been. He wasn't perfect, but he wasn't a predator.

"I'm so glad you called." I had kicked him out of his own house, and yet he sounded genuinely happy to hear my voice.

"Jason, Kerry Lynch is missing. Please tell me you didn't do this because of me."

# 44

From: Jason Powell
To: Olivia.Randall@ellisonrandall.com
Re: Discovery from NYPD/DA
Date: June 7

Hi Olivia. Sorry for the delay. Needless to say, a lot has happened since you sent me the discovery you got from the DA yesterday. (I also just left you a voice mail message about Det. Duncan going to the house today to question Angela. Angela said she left you a message, too.)

Apparently Kerry is "missing," whatever that means. As you can imagine, I am deeply disturbed that their first instinct was to show up at our home. Make sure you read to the end for notes on this.

In response to the questions from your earlier e-mail, here are my thoughts, followed by—more importantly—new developments:

1. Regarding our argument that night at the W, we should discuss this further, because the dynamics are complicated. Here's the short version: After dinner on 4/10, we were intimate in her room. She wanted me to stay the night but of course I could not (that never stopped her from asking).

In an act of very bad timing, I decided to talk to her again before I left about my concerns regarding Oasis. She knew I was in a conflicted position, not only because I had investors with them, but also because she worked for them and I cared about her. I had talked to her about the possibility of becoming a whistleblower, and brought it up with her again. At that point, I thought the problems were limited to projects in Tanzania and Mozambique, which could mean that someone handling their operations in Africa was responsible. But that night, she said my concerns shed new light on some internal memos she had been cc'd on. She's the one who made me suspect that corruption might be par for the course for Oasis. I pressed her for details, but she shut down. From that moment on, she was basically promising to give me the documents and help me "go whistleblower" if I left Angela for her—a test of my commitment to fulfill promises I never should have made. If the video shows us fighting, it's because I was telling her that she could not be complicit if she knew Oasis was in bed with dictators and warlords. I remember thinking when I stepped into the elevator, "What have I done?" I knew I had messed up getting tied up with Oasis.

2. Regarding the clothes Kerry was wearing, she wears knee-length skinny black skirts more often than not, and almost always wears a black lace thong (to my knowledge). If I had to guess, whatever clothing she was wearing our last time together at her house will line up with what she was wearing in the hotel video. She's not stupid.

3. Regarding the "injuries" to her wrists: Yes. We engaged in that activity multiple times. The last time we were together, she specifically asked that I use my belt. I remember she said "Tighter"

twice. I was worried it was too rough, but she was encouraging. I now realize why. I'm a fool. There's no doubt in my mind those photos are from 5/19 at her house, not 4/10 at the W.

4. Regarding your attempt (once again) to put Angela out front, as we've discussed, this is a deal-breaker. Angela has been through enough. Mention this again, and I'll need to find a different lawyer. You indicated yesterday that their attorney was open to a settlement. If it will put all this behind us, I'll pay. Just tell me the number.

*****IMPORTANT: While I was at work today, Det. Duncan questioned Angela without counsel at our home regarding my whereabouts last night (I assume this must be when Kerry went "missing"). As she explained, we were home together from the time I finished client meetings (got home around 6:15) until we fell asleep. Our son called from camp shortly before 7:30. We ate takeout from Gotham, then stayed up late and watched La La Land. I am attaching the following documents should they prove helpful: (1) photo of Angela's phone (as you know, we have no landline), showing call from Spencer's camp (ending 7:23 pm); (2) receipt from Gotham (Colin brought us food for the whole day); (3) printout from Amazon Prime movie rental, showing streaming time (starting at 11:02 pm). What more could they want from me other than a webcam in my house (which I would have agreed to if I had known this nonsense would happen)?

I have no idea what Kerry's trying to pull, but trust me: it's about money and getting back at me. You saw that movie Gone Girl, right? She's that batshit-crazy about me not leaving Angela for her. Granted, I was a shit head, but I don't deserve this. Give me a call to discuss. Thanks, as always, for everything. I still can't believe this is happening.

# 45

Corrine found out Kerry Lynch was missing when a sergeant with the Port Washington Police Department called. According to him, Kerry Lynch's dog walker showed up to her house to walk Kerry's bichon frise, Snowball. The Long Island cop must have been a dog person, because he couldn't just say "dog." He had both the breed and the name at his fingertips. The dog walker did her usual routine with Snowball, but noticed as she returned his leash to its hook in the mudroom that Kerry's purse and briefcase were both on the bench. She called out for Kerry, then looked in the attached garage and saw her car. When she walked into the kitchen, she found takeout containers on the counter and dishes in the sink. She had never seen a spot of dirt in Kerry's house before.

Growing concerned, the walker called Kerry's cell to make sure everything was okay, and heard her own call come through on a cell left on the living room sofa. When she tried Kerry's office, they said she hadn't come in to work that day and that they had been trying to reach her. The walker's next call was to 911.

When the sergeant who got the call-out realized Kerry was the woman who had accused Jason Powell of sexual assault, he contacted Corrine.

Corrine's first call had been to Brian King. The second was to Janice Martinez, who had not bothered to get back to her until now, after a full day had passed.

"Sorry, Detective. I've been swamped."

"All I needed was a phone call to find out the last time you spoke to Kerry Lynch."

"My communications with my client are—"

"Give it a rest. I'm not asking about conversations. When I first called you, Kerry had only missed one day of work. We're now on day two. She left behind her wallet, cell phone, ID, car, and dog. It's not looking good."

The local police had called Grapevine, the Italian restaurant whose takeout containers were found in Kerry's kitchen. According to the restaurant, her order—eggplant parmesan and a chicken Caesar salad—went out at 6:30 the evening before the dog walker found the house empty.

"Fine," Martinez said. "I haven't spoken to her since Wednesday."

That was two days ago, the last time she was seen. "What time?"

"Hold on." Following a short pause, she said, "Three o'clock to three fifteen."

"This was a phone call?" If Corrine had to guess, it was an eight-minute call rounded to the nearest quarter hour for billing purposes.

"Yeah, her cell. I heard her tell someone she was on the phone at one point. I got the impression she was in her office."

So Kerry had been at work until at least 3:15. She was likely home by 6:30 to order takeout. Then nothing.

"Did you discuss anything that might explain why she's gone now?" Corrine asked.

"Nope, that's off-limits."

"There are exceptions to privilege," Corrine said. "Your client could be in danger."

"'Could be' are the key words. I need to talk to bar counsel for advice. I really am not sure what to do under the circumstances, and that's not something you're going to hear me say too often."

"It sounds to me as if you're confirming that something happened Wednesday that might be relevant."

"I'm not. Because I can't. Let me figure out what the options are, and I'll get back to you. I promise."

Corrine hung up and called the Port Washington sergeant again. His name was Mike Netter. She wondered if he got as many cracks about his name as she did.

She started the conversation by letting him know that Janice Martinez had finally gotten back to her. This, after all, was his case, not hers. "She hasn't talked to Kerry since fifteen fifteen on Wednesday. Any new information on your end?"

"Talked to a friend of hers at work—girl named Samantha Hicks. She said Kerry was in on Wednesday, out yesterday and today. She didn't know much more. She said she couldn't think of any reason she'd be gone except the stress of everything that was happening—first the work trouble, plus the rape, then the media attention, not to mention a breakup. Believe me, I got an earful."

Corrine's mind was swirling with questions. She scribbled key words on her notepad so she wouldn't forget them.

"She told this friend Samantha about the rape after it happened?" Kerry said she never spoke to anyone about it until she reported it to Corrine.

"No, sorry. I didn't mean to suggest that. Samantha only heard about it when everyone else did, at that big press conference the lawyer held."

"Did she say what the problems were at work?"

"Nah. Pretty vague. Something about Kerry being in the

doghouse—quote, unquote—for the last few years."

That timing lined up with what Kerry had told Corrine about her affair with the company's CEO, Tom Fisher.

"And what about the breakup? Was that also a few years ago?"

"She said Kerry started talking about the dude maybe five months ago. She referred to him as Jay, but never gave a last name and kept blowing her off about getting to meet him. Samantha even asked her once, point-blank, if the guy might be married. I heard all about how Kerry was smart in every way, except she falls head over heels for the wrong guys and lives her whole life around them. I've got a sister like that—anyway, Kerry stopped talking about the guy around the time the news of her complaint against Powell came out. So now I got to figure out who Jay is. Didn't find anyone by that name in her cell phone, and that seems weird. I'll have my tech guy look at it to see if maybe it all got deleted. And, oh shit—I still need to find that delivery guy from the restaurant."

Corrine hung up, trying to quell the worry building in the back of her mind. Kerry was a beautiful, successful single woman. Of course she probably had a boyfriend. There's no reason that would have come up in conversation with Corrine. And maybe Kerry was secretive about him at work because she'd already been churned through the gossip mill over her affair with Tom Fisher.

But she couldn't ignore the warning signs. If Jason Powell was telling the truth about an affair with Kerry, she might have referred to him as "Jay" around the office to keep the relationship on the down-low.

She had told Brian King that it really didn't matter to her whether Kerry had had an affair with Jason, but now that the evidence was sitting there, she wanted to know the truth. But the missing-person case belonged to Port Washington Police, and her case against Powell was on hold. Corrine didn't have an angle to work.

Corrine walked the twenty feet to her lieutenant's office and tapped on the open door. After she filled him in on what she knew about Kerry's disappearance, he said what she expected: Let Port Washington handle the investigation, and in the meantime hope they find her, alive and well.

She couldn't argue with his logic, but she was still standing in his doorway.

"Damn it, Duncan. I got detectives I have to yell at to do more work, and now I'm yelling at you to give it a rest. Go home."

"It's only two o'clock."

"Not literally. I mean—Jesus, get out of here. If she doesn't turn up in the next day or two, we can talk again. Until then, she's Long Island's problem."

*

Corrine was at her desk an hour later when the number for the main switchboard at the district attorney's office appeared on her cell phone screen. "Duncan."

"It's King." He was back to being King now, not Brian. She preferred it that way.

She started to fill him in on her conversation with Sergeant Netter, but he interrupted.

"The pictures of Kerry's wrists—how do we have those files?"

"What do you mean?"

"I mean, how did we physically get them? She took the photos herself, right?"

"Yeah."

"So how'd she send them to you? E-mail? Text? Did you plug

in her phone? Like, technically, how did we get them? You gave them to me as jpeg files."

Corrine woke up her computer and looked through old e-mails to jog her memory. "Yeah, she e-mailed them to me as attachments."

"Straight from her phone? Right in front of you?"

"No. She showed them to me on her phone and sent them to me when she got home. Why?"

"Because Olivia Fucking Randall swears there's a problem with them, but won't tell me how she knows that. Specifically, she wants to confirm the date the photographs were taken."

"I'm looking at the files on my computer. The date on my files is May 19, but that's when she sent them to me."

"Well, I just learned way more than I wanted to about digital photographs from our geek here. It looks like Kerry exported the original photograph into a jpeg file before she sent it to you, which is why the date on the *file* is the day she filed her complaint. But if you look at the photo's *properties*, it says the image is from the night of April 10, which is the night she says he assaulted her at the W. No problem, right? Except Olivia's saying you can easily change that on any Mac. She's demanding that we produce the actual device used to take the photographs so she can examine the microdata to see if the date was changed."

"She thinks Kerry took the pictures later and lined them up with the date we'd have hotel footage."

"That's my guess. Please tell me you looked at Kerry's wrists the day she made the complaint."

Corrine closed her eyes. "Of course not. She said the assault was six weeks earlier. And before you ask, she was wearing a long-sleeved dress. I wouldn't have noticed if she'd still had the marks."

"Damn it."

"I found out something else that's not going to make you very happy either." She summed up her reasons for believing that Kerry's boyfriend, "Jay," might have been Jason Powell.

"And you said before, it doesn't matter."

"I didn't think before that she might be lying about the date of those pictures. The guy with the PD in Port Washington mentioned looking at contacts in Kerry's phone, so he must have gotten a warrant to unlock it. Let me call him."

Netter picked up immediately.

"You still have Kerry's phone there?"

He said that he did.

"Can you do me a favor and look through her photographs? I'm looking for April tenth."

"I don't see anything."

"Nothing?"

"No, I got a picture of a meatball pizza on April eighth, and a picture of Snowball four days later. What am I looking for?"

"Three pictures of injuries on her wrists. Scroll through and see if you can find anything. Maybe it's closer to May nineteenth."

"Nope, nothing."

"Are you sure?"

"You want to drive out here or what? I'm telling you, it's not here." Kerry must have deleted the photos after she e-mailed them to Corrine. "And I got hold of that restaurant guy. He's out surfing in Montauk today, but he's coming back tomorrow to work a shift. I'm supposed to talk to him at four."

Tomorrow was Saturday, her day off. Fuck it. What else was she going to do? "Do you mind if I come out and meet him with you?"

"No skin off my back."

# 46

"A jury would let me walk if I knocked you into a coma right now." The nice thing about Susanna was that I never needed to wonder what she was actually thinking. "No offense, but I want to run your life until you come to your senses."

We were in her apartment on Central Park South. It was Saturday, the only day when she didn't have studio obligations. When I arrived at eleven, she had her sideboard covered with Bloody Mary mix and vodka, lox and bagels, caviar and blinis, and a bottle of chilled and very expensive champagne. She told me she splurged because I had been living like a hermit for nearly a month. But now the caviar and blinis were gone, I was picking at the remaining lox and capers, and she was threatening to knock me out for defending Jason.

"For all we know, she's turned up by now," I said. "I mean, she slept with my husband. She could be hooking up with anyone for a night or two."

"'Turned up'? I don't think an NYPD detective would show up at your door if they thought she was off on a romantic sojourn."

I had filled Susanna in on Detective Duncan's visit to the house, as well as the alibi I ended up offering for Jason. Jason was back at the house with me now, and he, Colin, and I had gotten our stories straight. We even printed out evidence of

Spencer's call to my phone and the receipt from my movie rental for Olivia.

Susanna sounded like a prosecutor, laying out Jason's motive to kill Kerry Lynch. His criminal case was only paused for a month. The woman had filed a civil suit seeking millions of dollars in damages. His career, reputation, and future hung in the balance.

"I can't believe we're having this conversation. We're talking about Jason. He didn't *kill* anyone."

"People get pushed to the brink and do things you never expect. I mean, I never thought you'd lie to the police. You not only *lied* for him, you dragged Spencer into it. And you tripled down on it by giving all those documents to Jason's lawyer. It's one thing to stand by his side, Angela, but that's obstruction of justice. You're affirmatively doing something wrong to cover up for him."

"It's not 'covering up for him' if he was at Colin's house. Whether he was at our place or Colin's is irrelevant. The point is, he wasn't anywhere near Kerry Lynch's."

"Why are you so certain of that? You know Colin. He's convinced Jason is innocent. If he thinks vouching for him will put your mind at ease, he would totally lie for him."

If I had to bet money, I'd say Colin was telling the truth about being with Jason. But if I had to bet my arm? I wouldn't take that wager. I didn't *know* where Jason was Wednesday night, in that sense of the word.

"I can't explain it, Susanna. When you've got a cop standing right there, asking 'Where was your husband?,' you just start talking. I'm actually sort of proud of myself that I managed to lie so strategically. I could've screwed it up royally."

"Well, that's comforting. If this all goes south, maybe you can run a flimflam racket from prison."

"I'm not going to prison."

"You lied to a detective. How many times do I have to say that before it sinks in?"

"Maybe you should have bought less hooch if you wanted me to pay attention to reality." I refilled my flute, even though it wasn't empty yet.

"I'm not kidding, Angela. The last time we talked, it sounded like you were starting to realize Jason might have another side to him, including the way he treats you. Now you're back to being his biggest defender."

I put my glass down and looked her directly in the eye. "Trust me. I am not a fan of his right now. What he did to me was bad. Really bad. And he's no angel. But I'm not willing to use the word you want me to use for what happened between us that night. And he's definitely not a murderer. Just the thought of it is ridiculous. Are you telling me that you can picture Jason—*our* Jason—driving out to that woman's house, killing her somehow, and hiding her body in the woods somewhere?" I heard my own voice shake. I didn't want to let my mind picture the scene.

She held my gaze and then looked away and shook her head.

"Okay, good. We at least agree on that. My husband's not a murderer. Cheers!"

"I'm only looking out for you."

"For fuck's sake, Susanna, I know that!"

She flinched. I had never snapped at her like that before. I reached over and gave her shoulder a quick squeeze. "I'm so sorry. I just want this to be over."

"Well, what if it's not?"

"It will be at some point."

"You need to protect yourself before then. Just tell me this: If the DA pulls you into a grand jury and asks you where Jason was, what are you going to do?"

She kept pressing me until I finally answered. "I wouldn't lie under oath."

"You're sure? You promise?"

"Yes. I wouldn't cross that line. But they're not going to do that. Stop worrying. That girl—woman, Kerry, whatever—she'll turn up any second."

I was doing my best to sound confident, and the alcohol was helping. But inside, I knew my entire life was about to change. It had to.

*

After two cups of coffee and a cleaning frenzy, I was feeling nearly sober by the time Jason got home. The entire contents of the pantry were emptied on our kitchen table, countertops, and floor. I had purged a garbage bag full of half-eaten packages of nuts, chips, crackers, spaghetti, hot cocoa, oatmeal—everything that needed to go—and had a plan to organize what was left. Two boxes of Nicorette were set aside near the doorway.

"Are we having a food drive?"

"You didn't get my message?"

He checked his phone. "It was off."

His phone was always off.

"I want you to go to Colin's. He said he'll wait for you there." I finished wiping down the final shelf. Not a single bread crumb or grain of rice in sight.

"Are we fighting again? I thought we were fine." So much had changed in the three days since I'd thrown him out of the house to stay with Colin for the night.

"Just go talk to Colin. I don't want to have this conversation. He'll explain it to you."

"Is this about Kerry again? You can't possibly think I hurt

someone—"

I was focusing on my stacks of organic, low-sodium chicken broth as if I were constructing a landmark bridge.

"Please. It will all make sense once you're with Colin. If you don't agree with me, you can come back, and we'll talk it out."

"Angela—"

"Just go. I promise. Put on your economist hat. You'll see, objectively, it's the right thing to do."

I was already crying by the time I heard the front door shut, picturing the scene that was going to play out when Jason got to Colin's apartment.

I had called Colin as soon as I got home from Susanna's. He explained it to me once again: if I filed for divorce before a civil judgment against Jason was rendered, our divorce could proceed as if we were any normal couple going our separate ways. The burden would be on any creditor of Jason to come after me, arguing that we had only gotten divorced as a way to shelter assets from liability. I could play the finally-had-it-up-to-here-wife card. After all, the kindest version of the facts was that Jason had been a serial adulterer. Under the circumstances, who else would have put up with all of this until now except me?

To an outsider, it would sound cruel—asking my husband's best friend, the man I'd cheated with three days ago, to serve the divorce papers. But after what I'd learned about Jason in the last month, I didn't know what a "normal" process was for us anymore. Colin was exactly the right messenger, because he loved us both.

I had no idea what was going to happen to Jason, either in criminal court or civil. The only thing I knew was that I had to protect myself, and mostly I had to protect Spencer. I would take half of our assets, and I would take Spencer.

And if Jason asked about "us," I'd reassure him that he had been Spencer's father all these years without legal documentation. We could be whatever we wanted to each other, regardless of a piece of paper.

I was halfway done stacking the pantry when my phone rang. It was the realtor who had sold us the carriage house two years earlier, returning my call. She was coming over the next day to take a look around before setting a list price.

# 47

Corrine left Harlem at exactly 2:31 p.m. on Saturday for Port Washington, making a point to mark her time. She arrived at Kerry Lynch's house at 3:12 p.m. Departing from Greenwich Village would have been farther. Saturday-afternoon traffic was probably worse than a Wednesday night. So forty minutes minimum from Jason Powell's house to here was a good estimate, if he had traveled by car.

She had already searched the data from the license-plate readers on the bridges and tunnels, looking for any evidence that Powell's Audi wagon had left Manhattan on Wednesday. She didn't find a hit. In theory, he could have gone by train or used a different vehicle, but, in her gut, Corrine wasn't feeling it.

The first time she went to Kerry's house, she hadn't realized how isolated it was. Now that Kerry was missing, she was certain that someone could come and go without a neighbor noticing.

A marked Port Washington police car pulled to the curb behind her a few minutes after she arrived. The man who stepped out was younger than she had expected, based on their phone calls. He was probably in his late thirties, with dark brown hair and a neatly trimmed beard. "I brought you doughnuts, Duncan." He extended a half-dozen box of Krispy Kremes, and they each helped themselves to one. "Come on, humor me, tell me

I'm the very first person to make that joke."

She finished swallowing before answering. "You should know I hate puns, but I love a good doughnut, Netter, so you get a pass."

"Fair enough."

He led the way behind the house, removed two ribbons of crime-scene tape, and opened the back door. He held out an arm to stop her from walking any farther than halfway through the kitchen.

"Have you contacted her family?" Corrine asked.

"Mom's passed, Dad's got Alzheimer's in Indiana. Estranged from a brother there. From what we can tell, she was all about her job. Some friends at work, like Samantha, but just casual socializing outside of the office. Not anyone close."

"Where's Snowball?"

"You just had to ask me that, didn't you?" His embarrassed smile was sweet.

"Really? You've got her dog?"

"She's so cute."

"He." Corrine remembered Kerry correcting her when she was here before.

"Technically, but Snowball transcends labels. Kerry's brother wouldn't take the poor thing. And Samantha said she's allergic, even though I told her bichons are hypoallergenic."

"We're on day three. Don't you think it's about time you started processing this as a crime scene?"

"Well, seventy-two hours is our general rule of thumb, but there's been a development. When I went through her phone looking for our mystery man, Jay? I found phone calls to realtors. Apparently she was looking to list her house, and fast. She said she wanted it priced to sell."

"That could mean anything."

"Maybe she took off for a couple of days to go wherever she was planning to move. She did leave Snowball's automated food and water bowls totally filled."

"Without her purse and her phone?"

Netter shrugged. "I know. But those real estate calls have to be related. That can't be a coincidence."

"Just so you know, she told me herself she was kind of a crappy dog owner, leaving Snowball alone all the time. That's probably why she had those feeders. If I had to guess, she probably kept them full all the time. Do you mind if I take a look around?"

He obviously had no idea what was permitted under the current circumstances.

"I want to look in the living room. It's the only part of the house I saw when I was here before." She made her way to the threshold of the kitchen entrance and stood there for a full five minutes, scanning the entire room in small sections. She noticed only one thing out of place, but it was important. Once she told Netter, it would change the way he was looking at the case.

She asked him what the plan was for interviewing the person who had delivered food to Kerry the last night she was seen.

Netter looked at his watch. "Perfect timing. We're supposed to meet him at the restaurant in ten."

She climbed into her car, pulled a U, and followed Netter.

*

Based on what she'd gleaned about the delivery boy, Corrine was expecting someone around twenty years old—surfer by day, Italian food delivery guy by night. Instead, they pulled in front of the restaurant called Grapevine to find a guy older than either of them, probably fifty, a surfboard still strapped to the top of his Toyota Prius.

He introduced himself as Nick Lowe. "No, not the musician, if you've even heard of him. It's Dominick, legally. My parents called me Nick, and I figured, Yeah, let's go with that." She noticed the air freshener hanging from Nick's rearview mirror.

She let Netter take the lead. It didn't take long for Nick to confirm what they already knew: he had delivered a takeout order to Kerry's house on Wednesday night. If the receipt said the order left at six thirty, he estimated he arrived around six forty-five. Maybe seven, seven fifteen. "There's a lot of orders, plus suburban sprawl. Carbon footprints are large around here."

"Do you remember anything about her demeanor?" Netter asked.

"I don't know. She took the bag of food, handed me a five for a tip, and that was basically it. She's a good person, you guys. She, like, works all the time and eats at home. She's kind of sad. Why are you asking about her?"

Corrine realized why it had taken this long to get a statement from Nick. Netter had never explained that they were asking because they were concerned about Kerry. Nick obviously thought she was a suspect.

Netter struck her as a decent guy, but she was done letting him call the shots. "You deliver to her house regularly?" Corrine asked.

"Oh, yeah, sure. Every couple of weeks or so, I'd say."

"Nick, to our knowledge, you were the last person to see Miss Lynch," she said. "We can't find her and are concerned about her safety."

His brow furrowed.

"What else did you notice that night?" she asked.

"Well, her boyfriend was there." His tone was more serious now, focused. "That was different."

Fuck. They could have found this out two days earlier. She pulled out her phone and searched for a photograph of Jason Powell. "This guy?"

"No, not him."

Something about the way he said it. "But you've seen him before?"

"Yeah. I think so. I mean, wait, isn't he on the news?"

"He is, for various things, but did you see him with Kerry Lynch?"

"Um, yeah. Maybe once. Twice at most. He definitely looks familiar. Like he's British or something. Not an accent or anything. I never spoke to him. But that kind of vibe. I'd say he was there, maybe three or four months ago."

Netter interrupted. "You said a man was there on Wednesday. Was his name Jay?"

Nick shrugged. "I don't know any name other than what's on the order. Customers make shit up, too. Hugh Jass. Seymour Butz. People kind of suck."

"But you said she had a boyfriend over," Corrine said, trying to get Nick back on track.

"Yeah. Or at least, he used to be. But it was a long time ago—like, more than a year. Two, maybe even three years ago. He used to be there a lot. Would answer the door and tip me and everything. I thought he lived there. Then I stuck my foot in my mouth and was like, 'Hey, where's your husband?' And she said he was a scumbag. And all of a sudden on Wednesday, he was back again. That same guy."

Corrine googled "Tom Fisher Oasis" on her phone and hit "Images." She clicked on the first image in the results. "Does this guy look familiar?"

"Yeah, that's the guy. He's the one who was there on Wednesday. She's okay, right? She's a nice lady."

*

Corrine and Netter walked together to the far corner of the parking lot, where they had left their cars side by side.

"So who's the dude?" he asked.

"Her boss. They had an affair three years ago. She told me it didn't end well. He stayed with his wife."

"Oh shit. And she kept working for him?"

"Yes, but it wasn't comfortable, at least that's what she said. She threatened to sue, so she was able to keep her job."

"Like a cop who barely makes it out of a beef with his badge. It's never quite the same again. That would be the work trouble her friend mentioned."

"And the reason she said Kerry had a weakness for the wrong guys," Corrine added.

"So this might not be related to your case at all?" It was barely a question, the way Netter said it.

"Hard to say, but I don't think she left on her own. When I was at the house, I did notice one thing. She had a big crystal egg on the coffee table. My guess is around ten or fifteen pounds. It's gone."

"The dog walker didn't notice."

"It's not the dog walker's job to notice." Corrine could already picture it. The dining room table cleared, the dirty takeout containers on the kitchen counter. The glass egg smashing against Kerry's head. Blood in her dark hair. Moving the body, no neighbors in sight. Someone cleaning blood from either the hardwood floors in the living room or the terra-cotta tile in the kitchen. Maybe even leaving all that food and water for Snowball.

"I'll call the crime scene now," Netter said again. "Why didn't you say something at the house?"

"I wasn't sure what to make of it until we talked to the delivery guy."

"Or you wanted to make sure you still got to tag along while I was still assuming she'd turn up."

"You should make that call, Netter."

*

It took Corrine nearly two hours to tell Netter everything she knew about Kerry Lynch, including Jason Powell's suspicions that Kerry might have known more than she was admitting about Oasis's international dealings. She spent another hour giving him advice on the various steps he might take to work the case, now that it was becoming clear that this investigation belonged in Long Island.

She had just pulled onto the LIE when her phone rang. She didn't recognize the number, but the area code was Manhattan.

"This is Duncan."

"Hey, it's Brian."

He was Brian again. "From your cell phone on a Saturday. No, I won't go out with you."

"You should be so lucky. Any updates on Kerry?"

She hadn't spoken to King since Thursday, when she first found out Kerry was missing. She told him she was driving back from Port Washington and gave him a quick summary of what she'd learned there.

"So you think Jason Powell is this boyfriend she called Jay? The surfer guy saw them together?"

"Unclear. There's a Jay of some sort, who might or might not be Powell. I wouldn't bet my life on surfer guy as an eyewitness."

"And yet you trust him about seeing Tom Fisher there Wednesday night."

She recognized the inconsistency. "He seemed certain about Fisher. Powell, not so much."

"So are you interviewing Fisher?"

"How can I? I was already stretching to say if Powell left the city to target her, we had a basis for jurisdiction. But Fisher? Their entire relationship was on the island. If my suspicions about that missing glass egg are right, that crime also happened in Long Island. Not to mention, I'm not even on duty."

"Like that would stop you. I can spot a fellow sucker for truth and justice."

She did, in fact, want to question Fisher herself, but she knew that she had outworn her welcome with Netter. The second she told him about that missing egg, he had kicked into a higher gear.

King was silent on the other end of the line, thinking. "Don't tell anyone I said this, because it's cold as hell—"

"Hell's not cold."

"Don't bust my balls, okay? I hope Kerry's fine, but shit, I'm actually glad this case is on hold. Gives me an easy out on this phone call I need to return."

"Which is . . ."

"I checked my office voice mail—which I should never do on a weekend, note to self. I had a message from Eric Jordan. He said he'd heard that Kerry Lynch was missing and was wondering if we had opened a grand jury to investigate."

Corrine let the information sink in. Eric Jordan was with *New Day*. His cohost, Susanna Coleman, was best friends with Angela Powell. It couldn't be a coincidence. If the news of Kerry's disappearance were going to leak from someone on Long Island, she'd expect it to be to one of the local media outlets, not to a national network morning show.

"It's coming from the wife." Corrine explained the common

link between Angela Powell and Eric Jordan. "He specifically asked about a grand jury? That seems weird. I should have known something was off when she came to the door in her pajamas."

"I feel like you started having an entirely different conversation at some point."

"Sorry, I'm thinking out loud. The first time I went to the Powells' house, Angela was cool as a cucumber, even as I told her about her husband hiring a prostitute. There was something almost Stepford-y about her. The house was impeccable, despite a teenage son under the roof and her husband in the middle of an investigation. But when I showed up Thursday, she came to the door in her pajamas in the middle of the afternoon."

The more Corrine thought about it, the more convinced she was that Angela Powell had been "off" that day. She'd explained her appearance by saying she had a migraine, but Angela didn't seem like the type to reveal any kind of personal detail—let alone a weakness—to a stranger, let alone a police detective investigating her husband.

"A second ago, it sounded like you thought Kerry and Tom Fisher might actually have been framing Powell all along, just like he claimed. Now you think Powell's wife is lying about his alibi."

"I'm not sure what's going on at this point, except that Eric Jordan's phone call to you was no coincidence. He mentioned a grand jury? That almost seems like a suggestion. Maybe Angela has something to say, and her friend Susanna knows it will take a grand jury subpoena to get her to say it." Corrine had been telling herself that Angela's background had nothing to do with Jason's case, but now she was wondering whether Angela might be more submissive than she let on.

She passed two exits before King spoke again. "As far as I'm concerned, my case is on hold. Hopefully, by the time it's not, we'll have some answers, one way or the other."

"And what if Powell's been telling the truth the whole time?"

"Are you fucking with me? You were just telling me to open a grand jury to question his wife."

"Because I know we're missing something. I just don't know what it is yet."

"Work your other cases, Duncan. You really drove out to Long Island on your day off?"

"Port Washington. It's barely past Queens."

"You're still making me feel bad. I'm going to go drink a bottle of wine and tell myself that Kerry Lynch is on an island somewhere, reading a book."

# 48

By Sunday, the realtor had decided to list the carriage house for $7.5 million, half a million more than we paid for it. We would end up losing more than that to her commission, legal fees, and taxes, but if it all worked out as planned, we'd have about $1.7 million in equity to show for it—all of Jason's book money and then some—half of which would be mine, at least legally.

Jason had handled the news exactly as I expected: objectively and rationally. We were divorcing on paper only. From the moment he told me that his DNA would match whatever evidence Kerry Lynch had provided to the police, I had said I would stand by him, and we'd figure out where he and I stood later. This, objectively and rationally, was consistent with that plan.

On my behalf, Colin had served Jason with divorce papers at his apartment on Saturday. I had printed the documents off the Internet myself, trying to restrict Colin's involvement to the role of messenger. As it turned out, New York had only recently adopted a form of no-fault divorce, and even that wasn't exactly straightforward. It required at least one party to allege that the marriage had "broken down irretrievably" for a period of at least six months. I was certain we didn't meet the requirement, until I read further. The lack of any physical intimacy counted as "broken down irretrievably." We had been broken, as far as the law was concerned, for three years, and I hadn't even realized it.

My bare-bones documents weren't enough to actually render us divorced. The process required us to divide our marital property and reach an agreement on spousal support. One simplification was Spencer. He was my child, not Jason's, at least legally—and this entire arrangement was about legalities.

Only two hours after Colin broke the news to him, Jason had come back home. We went through our financial statements and filled out the affidavits that we'd need to give to the divorce lawyer Colin had recommended. It felt like the paperwork we filed when we got the loan for the carriage house we were now selling.

He held me all night as we slept, but we were practically silent as I helped him pack the things he'd need for a while and drove him the few blocks to Colin's apartment. He reached for the car handle and then stopped. "It's only on paper, right?"

"Jason, we talked about this—"

"I know. You need time. I hurt you. But Angela, I love you. I always have, and that's not changing. I really screwed up. I don't know how to tell you how sorry I am for where we are right now. But you are everything to me. Always. If this is your way of telling me—"

"No. It's like I said, we're doing this for us, Jason. All three of us." I had a good shot of protecting at least half of Jason's money in the event he was hit with a major damage award. Colin said Kerry's case would get dismissed if she remained missing, but we had no guarantees of that. I was being practical.

"You're amazingly strong, do you know that?"

I gave him a sad smile. "A little bit."

He kissed me on the cheek. As he made three trips into Colin's building, I sat alone at the wheel, frozen.

# 49

Corrine watched from her unmarked vehicle on Union Square West as Jason Powell made a second trip from the Audi into the sleek glass building around the corner on Fifteenth Street. Angela remained in the driver's seat of the station wagon, hatchback popped open, the engine idling. From Corrine's vantage point, it appeared as if Angela were staring straight ahead, both hands still on the wheel.

She had spotted the Powells' Audi backing out of their driveway when she was still a block from their house. She had hoped to catch Angela alone, but decided to follow them instead. The delivery of boxes a few blocks away could mean anything, but something about Angela's gaze into the distance told Corrine that the boxes weren't the only thing being dropped off here.

As Powell made a third trip into the building, he paused and turned back toward the curb. Corrine couldn't make out his expression, but the moment struck her as sad. Angela drove away alone.

Thanks to the direction of the one-way streets involved, Corrine had a head start. When Angela pulled into her driveway, Corrine was standing in front of the garage door.

Instead of asking Corrine to move, Angela parked the car in the driveway and stepped out.

"It's not a good time, Detective."

"I'll be quick. Is your migraine gone?"

"Yes, thanks. I actually tried that vinegar-and-honey trick. I think it may have helped."

It was a good answer, but Corrine noticed the pause when she first asked the question.

Corrine was certain now. There had been no migraine, and Angela Powell was not the kind of woman who stayed in her pajamas all day without a reason. What else had she been lying about?

"Did you keep my business card?" Corrine asked, following Angela to the front stoop. "I told you to call me twenty-four/seven, for any reason."

"I know, and I didn't call. And yet here you are on a Sunday afternoon. What am I missing, Detective?"

"If you're called in to a grand jury and asked what you know about your husband, what are you going to say, Angela?"

"That's a strange question."

"Do you want us to subpoena you? I know you don't believe me, but I really am trying to help you."

"By asking me whether I want to testify about my husband in front of a grand jury? That's an odd form of assistance."

"I know you had your friend Susanna send a hint to the DA's office. If you have something to say and want the cover of a grand jury, I can arrange that. If you're afraid of Jason—"

"I'm not *afraid* of my husband."

"Maybe not now. Now that he's moved out."

Angela's face fell as she realized the implication of Corrine's statement. "You were watching us?"

"You might think this is over, but it's only just beginning. Kerry Lynch has been missing for four days now. She left her dog, her ID, her credit cards—everything. Based on other evidence at the house, I don't think she left of her own accord. If

Jason wasn't here Wednesday night, we need to know that."

"I have nothing else to say to you, Detective."

"You told me he was home having dinner with you and watching movies that night, like any normal couple. But now he's moving out. Something's not right here."

"Leave, Detective, or I'll report you for harassment."

"All right, but like I said, call me whenever you want."

# 50

I didn't bother with a hello. "What did you do?"

When Susanna asked what I was talking about, I could tell immediately she was feigning confusion.

"You're the one friend I can trust right now, and you're lying to me. Stop it. That detective was here again, saying you sent some kind of hint to the district attorney. Something about me testifying in front of a grand jury. What did you do?"

"I'm trying to protect you, Angela."

"By sending a cop to my door? By forcing me to go to court?"

"I asked you point-blank yesterday whether you would lie for Jason if you got subpoenaed. You promised me that you wouldn't."

I had hoped my suspicions were somehow wrong. "And so you tried to make that happen. I can't believe you did that to me."

"*For you,* Angela. I did it *for* you, not *to* you. All I did was ask Eric to make a call to see if they were opening a grand jury. Frankly, it wasn't easy for me to ask that jerk for a favor."

"Don't make it sound like I should be grateful to you for this. You stabbed me in the back. You have no idea the kind of danger you're putting me in."

"Danger? Are you kidding me? Do you know the ethical compromises I've made over and over again since this happened, completely out of loyalty to you? I work for the *news* division of a major network, and I'm keeping company with an accused rapist, one whose career I helped launch. Then you go and falsify an alibi for him to the police. Never once have you acknowledged the position that puts me in."

I was furious at her for trying to manipulate the situation, but even I could see she had a valid point. This entire time, I had been leaning on her for support, knowing that she would put our friendship over her job. I tried to set aside my own emotions to thank her now. I also apologized for only thinking about myself.

"I wouldn't be upset if you were actually looking out for number one," she said, "but you're not. You're protecting Jason, at your own peril. Spencer's too. So, yes, that's why I tried to get you back on track with that call to the DA's office. I thought that if they opened a grand jury to look into Kerry's disappearance, it would give you a chance to come clean."

"He moved out today," I said suddenly. "Jason. He went to Colin's. And I served him with divorce papers last night. So you can stop trying to take care of us. I'm doing what I need to do. I made the decision on my way back from your house yesterday, so you had already helped, Susanna."

"Why didn't you tell me?"

"I don't think I was ready to say it out loud yet, and it's all moving so fast. We packed what he needed for now. We're going to sell the house." I still couldn't believe I was in this situation, and the drastic steps I'd need to take to get out of it.

"You're doing the right thing."

"I know," I said quietly.

"I'm sorry about the call to the DA. I was just so frustrated when you left yesterday."

"It's okay, Susanna. I understand."

"I won't ever stop trying to run your life, you know." Her voice was softer now. "We're okay?"

"Of course."

"So, at the risk of prying again too soon, is this breakup for real, or strictly on paper?" She had been the one to suggest a technical divorce, if only to protect us financially.

"He told her he would leave me for her." The words surprised me once they were out of my mouth.

"He admitted that to you?"

"No, to his lawyer." Now that I'd opened that door, I owed her a more complete explanation. "I've been reading his e-mails. All that nonsense about her company and kickbacks and whatever? He told Olivia he thought Kerry was pissed because he hadn't left me yet."

"So she framed him for a sexual assault?"

"Apparently."

"So you still think he's innocent?"

"Of that? Yes." When I first saw the police reports Olivia sent to Jason, I believed he was guilty. It was the photographs of her wrists that convinced me. Her description of the way he suddenly seemed like a different person. With that one e-mail, I became convinced that he had done to her what he had done to me, and she was willing to label that as rape, precisely as Susanna had argued. That was why I had kicked him out of the house that night.

"But how can you be sure?" Susanna asked.

"Because I read the explanation he gave to his lawyer. Just trust me, Susanna. It all makes sense. She set him up. I'm sure of it."

Normally, she would have pressed me for details, but she let it go, no doubt sensing that she had pushed me far enough for the day.

"Are you okay? Do you want me to come over?"

"No, I'm fine. I'm actually looking forward to being on my own for a while. You know I've never lived alone before? Not once. This might be good for me."

*

Spencer called me that night. I couldn't believe how much had changed in the two weeks since I drove him to camp.

"How's the arm? Still there?"

"Yeah. It's actually getting better already, but don't tell Kate. She's been, like, super nice to me. It was sort of her fault I got it. She was all, 'That stuff looks like poison ivy, but it's not.' That's worse than not noticing in the first place, right?"

"Are you doing okay up there otherwise?"

"Other than getting poisoned by nature under a counselor's watch? Yeah, I'm fine. It's pretty fun up here."

"It's only another week, huh?"

"Um, is it? You mentioned before it might be six weeks instead of three."

I shut my eyes and took another drink of wine. I couldn't believe I had ever thought that this would all be over by then. "No, unless of course you want to stay." I'd have to put the rest of the fees on a credit card.

"I'm actually kind of ready to come home, but I like it here too. Mom, what's going on? Did Dad's thing get taken care of? Is it over?"

I closed my eyes, searching for an honest response. "It's going to take longer than we thought, and Dad's going to stay at Colin's for a while. After what happened, we thought we'd have a better chance working things out if we lived apart for a while."

"You kicked him out."

"No—"

"Mom, he cheated on you, and you need a break. You can tell me that."

"It's more complicated, but, yes, we're on a break."

"Good."

"He's still your father." They had finally talked Friday night when Spencer called, the first time since Jason told him about the affair.

"I know, and I'll be fine with him someday. But he's the one who screwed up, not you. You can stop protecting me."

"I didn't want you to spend your whole summer hearing bad things about your family."

"Well, the stuff I've been imagining is probably way worse than what's really happening."

I couldn't believe how smart my kid was.

"Mom?"

"Yeah?"

"Do you want me just to come home? I can handle it. I promise."

I sucked in my breath. I had given myself so many pep talks about finally living on my own. I didn't need Jason. I didn't need anyone. "You don't mind?"

"Definitely not. Everyone's starting to stink up here. We take showers, and somehow we get smellier every day."

My laugh was more of a snort. I missed my kid. I told Kate I'd be picking Spencer up tomorrow.

# 51

Corrine woke up Monday morning to a call out at Columbia University. What was her early morning was the middle of the night for a college student. For all the headlines about college responses to sexual assaults on campus, universities seemed to be getting worse, not better, in their procedures. By the time Corrine arrived, the victim had already spoken to three friends, a student residence adviser, a faculty mentor, a student services counselor, and a university health clinic nurse. Only the nurse had encouraged the woman to call the police department. From what Corrine could gather, the rest of the crew spent that time convincing the woman that the police would arrest her for using Ecstasy with the suspect the night before, that she could file a complaint through the university system, and that criminal charges could ruin the suspect's life.

By the time Corrine got to SVU, it was a little after noon. She found a thick mailing envelope on her desk chair. It was from the Pittsburgh Police Department. She opened it to find the reports she had ordered when she first learned that Angela Powell had once been Angela Mullen, the girl recovered after police fatally shot Charles Franklin near the Canadian border.

Corrine flipped through the pages. Photographs of the house that had been Angela Powell's prison for three years, including two unmade twin beds and a crib with soiled linens. A doctor's report, describing Angela's refusal to let anyone else hold the baby until her mother showed up. An FBI agent's report, detailing Daniel and Virginia Mullen's threat to sue if their daughter and grandson weren't released to come home immediately. Background on Charles Franklin: one arrest for indecent exposure outside a public restroom, but no conviction; child pornography found in the house; the typical statements from neighbors saying he seemed so "normal." A printout of a photograph of him on a gurney, his face already gray and bloated, blood clotted in his dark brown hair.

Even in death, Charles Franklin exhibited physical traits Corrine recognized from photographs of Angela's son, Spencer: the dark hair, wide nose, low forehead. She hoped that there was some part of Angela's brain that protected her from seeing the resemblance.

Toward the bottom of the pile, she found the documents describing the discovery of the second victim, the one Angela had been instructed to call Sarah after Franklin brought her back to the home two years earlier. Franklin told Angela he finally got lucky on a trip to Cleveland when a girl "even dumber than you" accepted the offer of a ride home while waiting for a bus across the street from a shopping mall. He threatened to kill them both if they spoke a word of their previous existence under his roof, but Angela remembered Sarah telling her once that the only thing worth seeing where she grew up was the Rock & Roll Hall of Fame. She was fourteen years old when Franklin abducted her, making her about sixteen when it was all over.

The girl's decomposed body had washed up near the Pennsylvania–Ohio state line nearly two weeks after Franklin dumped her in Lake Erie. Two bullet wounds at the base of her skull. Putrefication had taken its toll. She was unrecognizable.

A tattoo approximately three inches by two on her right hip was unidentifiable, too, other than the fact of its existence.

The most recent document in the file was written almost a year and a half after Franklin was fatally shot during the rescue. The police and FBI had searched all missing-person reports from Ohio and the surrounding states, but nothing matched the description they were able to provide of "Sarah." The case, for all practical purposes, was closed. As far as Corrine could tell, no one had ever come forward to claim Sarah as their child. The parents who had allowed a fourteen-year-old to get a tattoo must not have looked especially hard when she disappeared.

Corrine felt empty when she had finished reading. Death wasn't a good enough punishment for a savage like Charles Franklin.

Corrine started to carry the file to the shredder, but stopped herself. She found space at the back of her bottom desk drawer. She'd keep it there for a while, just in case she needed it.

# 52

*Two Days Later*

"The *Long Island Press* has the story." It was Brian King on the phone. Corrine didn't need to ask which story he meant. "They called me to see if I consider Powell a suspect in Kerry's disappearance."

"And what did you say?"

"That any questions concerning Ms. Lynch should be directed to the police department where she lives."

"Very diplomatic."

"Except the reporter's no idiot. Her follow-up was whether we were still prosecuting Powell."

"And?"

"I said the case was on hold, pursuant to a court order."

"So why are you calling me?"

"Who else am I supposed to vent to? Don't you want to know what I found out?"

Of course she did.

"That guy you met out there is still the lead: Netter. He said Tom Fisher refused to answer any questions—about the affair, about where he was last Wednesday night, about Kerry's work for the company, about Oasis's international operations. Blanket invocation of the Fifth. And the realtor who was going to list

Kerry's house said Kerry wasn't interested in looking for a new place. She said she wanted to—quote—'take her money and get out of Dodge.'"

"But why would she leave without her stuff, or even her dog? And what's Fisher hiding?" Kerry had been missing for a week.

"Exactly. So I called Janice Martinez, who said she was about to contact me, because the same reporter had reached out to her. She wouldn't give me exact conversations with Kerry, but she said Kerry had been missing long enough that she was willing to share information she believed I needed. Apparently, Martinez notified Olivia Randall on Wednesday that Kerry was amenable to settling the civil case—with an eye toward dismissing the criminal case—if the price was right."

"She was going to take a payoff, just like we suspected."

"Exactly. But Martinez was also working out a settlement with Oasis, negotiating directly with Tom Fisher, not his counsel. In theory, it was to settle potential discrimination claims arising from Kerry's affair with Fisher, but the settlement would include a blanket nondisclosure agreement as to all matters involving her work at Oasis. Martinez said she got a feeling from both Kerry and Fisher that there was some subtext she was missing."

Corrine filled in the blanks. "Kerry would keep her mouth shut about the company's kickbacks. She was basically shaking down two different men—one for sexual assault, one for whatever's been going on at that company."

"Except now it's starting to look like one of the men is innocent. Jason Powell has been trying to convince us the whole time—telling us about Fisher, even sending us his movie rental receipts. Meanwhile, Fisher's the one invoking. So if one of them is responsible for whatever happened to Kerry, I know where I'd put my money. Maybe Fisher decided her price was too high, or thought Kerry would keep coming back for more."

"When are they running their story?"

"Any second. They'll go online first. Front page tomorrow. The other news outlets will follow. I sat down and took a fresh look at it all. The fact of the matter is this: If I had known at the outset everything I know now, I never would have charged Powell."

"So what should you do about that?"

"I know what I *should* do—dismiss this case immediately, at least until they find Kerry. What I'm allowed to do by my boss is another question."

*

Corrine finished the next paragraph of the supplemental report she'd been writing, but couldn't stop thinking about what she had learned about Tom Fisher. Nick Lowe, the restaurant delivery guy, said he'd seen Jason and Kerry together at her home months ago, in which case Powell was telling the truth about their affair, and yet there were no text messages or e-mails to suggest a romantic connection. According to him, Kerry was paranoid about her phone and computer usage because she thought her company was looking for an excuse to fire her. But what if she had other reasons for concern?

She opened her browser and searched for "Oasis Water Africa." She learned from press releases on the company's website that Oasis had been granted contracts in Tanzania and Mozambique a little more than three years ago—which would have been around the time Kerry was dating her boss.

Corrine picked up her phone and called Netter. "I was wondering if that might be you when I saw the number," he said once she identified herself. "I spoke to your ADA not an hour ago."

"Sounds like you're making progress with Fisher."

"That's overly generous. He's not talking."

"I assume you've got Kerry's financial records by now?"

"Yep. No recent large withdrawals. It's looking less and less like she left voluntarily."

"What about deposits?"

"Just direct deposits from work. Are you talking about the settlements her lawyer was trying to work out with Powell and Fisher? She said they hadn't talked final numbers yet."

"But Nick Lowe says Fisher was at Kerry's house that night. Given their history, maybe they were trying to work something out directly—without their lawyers."

"We're working on the same theory here. Only thing is: he's a rich man. Buying off an ex-mistress wouldn't have cost much."

"Unless she was in a position to make him a much less rich man—or get him in trouble with the feds."

"You're talking about all that foreign-country stuff with the company?"

"Powell claims that Kerry kept promising to help him prove his suspicions. But maybe she wasn't merely going to snoop around on his behalf. She was sleeping with her boss when the company got those contracts in Africa."

"You think she actually knew about kickbacks?"

"Or was even involved. That's why I was asking about her bank records. You mentioned her paychecks were on direct deposit. Can you go back a few years and look for anything unusual?"

"Yeah—I've got the bank info right here. It shouldn't take long."

She managed to type another section of her report, phone tucked between shoulder and ear, while Netter did the research.

"It looks like you might've been onto something. She got a huge raise about three and a half years ago." As he recited the numbers, Corrine figured out that it was about a 20 percent raise, issued only a month before Oasis announced new projects in Africa. Corrine pulled up Kerry's profile on LinkedIn.

"I don't see a corresponding promotion listed on her résumé," Corrine said. "She's been the VP in charge of global marketing for five years."

"Plus her year-end bonus was an even hundred grand, when it was twenty the previous two years."

"And since then?"

"Fifty."

The financial information wasn't a smoking gun, but it was consistent with Corrine's current theory. If there was corruption involved in Oasis's international projects, Kerry Lynch could have been complicit. She had told a realtor that she wanted to sell her house and leave town. Corrine had a feeling that the money Kerry's attorney was seeking to settle a sexual discrimination claim was nothing compared to what Kerry might have tried to extract from Tom Fisher directly when he came to her house.

The images Corrine had been seeing for days flashed in her mind again, but this time she saw the face of the man holding the crystal egg over Kerry's head. It belonged to Tom Fisher, not Jason Powell.

She told Netter she thought he was on the right track and ended the call. She immediately dialed Brian King. It only took a few minutes to lay out what she had learned.

"I feel better about my decision now," he said.

"Which is?"

"I need to dismiss our case against Powell. Maybe he did it, maybe he didn't. But I have too many doubts to continue the prosecution any longer."

As Corrine hung up the phone, she said a little prayer for both Angela Powell and Kerry Lynch.

# 53

"Spencer, you weren't kidding. These clothes smell like rotting fish." I had just pulled Spencer's camp laundry from the dryer, and every single item was still saturated in the same putrid scent. "Seriously, how is this possible?" I threw them back into the washing machine for a second tour, adding another capful of detergent.

Spencer had come home from camp two days earlier. His presence, more than anything, made the house feel as close to normal as I could remember in the last month. I had told him that Jason had been charged with a crime, but the case had been placed on hold to reach a settlement. It made it all sound so nice and neat, like an ordinary transaction to be resolved by contract.

To be safe, I had also mentioned that "the woman" had apparently "gone off the grid," and the police had "come by" to make sure that Jason's whereabouts could be accounted for the night she'd been seen last. "Your dad and I had an argument Wednesday, and he stayed with Uncle Colin for the night. I didn't want the police to read into it, so I said he was here at the house when you called. But he was with Colin, so it's the same thing."

Spencer seemed to take it all in stride. He was more upset at the thought of moving, but I had enlisted him in searching Zillow and StreetEasy for a rental apartment he might like. "It has to be walkable to school. And I was thinking we should find something pet friendly. Maybe it's time we got a dog."

Cliché, I know, to offer my kid a puppy to make up for a divorce, but I was willing to try anything.

When he asked me how big an apartment we were looking for, I realized I still pictured a home office for Jason and enough closet space for both of us.

"Let's just get a two-bedroom, since it's temporary."

Spencer had immediately volunteered to transfer to a public school if we needed to save money. I fibbed and told him that I was only keeping our rent low because rent was "money down the drain." Once we were ready to buy, I assured him, we'd get something better.

I had hit the wash button on the machine when Spencer came rushing from his room, iPad in hand. "Mom, that lady's missing."

"I told you that, Spencer. With all the media attention, she probably took a break for a while." God knows I had thought a few times about running off to a beach on the other side of the world until this all blew over.

"No, but it's in the news now. You need to read this."

"It's better to ignore that stuff." In truth, I was fairly certain I had read every single article, tweet, post, or comment written on the Internet about Jason since I first heard Rachel Sutton's name. My skin had gotten no thicker as a result. "They never know what they're talking about."

"No, they *do* know. Listen to this: 'Despite Lynch's role as the complainant in the pending sexual assault case against renowned economist and author Powell, law enforcement sources say that the current investigation does not implicate Powell as a suspect in Miss Lynch's disappearance. In fact, the ongoing investigation has cast doubt on the veracity of Miss Lynch's original claim against Powell."

"What?" I stood next to him and read the article myself. An unnamed former boyfriend of Miss Lynch was believed to be the last person to see her and had invoked his right to silence rather than answer police questions. The article closed by noting that the New York District Attorney's Office still had a case pending against Jason Powell, but quoted ADA Brian King as saying, "We are taking a close look at developing facts that may affect our decision making. For now, we want to make absolutely clear that Dr. Powell is not a suspect in the investigation currently ongoing on Long Island. His whereabouts on that night have been accounted for."

By me, I thought, completing the sentence. Spencer was running toward his room. "I'm calling Dad to make sure he knows."

It occurred to me that my son hadn't stopped—even for a second—to worry about what had happened to Kerry Lynch. Was empathy developed by nature or nurture? I pushed away the idea. Despite his biology, Spencer was nothing like Charles Franklin.

A few minutes later, he was back in the laundry room, cell phone in hand. "Dad wants to talk to you."

"Hey, did you see it?" I asked.

"Olivia just texted me about it right before the phone rang. They called her for a comment earlier today about Kerry's disappearance, but she decided it was better to say nothing. She sensed that the tide was on our side."

*Our*. I didn't know who that was anymore.

"Congratulations." It was an awkward response.

"I don't want to get my hopes up, but this might actually be over. Maybe she blackmailed her boss and got enough money to start over somewhere new."

"Without telling anyone?" Spencer hadn't seemed worried about Kerry, but Jason obviously was. "Are you okay?"

"Yeah." He sounded sad. "I miss you, though. Spencer said he wanted to see me, so that's good news."

I was tracing the herringbone pattern of our oak floors with my big toe, wondering how much longer we'd have this amazing house.

"Do you want to come over for dinner? I can cook."

"Really? I would love that."

"That should be okay, right? It's for you to see Spencer."

"I think it's perfectly normal for two separated coparents to meet for dinner with their son."

"Good. We'll be here."

I went to Agata & Valentina and bought lamb chops, his favorite. On the way home, I called Susanna to cancel our plans to get takeout and watch the next two episodes of *Billions*. We were binge-watching together. She was rooting for Axe, while I was on the side of the government.

"And this has nothing to do with that article in the *Long Island Press*?" she asked.

I couldn't put anything past Susanna. "Jason's coming over. For the record, Spencer's the one who invited him. He hasn't seen his father for more than two weeks. He seems ready to forgive him."

"*He's* ready to forgive, or you are? Angela, please tell me you're not rethinking this."

"I told you, we already filled out all the paperwork and have a rough agreement sketched out. That lawyer's crunching the numbers. You wanted me to protect myself and Spencer, and I am. We're getting divorced. The house is for sale. And I haven't forgotten what Jason did to me. But I never said I didn't love him."

While the lamb was roasting, I put on the pale-yellow linen dress that Jason had bought me last summer as my anniversary gift, hoping he'd recognize it.

He had told that woman—a horrible woman who had been willing to destroy his life and mine—that he would leave me for her. Maybe it was cruel, but I wanted to make him want me.

By the time he arrived for dinner, he had gotten another piece of good news: the district attorney's office was dismissing the charges against him.

# III

# ANGELA

# 54

*Five Weeks Later*

That day's appointment with Dr. Boyle was a joint session, without Spencer. We all had individual sessions, in addition to our couples therapy, and the occasional joint family discussions. Basically, we had been living in Dr. Boyle's office for the last month.

We were also living in two apartments in adjacent towers on Mercer Street. His two-bedroom was in 250 Mercer, mine in 300. Spencer had rooms in both.

Our most recent couples session had been spent going over finances. If all went according to plan, we'd close on the carriage house next week. Jason referred to the thirty-year-old buyer, who was paying cash with his hedge-fund money, as Satan. All I cared about was that, after a bidding war, he was paying $250,000 more than asking. We'd walk away with nearly $2 million in cash, after the mortgage and taxes.

To maximize the amount of money going to me, I was taking not only my half but also a lump-sum alimony payment, which meant I'd get almost all of the proceeds from the house. Our divorce decree also gave me half of Jason's retirement account.

Now we were back here with Boyle again. "You're about to end your marriage," Dr. Boyle said. "How do you feel about that, Jason?"

"Terrible. Obviously. I know this is my fault. I never would have left you, Angela."

I looked down at my lap to avoid crying. "I know."

"Angela, you've been very clear that you initiated this divorce for practical reasons more than emotional ones. But the circumstances have changed since you first reached this decision, have they not? And yet you're still going forward with the divorce. Would you like to talk about that?"

After Jason's criminal case was dismissed, Olivia got Kerry's lawsuit dismissed too, based on her unavailability. Rachel Sutton had accepted a $7,500 settlement in exchange for dismissing her claims and a mutual nondisclosure agreement over what I still believed was a genuine misunderstanding in Jason's office—a combination of a mistimed change of clothing and a habit Jason may have formed of being a little too cute around attractive women.

"Maybe it's from living all those weeks under a microscope," I said, "but we still have no idea how this is going to play out. Kerry's still missing." The case dismissals were "without prejudice," meaning they could technically be reinstated later. "They haven't officially named Tom Fisher as a suspect. Any way you look at it, this is the sensible thing to do."

Jason was still on the faculty at NYU, having agreed to a one-year research leave at half pay for the coming year. He also still had FSS Consulting, where he had lost some clients but was developing others. A week earlier, FSS and two of Jason's investment clients had filed a lawsuit against Oasis for fraud, arguing that Oasis had failed to disclose material information about deals they had closed for water projects in Africa. Jason's decision to back what he now alleged was a corrupt corporation was a minor dent in his reputation, but it paled in comparison to the earlier allegations. Meanwhile, the news coverage of his lawsuit against

Oasis fueled media speculation that Kerry's disappearance—as well as her seemingly false accusation against Jason—was tied to her work with Tom Fisher. It also sold a lot of books. *Equalonomics* was back on the *New York Times* list.

I was taking the bulk of our money—at least technically—but Jason would be back on his feet in no time. Olivia Randall was confident that the DA's office would never agree to reissue Jason's charges when (and if) Kerry reappeared. As for Kerry's civil charges, the statute of limitations was a year. If they weren't brought again by then, we wouldn't need to worry any longer about her shaking us down for money, and Jason and I would be free to marry again.

"Did you tell Spencer you were signing today?" Boyle asked.

Spencer was spending the week with my mother in East Hampton, enrolled in sports camp. "We'll tell him this weekend in person. We're both going out to pick him up."

"I have to ask you, Angela: Do you think it's possible you're using this arrangement to avoid saying that what you really want is to end your relationship with Jason?"

I shook my head. "Jason knows how I feel about him."

Before we left the office, Dr. Boyle called in his receptionist, who acted as a witness to our signatures. Once the lawyer filed the papers, it would be official: we were getting divorced.

*

We walked the six blocks back to our apartments together, reaching his building first.

"Do you want to come up?" he asked.

I didn't have Spencer as an excuse to go home. I could almost feel the papers tucked into my purse, pressing into my side. They weren't filed yet. "Yeah, that sounds good."

"You're sure?"

"Yes. And if I'm ever not sure, I'm going to tell you."

The first time was right after we accepted the offer on the carriage house, when it became clear we were really going through with the divorce. He came over to say good-bye to our home. He held me while we both cried, and when he kissed me, I could tell where it was heading. When I took a step back, he started to apologize, but I told him not to stop. Before I led him to our room, I asked him to let me set the pace. In return, he asked me to promise to stop if at any second I was feeling uncomfortable.

This would be my third time up to his apartment since.

When we were done, he asked me what had changed.

"We need to go back to Boyle to have that conversation."

"Please don't ever say his name while I'm naked."

"Come on, Jason, what do you mean? *Everything* has changed."

"I know." He pulled me into the crook of his arm, and I curled up against him. "I meant, what's changed about *this*? You were never like this before."

Wasn't I? I suppose not. Maybe it was that day with Colin, which I would never tell anyone about.

"Yes, I was," I said. "You just don't remember."

"I'm so glad we're back together again."

I felt a wave of nausea—not like the flashbacks; to my surprise, I hadn't experienced anything close to one of those. I felt sick, not about the past but about the present. Jason believed we were "back together," only minutes after signing divorce papers, all because I had slept with him a few times. Those three years when we had stopped doing this—were we *not* together?

"Me too," I said. "The next year's going to feel like an eternity."

"There's something I haven't told you, and I don't want there to be any secrets between us anymore."

I swallowed, knowing there would never be an end to the lies.

"I told her about you," he said quietly, staring up at the ceiling. "About what happened to you in Pittsburgh. Not everything. I didn't tell her about Spencer, but she knows about Charles Franklin."

I clenched my eyes shut, not wanting to process the implications of what he was telling me.

"I'm so sorry, Angela. She was making you out to be an awful wife, and it just came out. I don't know what I was thinking. But I owe you the truth. Kerry's still out there somewhere, and she knows."

My whole body began to shake. I didn't want to think about where Kerry was now. The apartment's air conditioning was struggling against the heat outside, but I felt as if I were standing in a freezer. I pulled the blankets up to my neck and forced myself to regain control.

"You didn't tell her about Spencer? Only about me?"

I would never have told Jason the truth about Spencer except for the problems I had carrying a baby after we got married. My condition wasn't temporary. It was structural, according to the doctors—an anomaly in the uterus. Not insurmountable, but how could I explain my difficulties bringing a child to term under the most privileged medical conditions on the literal planet, when I had supposedly given birth in captivity as a crime victim? He didn't understand why I wouldn't keep trying.

So I had to tell Jason. A year after Charlie kidnapped me, Sarah showed up. Spencer was born the following year. When we had to leave the house after the police came, Charlie decided that two girls and a baby was too specific a description. He killed Sarah, and kept me and Spencer.

Most of what I told the police was true, I explained, except Sarah was the one who got pregnant, not me. But she was younger, and always a little bit off, and I had taken care of the baby at least as much as she had. That was Charlie's logic, at least.

When the rescue team descended on Niagara Falls, my only goal was to protect Spencer and keep him with me. I said he was mine. That's why Mom said she'd sue everyone on-site if they tried to examine us physically. Spencer didn't have my blood, but I was the only family he had left.

"I swear on my life," Jason promised now, "I will take the truth about our son to the grave. But to have spoken even a word about your past to her was a terrible betrayal. It wasn't my story to tell."

I nodded, imagining their conversation—Kerry running me down, trying to convince Jason to marry her. Jason explaining that there were things about me she didn't understand.

But he had stopped short of telling her everything.

"Well, there's nothing we can do about it now, I guess." The cavalier words were overcompensation for the emotions I was fighting to control. "Maybe she has one ounce of decency and will keep it to herself."

"I'd do anything to turn back the clock and change all this," he said.

He had no idea how much I wanted that, too.

The room became quiet, and I stood up to get dressed. "I meant what I said before," he said softly. "I would have never left you."

Maybe not, I thought, but that's not what you told Kerry.

When I left his building, I crossed Eighth Street. Inside the mobile store I bought a prepaid phone, the kind a European tourist might buy on a visit to New York City. In some circles, it would be called a burner. I was going to need it. I had made my decision weeks ago. I would never be Jason's wife again, which meant I needed a longer-term plan.

# 55

*Three Days Later*

I remember when I used to think of the reserved cars at the front of the Cannonball as the equivalent of a private jet, the way the rich folks arrived to the Hamptons in the summer. A couple times a week, an express train ran between Manhattan and the Hamptons, shaving the ride down to about two hours. The big splurge was a booked seat during peak season, at double the price, with bar service and no anxiety about having to find room on a train carrying twice the number of people intended.

Now, our $51 tickets felt like slumming. The Audi had been sold, along with the carriage house, so driving was no longer an option. Last summer we had gotten into the habit of using the helicopter service to save time, because in Jason's world, time was money. Now we were the kind of people who rode the train, springing for the reserved seats.

"You sure your mom's okay with me staying there? Susanna offered me a guest room."

I was too busy waving down a taxi in the crowd to have this discussion with him again.

"We've talked about this a hundred times. If I could get away with staying with Susanna instead of Mom's, I would totally do that, but Mom would kill me. And Spencer wants you at home with us."

The plan was for Jason and me to take the twin beds in my childhood room, because Spencer asked to sleep in the living room, where I knew he'd stay up all night watching YouTube. This was going to be our first weekend as a family under one roof in more than a month.

*

"Angela?"

The cabdriver was looking at me in the rearview mirror.

"Hey, yeah. Sorry, I can't see you from back here."

I leaned over the bench seat to get a better view of the driver. The man was probably about my age, but didn't look great. Something about him seemed familiar.

"It's Steve."

Steve. Right, Steve.

"Yes, of course, it's so great to see you." I searched the recesses of my memory for the local Steves. Clerk at IGA. Bartender at Wolfie's. Trisha's cousin. Yep, Trisha's cousin, that was the one. "How are your parents?"

Steve's father was the least horrible brother among the Faulkner men. He was a mechanic at the shop on Springs Fireplace. His mother used to sew tablecloths and napkins to sell at the farmer's market.

"Dad passed last year—a stroke. Same with yours, right?"

"Five years ago. I'm so sorry."

"Mom, she's okay. Needs a walker already because of swelling in her legs, but otherwise, she's doing good."

Jason was looking at me, obviously wishing we had taken Mom up on her offer to meet us at the train station.

"Well, it's real nice seeing you. We're only out for the

weekend." For some reason, I needed him to know we didn't own a house here. "My son's been out, staying with his grandmom. We're here to pick him up."

"Don't suppose you heard from Trisha this summer?"

I shook my head. "I haven't talked to her since—wow, high school, I guess."

"I figured. I thought maybe with you being in the news and everything, she might have reached out—"

He was looking at Jason, not me, in the rearview mirror.

"Nope," I said. "She may not even know I got married. How's she doing?"

"No one knows. She always said she was going to get away from here and never speak to another member of the family. I guess she meant it."

"I'm sorry to hear that."

"The two of you were always the same—wanting to get as far away as possible. Hell, if she had stuck around, you probably wouldn't give her a second thought, the way you've moved on."

Next to me, Jason nudged my leg with his knee. Instead of ending the conversation, though, I leaned forward to make sure Steve could hear me. "That's not true."

"Yeah, well, I guess there's no way to know."

Jason rolled his eyes and began reciting a turn-by-turn guide to Mom's place to fill the silence.

The house was empty, a note left on the laminate-topped breakfast table: "Went to IGA. Back soon. I'll cook!"

"I thought you told her we wanted to take her to the Grill tonight."

I had. She responded by saying she'd rather eat corn flakes than put up with the "crowds of summer sewage."

"I figured she was less likely to give me the riot act in public," Jason said.

This would be the first time my mother had seen Jason since I found out about his affair. "She promised to be on good behavior." In reality, her only assurance was that she wouldn't run Jason down in front of Spencer. "Do you still think about her?" I asked.

"Your mom?"

"No. About *her*." Kerry, I thought. "I asked you once, in our room, if you loved her. You never answered me."

The kitchen was so quiet, I didn't want to breathe. The only sound was a lawn mower in the distance.

"Yes, but not the way I love you. And she obviously didn't love me back, or she never could have done what she did."

*

The next morning, I woke up thinking I had heard a phone ring.

I opened my eyes to see Jason in the twin bed three feet from mine, ear already to phone. I heard muffled voices and dishes clanking in the kitchen and fumbled to find my own phone in the blankets wrapped around my legs. It was nearly nine. Jason never slept in this late. I suspected he had been waiting for me to get up before venturing anywhere near my mother.

I listened to a series of "uh-huhs," a "Where?," and a "Do they know anything else?" before he hung up.

He was staring up at the ceiling, absolutely still.

"Is everything okay?"

"That was Olivia. A cop she knows called her. They found Kerry."

"Where was—" I didn't finish the question. He was covering his face with his hands.

"She's dead. Kerry's dead."

I joined my mother and son in the kitchen, leaving Jason alone to cry for a woman he had once loved.

*

After breakfast I asked if anyone wanted to take a walk up to Gerard Point with me, knowing that Jason would want to go for a run, and that Spencer shared my mother's view that walking was for people who didn't have cars.

I waited until I had made the turn from Springs Fireplace Road onto Gerard Drive to remove my burner phone and a single Post-it note from my skirt pocket. Sitting on my favorite boulder, a few feet from the water, I called an international number and then used the keypad to follow the automated instructions. As a final step, I entered my eight-digit PIN, already committed to memory.

The computerized system on the other end of the line confirmed that I had a balance of $100. It was official: I had an offshore account. We'd be closing on the carriage house on Tuesday. Our lawyer was planning to take care of the checks for alimony and my half of Jason's retirement account at the same time.

I looked out over Gardiners Bay, realizing this might be the last time I saw it. I was actually going to miss this place.

# 56

Corrine leaned close to her bathroom mirror to apply a second coat of mascara and then stepped back to make sure it wasn't too much. As a final check, she used her compact to inspect the back of her hair, which she sometimes forgot to tend to. Not too shabby. She had a seventh date tonight with a sports producer named Andrew who made specials for ESPN. He was the first man she'd been willing to see that many times since the divorce. Even more surprisingly, he had asked her to go with him next weekend to a wedding in South Carolina, and she hadn't hesitated. It dawned on her that she—who prided herself on being at least one step ahead of everyone—may have gone and gotten a boyfriend without realizing it.

She was strapping on high-heeled sandals she knew she'd regret later when her cell phone rang. It was a 516 area code—Nassau County. Something in the back of her brain told her what was about to happen.

It was Netter. The body had been found late the night before by two teenagers who had wandered away from a beach party for privacy. "I'm sorry it took me so long to tell you. Been working nonstop. No autopsy yet, obviously, but it was clearly a head injury. You were right about the missing crystal egg."

She had known she was right the second she inspected Kerry's living room.

"What beach?"

"Ocean Beach. The task force is on it now, but I'm still lead." Ocean Beach was at least an hour east of Kerry's house, in Suffolk County, a two-hour drive from Manhattan with zero traffic.

"Anything new on Tom Fisher?"

"His wife and kids were visiting the grandparents on the Cape the night Kerry was last seen, so if he has an alibi, we don't know about it. The drive from Kerry's to the drop site and back to his place is about ninety miles. We're hoping he had to stop for gas and are checking all the stations off the Meadowbrook. And we're getting warrants now for his house, car, and office."

Married ex-boyfriend she was shaking down for money, spotted at the house the last night she was seen. Corrine could imagine a judge signing off on that.

"If you need anything from the NYPD, let me know?"

"Will do."

"And, hey, thanks for calling. Seriously."

Corrine made it all the way to dessert before she mentioned the case to Andrew. She could tell from the way he kept looking at his napkin that he would have preferred to discuss anything else, and she knew that he would find a reason that maybe she shouldn't join him in South Carolina after all.

# 57

Six days later, the nightmare began again. I was on my way home from Dr. Boyle's office when my cell phone rang. It was Susanna.

"Are you okay?" She sounded rushed.

"Yeah, I'm fine. What's up?"

"You don't know?"

"What are you talking about?"

"I need you to sit down."

"I'm on the street, covered in sweat." Last weekend at Mom's had been a break from the city heat. I was counting down the days before I could sit on a beach again. "Just tell me."

"I got a call from our crime beat guy. Jason's in custody. They arrested him at his apartment."

I turned to face Jason's building on Eighth and Mercer, and remembered the three police cars I had seen pulled to the curb on Eighth Street on my way to therapy. I'd thought nothing of it at the time. "Is it another woman?"

"No. It's Kerry. They're charging him with murder, Angela."

I reached out for something to help me stand. I was leaning against a trash can. "That doesn't make sense. She was found all the way on Ocean Beach. That's at least two hours away, and we gave them a timeline for the whole night."

"Are you listening to yourself, Angela? Have you forgotten

that Jason wasn't actually with you? If they arrested him, they must have evidence. And they know you lied to the police about his alibi. I told you to come clean by now."

Her words were still ringing in my ears when I walked into my lobby. It took a moment to register that the doorman was speaking to me. A police officer wanted to see me. He gestured to a man in a uniform, sitting on a bench by the elevator.

Technically, he was a sheriff's deputy, not a cop, and he was there to serve me with documents. It was happening: I was subpoenaed to appear in front of a grand jury in Nassau County.

# 58

Netter finally answered his phone the third time Corrine tried to reach him. He obviously knew why she was calling.

"Sorry, I wanted to give you a heads-up, but the ADA's on the warpath about leaks."

"I could've at least helped you pick him." She had learned about Jason Powell's arrest from a news report on her car radio only twenty minutes earlier. Netter had apparently gone through the Manhattan South homicide squad instead of contacting Corrine for assistance.

"I think our DA is pissed that your DA made a statement clearing Powell before all the facts were in."

"And what are the facts? Last I heard, you liked Fisher for it."

"You're won't be happy about this, either, but we matched a piece of physical evidence near the body to the DNA swab you took from Powell. Sorry."

Her swab; his case.

"What kind of physical evidence?" she asked.

There was a long pause, followed by another apology.

"Wow, it's like that. Okay. I guess the wife lied to me about his alibi after all."

"So it would appear. The ADA subpoenaed her. We'll see if that puts the fear of God into her."

"Assuming she lied, how'd he get to Long Island that night?"

"We're thinking he trained it out to her place, and then used Kerry's car to move her body to Suffolk County and back. Hey, I gotta run."

She heard voices in the background. "Wait. Did you find blood in her trunk? Or video from the train station?"

"Don't worry about it. We've got DNA. It's locked and loaded."

That was the problem with DNA. It made law enforcement lazy. If they convicted the wrong person years ago, they expected DNA to fix it. And if they had DNA to match? Forget about it; they were done.

As she continued to crawl through traffic, she realized that transportation was the one equalizer in New York City. Unless you were in a helicopter or a hovercraft, you had to deal with this bullshit in one form or another.

So how the hell had Jason Powell gotten to Long Island that night?

Netter didn't seem bothered by this hole in the case, but Corrine could picture a lawyer like Olivia Randall driving a long-haul truck through it.

Sitting behind the wheel of her own car, she started thinking of all the ways a person could get to Port Washington and back. The train, cab, the usual car rental companies, Zipcar, Uber, Lyft, Juno. The more she thought through the options, the more futile the search felt.

Forget the train; he would definitely use a car. And he would use his own car if at all possible to avoid a paper trail. His plates hadn't turned up on the readers from the bridges and tunnels, but a lot of city drivers bought blocking devices to protect themselves against red-light cameras.

Kerry Lynch was no longer her case, but Corrine wasn't the type to accept loose ends. Maybe she'd poke around in her spare time.

# 59

*Five Days Later*

Jason looked ten years older and ten pounds lighter. It was the first time Olivia had been able to get me access to him since he was denied bail after his arrest. I spotted what I thought was a bruise on his left cheekbone, but he swore I was seeing things because I was worried.

"How are you and Spencer holding up?"

I shrugged. "I mean, fine, under the circumstances. I'm doing my best to tell Spencer this will all get worked out, but I see him on his computer all the time—trying to figure out why exactly his father is here."

"He thinks I'm guilty."

"No, of course not." I was unable to meet his eyes. If it weren't for me talking Spencer off the ledge, he'd be on the news telling anyone who would listen that Jason killed Kerry Lynch, was a horrible father, and had been on the grassy knoll with Lee Harvey Oswald. Dr. Boyle said I should expect his loyalties to swing wildly for the foreseeable future.

"There is one thing," I said, as if it had just come to me. "A *New York* magazine reporter called me last night. I looked at her stuff. She's not just some blogger. She writes these long, intense pieces. She left a message for Mom, too. And right when I was coming in, Mom texted me. Three different people out East got calls, including my old boss at Blue Heron."

"What did you say?"

"No comment, of course, but I don't know how long I can keep that up. She's obviously digging around. When she called Mom, she even mentioned that time Trisha and I got in that car accident with the BMW guy."

"And how do you feel about that?"

I liked that question when it came from Dr. Boyle, but from Jason, it was annoying. "Afraid. Terrified. It's only a matter of time before it gets out."

Jason's expression was blank.

"Oh my God, I'm so sorry," I said. "I'm rambling about myself when—I'll be fine. I'll figure something out."

I did my best to sound optimistic as Jason outlined Olivia's strategy to blame Tom Fisher for Kerry's murder. Already, she had confirmed that Oasis's marketing department—under Kerry's control—had spent millions more in Africa leading up to the finalization of their deal there than in other international markets. In combination with Kerry's pay records, Olivia planned to argue that Kerry was complicit in a kickback scheme at Oasis, had framed Jason to silence his concerns about the financial irregularities, and had finally been murdered when she tried to blackmail Fisher for more money.

But with each tactical point he raised, I reminded myself that Olivia's job was to get her client off, even if he was guilty. The police hadn't arrested Tom Fisher. They had arrested Jason, which meant they had evidence, and I had been racking my brain for five days, wondering what it could be.

"Olivia says a trial will take until at least November," Jason said. "Spencer will be in school by then. It'll be a media frenzy. You guys should go."

"Where? My mom's? No thank you. And we can't keep sending Spencer to camp."

"No, like actually *go*. You have enough money. Find some place where you can get some peace and quiet."

"We need to stay here with you."

"Why? In case you haven't noticed, I'm in jail." He looked down at his orange jumpsuit. "I don't want you afraid of picking up your phone because some reporter is asking questions about you. And it's only going to get worse as the trial date gets closer. Seriously—I insist on this. I'm going to call Colin and literally *make him* find you guys somewhere to stay until the trial."

I was shaking my head.

"Just promise me you'll think about it."

"Fine, I'll think about it and then not do it. I need to go now."

It was an abrupt end to the visit, but we both knew I had somewhere else to be. I was testifying in front of the grand jury.

# 60

I did a quick scan of the room. Eighteen grand jurors from my quick head count, seated in two rows. No judge, as Olivia Randall had warned me to expect. The only other person in the room, besides the court reporter, was the prosecutor, a woman named Heather Rocco.

The background information moved quickly—dates of the marriage, separation, divorce, and Kerry Lynch's rape allegation. From an outsider's perspective, my entire life had boiled down to those four dates.

Once introductions were done, ADA Rocco asked me if I understood the conditions under which I was testifying. She explained what Olivia Randall had already told me: any witness, like me, subpoenaed to appear before a grand jury was automatically granted immunity in exchange for his or her testimony. That explanation sufficed for the ADA's purposes, but I knew far more than the grand jurors about what that meant. Unlike most states, in New York, the state's decision to force me to be here entitled me to something called "transactional immunity." Olivia had called it the "golden ticket" of deals with the government. In short, the police could find a videotape of me helping Jason move Kerry's body to Ocean Beach and they still wouldn't be able to prosecute me. I had blanket immunity from anything involving Kerry Lynch—full stop.

On the other hand, I could not claim the Fifth. Because I had immunity, nothing could actually "incriminate" me. The only basis I had to refuse a question was spousal privilege. Olivia had wanted me to hire a lawyer to stand in the hallway in case I needed to ask someone what I could or could not do, but I wasn't about to start cutting checks to yet another attorney.

After ADA Rocco had assured the grand jurors that I understood the ground rules, she dove immediately into the subject of Jason's relationship with Kerry. "Isn't it true that Jason claimed he'd had a consensual affair and that Ms. Lynch fabricated the criminal allegation as an act of revenge?"

"I apologize if I'm mistaken, but I was told that anything Jason actually said to me while we were married was privileged."

"Very well, then." Rocco paused to remind the grand jurors that they'd already heard testimony from a previous witness regarding Jason's defense. My guess was that either Detective Duncan or Brian King, or both, had already testified regarding the facts of the original case against Jason. "In addition to the criminal case, Ms. Lynch was also pursuing a civil suit, demanding five million dollars in damages. Is that correct?"

"Yes, that's my understanding."

"And both the criminal and civil cases were dismissed after Kerry Lynch went missing?"

"That is what I was told after the fact."

"What were the grounds for your divorce, Ms. Powell?"

"I believe the exact terminology is that our marriage had 'broken down irretrievably.'"

"Was your husband unfaithful?"

"Yes."

"Allegedly with Kerry Lynch?"

"Yes, among others." I saw two different grand jurors—both women—shift in their seats. I sensed that they didn't like the idea of my being here, forced to discuss my husband's infidelities.

"But you were still married to Mr. Powell when Detective Corrine Duncan came to your home on June 7 and informed you that Kerry Lynch was missing?"

"Yes."

"Did she ask you where your husband, Jason, was the previous night?"

"Yes." Olivia had instructed me only to answer the question presented. If Rocco asked me if I knew the time, the correct answer was yes. It wasn't my responsibility to make her job easier.

"And what did you tell her?"

"That Jason was at home with me." It was a truthful response to the question she had posed.

"What specifically did you tell her about your activities that night?"

"Well, there was dinner. And a phone call from our son. And watching *La La Land* before going to sleep."

"And was that true?"

I paused, focusing on her precise wording. "Yes."

"I'm going to remind you, Ms. Powell, that you're under oath, under penalty of perjury."

"I understand that."

"I can ask your son under oath about that phone call if you'd prefer."

"I answered the question you asked, Ms. Rocco."

A heavyset woman toward the end of the second row—one of the women who had seemed uncomfortable at the mention of Jason's affairs—held up her hand sheepishly. "It's the way you worded it," she said. "You asked about *her* activities, then asked if that was true."

The prosecutor looked confused, and then embarrassed.

"I didn't realize we were playing semantics, Ms. Powell."

"I'm answering your questions."

"Was your ex-husband, Jason Powell, with you the entire night during those activities?"

"No."

I said it in such an offhand manner that Rocco marched forward with the first few words of her next question before registering my response. The entire room fell silent until one of the jurors coughed. Rocco stared at me, as if expecting me to retract my answer. I returned her gaze but said nothing.

"So, you weren't telling the truth to Detective Duncan when you said Mr. Powell was with you at home?"

"No, I was not." I had made Colin call two other defense attorneys to make certain that I had immunity. The law was absolutely clear: because I was subpoenaed as a grand jury witness, I could not be charged, not even for my dishonesty to Detective Duncan about Jason's alibi. I could, however, be prosecuted if I lied to the grand jury, so I was determined to be truthful.

"Do you know where Mr. Powell was that night?"

Technically, the correct answer was no, but I still wanted to protect Jason. "He was with Colin Harris."

Once again, I had caught Rocco off guard. "If you knew where your husband was that night, why did you lie to Detective Duncan and say that he was with you?"

I did my best to make eye contact with each juror as I told them about the stress we'd been under since Jason's mistress had framed him for a sexual assault as punishment for not leaving his family to be with her and to curry favor with her corrupt employer. Rocco tried to cut me off, but I reminded her that I was only answering her question. The same grand juror who had pointed out Rocco's earlier imprecision said she wanted to hear my explanation.

"We'd spent weeks feeling like everything we did got twisted around, to where no one believed anything we said. On that particular day, Jason and I had gotten into a fight because I finally realized the extent of his infidelities. He wasn't a criminal, but I wasn't exactly happy with him either. I didn't want to explain all of that to Detective Duncan—this is hard for me today, in fact, but I don't have a choice—so I said he was home with me instead."

"But you don't know for certain that he was with Colin Harris all night, do you?"

"I know that Colin told me he was, and Colin Harris is the most honest person I know. And I'm sure the police have our phone records. You'll find a call from Colin's house to my cell phone that afternoon. That was from Jason right after he left the house."

"Please answer the question: You don't know firsthand where he was for the rest of the night, do you?"

"No, not firsthand."

I had no idea what evidence the police had used to obtain their arrest warrant for Jason, but this sudden change in his supposed alibi, courtesy of his own wife, was not going to help matters.

I knew that, as I spoke, Olivia Randall was taking Colin to ADA King, so Colin could provide a sworn statement regarding Jason's whereabouts, but we had no real way to prove where Jason was that night. Olivia had sent an investigator to Colin's building: they no longer had camera footage to establish that he and Jason had stayed in the apartment that night; on the other hand, there was no footage to prove that they had *not*.

"Please don't punish Jason for this," I said. "I just got nervous under pressure and blurted out that he was with me. But he was with Colin. The point is, he was nowhere near Long Island."

I looked again to the grand jurors for signs of support, but found nothing but eyes avoiding my gaze. Not only did I not have an alibi for Jason, but the fact that I had initially lied for him made him look even guiltier.

"That's enough," Rocco said. "I think your testimony speaks for itself."

*If they arrested him, they must have evidence.* These people had heard the evidence, and they had concluded that Jason was a murderer, and I was the idiot trying to protect him.

I thought she was about to excuse me from the room when she asked another question. "Does your ex-husband smoke, Ms. Powell?"

"No, he quit at New Year's."

"Does he use anything to help control the cravings?"

"He chews Nicorette."

"Very good. Thank you."

I could still feel my heart pounding in my chest as I stepped onto the elevator.

I had planned to take the Long Island Railroad back to the city after testifying, but decided to board an eastbound train instead. I'd be in East Hampton within ninety minutes, give or take.

# 61

Mom walked in about half an hour after I arrived at her house.

She flinched when she saw me sitting on the sofa. "Jesus H., you scared me. Did you call?" She was fumbling in her purse for her phone.

"No, I had grand jury in Mineola. Figured I was already halfway out."

"Well, there's a silver lining, I suppose. Where's Spencer?"

"Spending the night with a friend."

"Someone I'd approve of?"

"He has two nannies and a driver," I said.

She rolled her eyes, and I gestured to the bottle of white wine I had already opened on her coffee table.

She went to the kitchen for a glass and filled it halfway. "You going to tell me why you're really here?"

"What did you do, Mom?"

She set the glass back down on the coffee table and stood up, ready for a fight. I shook my head, too tired to argue. "You didn't need to do that," I said.

"Of course I did. Someone had to protect you. You were obviously out of your mind."

"You already *did* protect me, Mom, but Jason doesn't deserve this."

"That's not how this works, baby girl. They don't just leave murders unsolved. And if someone was going to be blamed, of course it should be him."

"Where'd you get the gum?" The ADA's question about Jason's Nicorette habit had been the giveaway. There was only one reason she'd ask. I now knew at least one big piece of evidence in the case against my husband.

"Your rental."

I was searching my memory. Jason had been the one to drop off the Audi to the dealer after I took Spencer to camp. He drove the loaner back to the garage at the carriage house. He must have left gum in the ashtray. I never even noticed.

"He has one of the best defense attorneys in the city," she said. "And your husband spits that nasty gum out everywhere he goes. The lawyer can argue that anyone could have planted it there, including Tom Fisher. All she needs to do is create reasonable doubt. Jason will be fine. He deserves to be put through the wringer for a while. Maybe he didn't tell that woman every bit of your business, but this is still on him."

"You really shouldn't have done that."

"Well, too late now. You told him about that magazine reporter?"

I nodded, realizing that my mother was right. I could no longer help Jason. "Yeah, he insisted that I take Spencer away until it's over." It was exactly the response I had anticipated. After all, when he said he would love us forever, he had meant it.

# 62

*One Month Later*

The timing for the move couldn't have been better. In August, there was hardly anyone around to notice that a young widow had moved to the island with her mother and thirteen-year-old son.

I heard the wheels of the gate out front start to move, followed by the sound of the Jeep engine cutting in the driveway. It was just like my mother and son to drive the five blocks to the ocean.

Spence still had patches of sand stuck to his bare skin when he burst through the door.

"Outdoor shower, please!" I met him out back and turned on the grill while he rinsed off. When I returned to the kitchen, my mother was inspecting the fish that I had left marinating in the refrigerator.

"I don't know why you have to be so fancy about things. Spencer and I would be just as happy with some hot dogs and potato chips."

"Well, I wouldn't. And it's Spence, Mom."

"Because that's really going to fool anyone."

Susanna's story last summer about the underground market for government documents had come in handy. My name, according to my UK passport, was Susan Martin. Mom was known as Rosemary Parker. And Spencer now went by Spence, last name Martin, same as mine.

My hair was now cropped short and bleached nearly white. Sometimes I barely recognized myself in the mirror. Spence says I look "punk rock."

Susanna understood my decision to leave, but thought my refusal to tell her where we were going was overkill. She eventually relented when I broke down in tears, telling her how paranoid I was that the *New York* magazine writer was going to find out about my past.

"Think about Spencer," I had pleaded. "I don't want the whole world to look at him and see Charles Franklin. I can't risk that. I'd rather be safe than sorry."

That magazine writer didn't exist. Well, she did exist, but she had never called me, and to my knowledge, no other journalist was looking to write a profile about the former Mrs. Jason Powell, not yet anyway.

I had promised Susanna that once we were set up somewhere new, I would let her know so she could visit. I still hadn't contacted her, and doubted that I ever would. I had learned my lesson. She had been a good friend to me, but friendship had its limits. From now on, I would only trust my family: me, Mom, Spence. Spence had been remarkably cooperative so far, because he was still convinced that Jason was guilty and that we were better off distancing ourselves. But eventually I was going to face a decision on how much to tell my son about the real reason we had come here.

Letting him have his way on his first name seemed only fair, given what I was putting him through. With a different last name, I didn't see the harm.

"You may not like my food," I said, "but someone else does."

"It went well?" she asked.

I had asked the broker who found us our house to let me

know if she heard about anyone who might need catering. As it turned out, she knew the owner of a modest little oceanfront restaurant with twelve four-tops whose chef had left for Anguilla to open his own place. Customer ratings on TripAdvisor were already starting to decline, even off-season.

"You're looking at the new head chef at Margo's."

My mother hugged me and told me how proud she was of me.

When I went to bed that night, I reached for the notebook on the nightstand. Dr. Boyle was the one who suggested that I start keeping a journal when I told him that Spencer and I were leaving New York for a while. It was no substitute for regular sessions, he warned, but might prove therapeutic.

I hadn't decided yet whether it was helping me, or even if I needed the help. But I tried to write once or twice a week anyway, burning the pages afterward when I used the grill, just to be safe.

*

What if . . . ?

What if I hadn't gone to the bonfire that night? What if I hadn't accepted Charles Franklin's offer of a ride? What if I had run out the front door instead of checking his garage to see if it was safe to leave? And what if I had never gone to Kerry Lynch's house that night?

When I feel my thoughts move in that direction, I shut them down, because asking what if can lead to regrets, and regrets are dangerous. You make the best decisions you can make in the time you have to make them, and you move on. It's instinct. It's survival.

I got in that car with Charles Franklin because it seemed safer than walking alone on a dark road at night.

After a year of learning how to survive in that house—earning tiny privileges like time away from my room, use of a toilet, fresh-squeezed juice when I was really good—he told me he was bored. He needed another girl. He had tried offering rides, the way he had gotten me, but it wasn't working. He made my choice clear: either I had to help him get another girl, or he would kill me. What else was I supposed to do?

We tried a few times—once at a mall in Cleveland, once in Philly, one time we drove all the way to Buffalo. As it turned out, not everyone was as trusting as I had been as I walked away from a bonfire party, even when there was a sweet girl in the passenger seat.

Sometimes I thought about those girls, wondering how their lives turned out. They had no way of knowing that their entire futures had rested on a decision to turn down the offer of a ride from a nice-looking young couple in a white SUV. The girl from Cleveland had been the basis for "Sarah" when the police asked what I knew about her. I remembered passing signs on the highway for the Rock & Roll Hall of Fame, so I added that detail, too.

Charlie didn't like the idea of taking two girls from one location, but his desire to have someone new had bloomed into an obsession, and he was blaming our failures on me. I begged him to give me one more shot, but on my terms.

We went back home—to my home, in East Hampton. I told him I knew a girl who would trust me.

I didn't actually expect to find her, not really. I crossed my fingers beneath my legs, hoping she was off on one of her excursions. It felt so surreal to be back again. The new chain drugstore whose construction my parents complained about was open on Main Street. We passed the bus stop where I'd been headed the night he took me. At the windmill, I looked longingly at the turn that led to my house. I felt my hopes drop as we reached the post office. We had gone all the way through East Hampton—the town where I was born and raised—and no one had recognized me. My plan had failed.

It felt as if we were picking up speed with every block until his SUV was barreling east on 27. Pretty soon we'd reach Montauk, right around sunset. We had been cruising the area for three hours, not to mention the drive from Pittsburgh. He said if we reached the lighthouse without another girl, he'd drown me in Napeague Bay. I thought about honking the horn or grabbing the wheel and running us into a tree.

And then I saw Trisha. She had her thumb out, walking backward along 27. My best guess was that she'd been drinking on Fort Pond. I had to make a split-second decision. I justified it by telling myself that together, we would be stronger. With Trisha's help, I would find a way out.

What shakes me to the core to this very day is how happy she was to see me.

I told Charlie to pull over, and then I hopped out of the passenger seat. Trisha ran at me so hard, she literally knocked me over. We were like two puppies wrestling in the sand at the side of the road.

"What are you doing here, girl? Where have you been?"

"Get in," I said, pointing to the white SUV. "Let's go party."

Charlie put the cloth over her face, the same way he had when he had taken me a year earlier. It was the second worst thing I have ever done.

*

You might think that killing Kerry is the worst thing I've done, but it's not. Even so, I force myself to tamp down the what-ifs about that night, too.

What if I had never read my husband's e-mail? I wouldn't have seen those photographs just minutes before he came home to report the "good news" that Kerry's lawyer was open to settling.

Or what if I had recognized Tom Fisher as he left Kerry's house? If I had realized who he was, I might have known that something was off with Kerry's story. I would have come to my senses and gone home.

Instead, I watched him drive away, and then I knocked on her door. I wanted to hear the truth about my husband, once and for all, straight from the source. She almost didn't let me in, but I told her that I had seen the pictures of her wrists. During the entire ordeal—the police visits, the arrest, the arraignment, the lawsuit—no one had ever told me the details of the alleged assault. It wasn't until I read that e-mail from Olivia that I knew, or thought I knew, the truth.

"He did the same thing to me," I said. "I believe you."

When she let me inside, I asked her to tell me exactly what had happened.

She was holding a glass of red wine. It was so bizarre standing there in her living room—two women on either side of her coffee table, with nothing in common except what Jason had done to us.

And then she laughed at me.

"You're even crazier than Jason said you were."

"I came here to be on your side, Kerry. I read the police reports." I thought I was being noble.

"You really don't get it, do you? He tied me up because I asked him to, and more than once, and I *loved* every second of it. We don't all have your hang-ups."

I felt my mouth moving, but no words came out.

"Oh my God. Catch up, honey." She snapped her fingers for emphasis. "I know your whole story. And I know it's why he'll never leave you. Jason loved me. No—he *loves* me. But he loves his persona more. And he can't be the good guy—Mr. Save-the-Planet, next mayor of New York—if he leaves his Little Miss Perfect with the tragic backstory."

"You're—a monster. Why would you tell me all this?" For all

she knew, I could have been recording her. I could testify to every word. "You admitted that you're lying. I'm calling the DA."

She grabbed my arm. "No, you're not. You do that, and I'll tell everyone what I know. You're that girl from the house in Pittsburgh. Who's the monster, Angela? Me, or the woman who makes a man stay with her out of sympathy? You wouldn't even let him adopt Spencer, so he has no choice. He's stuck with you. If he leaves, he loses his kid. I know all about you—"

The glass egg was heavy, at least fifteen pounds. I heard her skull crack the first time I hit her. She fell to the floor and was struggling to push herself upright. I hit her one more time and then another, until she stopped moving.

What if I had waited for her to finish the sentence? Maybe if I had heard her out, I would have realized that Jason only told Kerry about me, not that Spencer wasn't mine. But the sound of my son's name in her mouth made me certain she knew the whole story.

Or what if I had told my mother less about what really happened that night? I could have simply called her from that gas-station pay phone, told her I was in trouble, and given her the address. She had proven over and over again—first when I went missing, and then when I was found and ever since—that she would run through fire to protect me. And that is probably why I had trusted her, as always, with the entire truth.

She was at the house in a little more than an hour. Just like my instincts had kicked in the next day when Detective Duncan was on our stoop, I saw every piece of a plan. Cleaning the floor. Wiping down everything I touched. Getting rid of the glass egg.

The only thing I panicked about was the dog. I used a dish towel as a makeshift glove to fill his bowls, assuming that Kerry's absence would be noticed when she didn't show up to work the next day. I decided that if two days passed, I would make an anonymous call from a city pay phone to check on her. The funny thing is, I don't think I even saw her as a real person until I looked at that dog and wondered how he was going to feel when he realized his best friend wasn't coming back.

Mom would drive Kerry's body all the way to the East End. If anyone ever suspected me, I'd have an alibi of sorts: Spencer's phone call, plus the movie streamed as soon as I got home three and a half hours later. When that detective showed up at my door asking about Jason, I said he was home with me so both of us were accounted for.

It was a good plan, but apparently not good enough for Mom, who added her own touch by retrieving Jason's gum from the car and dropping it in the sand only three feet from Kerry's body on Ocean Beach.

It was already clear that Olivia Randall was planning to argue that Tom Fisher had framed Jason for the murder. It wouldn't be hard to find witnesses to testify that Jason was constantly chewing that stupid gum, leaving it like bread crumbs to mark his whereabouts. Kerry's own lawyer would testify that her client had been demanding huge amounts of money from both Jason and Fisher. Combined with the documents FSS had managed to get from Oasis about their Africa dealings, it would be easy to prove that Fisher had at least as much to lose as Jason.

Colin was sticking to his alibi testimony, and he'd be a good witness. Literally, all the state had was motive and a piece of gum. Olivia Randall would soak the courtroom with "reasonable doubt." As my son had said when he first heard Rachel Sutton's name: Jason wouldn't end up in prison; we were rich.

*

Do you hate me yet?

Maybe not. Technically, I was an accomplice to Trisha's kidnapping, which makes me—as a legal matter—just as guilty as

Charlie Franklin. But I was also his victim. He threatened to kill me if I didn't find him another girl. I had gotten boring.

There was a reason I chose her. From what she had told me, I figured her home life wasn't much better than what we could manage at Charlie's house together.

Even so, the first month was awful. He left me alone while she suffered the brunt of his attention. After that, it sort of evened out. When Charlie was at work, Trisha and I had each other. It was actually tolerable.

But then it became clear Trisha was going to have a baby.

Charlie punched her in the stomach three days in a row, trying to make it go away. Trisha and I made a vow to him and to each other that we would take care of the child growing inside of her. We would do anything and everything that Charlie wanted so that he would let us keep him. We made Charlie feel like we loved him, all for a little boy or girl we didn't know yet.

And the strangest thing happened: Spencer was born, and this horrible man who took so much pleasure in hurting us loved his baby. He would rush home to hold his son. He was nice to us, if that's imaginable. Trisha and I took turns going to his room every couple of days. He started letting us go outside, as long as we went one at a time, so each of us had to worry about the other as we walked around in freedom. We told the neighbors we were his nieces.

Considering what I'd been through the last three years, it wasn't that bad. Then a police officer knocked on the front door, and all four of us were in the SUV while an Amber Alert blast out on repeat across the airwaves. It was that Amber Alert that led to the very worst thing I've ever done.

I repeated the official story to law enforcement so many times that the horrific facts became rote. Charlie killed "Sarah" because he didn't want us to fit the description of two teenage girls and a baby. He pulled over at a boat slip two hours north of Pittsburgh. He ordered me to stay with the baby and Sarah to get out. He had a gun. I heard two shots. He came back to the car alone and told me to "look older."

It was so close to the truth.

I remember the sting of the splinter that worked its way beneath my skin when I dropped to my knees on the dock. When I wake up in the middle of the night, I still feel the cold metal of the gun barrel against the base of my neck and the warmth of my own urine on my thighs. The story unfolded just the way I told it, but I was the one Charlie had rejected. I was the one he had ordered from the car and marched to the end of that pier.

And once again, I chose to survive. The words seemed to come from nowhere as I stared out over the dark water. "I look older," I blurted. "I could pass for your wife."

It was true. I had always been the one who could buy us beer or talk us into a club. Trisha was a year older, but I looked at least three years older than her. And I doted on the baby at least as much as she did. And I had been the one who helped him get Trisha to come home with us. I was the one who didn't run away. I was smarter, and more cunning, and better behaved.

I was the one he could trust.

I try not to think about the momentary expression of relief that crossed her face when I returned to the car with Charlie. When I heard the two gunshots, I was holding Spencer in my lap, telling him that we were going to be okay.

*

So do I have any regrets? No. The choices I made brought us here, to this beautiful island, where I have my family, a new job, and enough money to keep us safe. But sometimes I do look out over the Atlantic Ocean and think about Trisha.

# 63

The woman who answered the front door at Virginia Mullen's house was probably around fifty years old. Her perfectly highlighted pixie cut was at odds with her outfit—an oversize Jets T-shirt, long denim shorts, and Crocs.

"I'm looking for the home's owner?" Corrine asked, holding up her badge to allow a closer inspection.

"She's not here right now."

"When do you expect her back? Her phone numbers have been disconnected."

The woman's brow furrowed. Like most people, she was uncomfortable with an unannounced police visit. "I'm not real sure. Her daughter was going through a rough time, so they left town for a little while."

Through the open door, Corrine saw that the television was on, but muted. Baby toys were scattered on the floor, and one of those portable playpens was popped open in the corner of the living room. A half-eaten sandwich waited on a plate on the coffee table.

"You're living here?" Corrine asked.

The woman wiped her hand against her shorts and offered it to Corrine for a shake. "Sorry, my name's Lucy. Lucy Carter. Ginny and I have worked together for years. Please, come in. Careful of the mess. Grammy's the babysitter when Mommy's at the hair salon. My grandson's only nine months, but he can take over a house within minutes."

The hairstyle made more sense now.

"So are you living here?" Corrine asked again. She tried to sound officious, as if the two women had broken some kind of city code or tax rule by not reporting a change in residency.

"Just staying here, really. She gave me keys and told me to treat the house as my own until she came back. She said it was better than leaving it empty."

"What about property taxes, insurance, that kind of thing?"

Lucy shrugged. "Hasn't come up yet. I assume she'll be back by then. Are you here about her son-in-law? Angela divorced him, you know. She's got nothing to do with him anymore. That's why they left town. Angela wanted to get her kid out of the city until the trial is over."

"Oh, I know." It was the same story Angela had given her super when she suddenly moved out last month. Corrine had now been searching for Angela for a week. No forwarding address. Bank accounts closed. No airline, train, or bus tickets purchased. She was a ghost.

And now her mother was gone, too, precisely as she had expected.

Corrine had a cover story ready. "It turns out Angela's entitled to some money from when she initially posted bail for him, seeing as how he's being held now. Do you mind if I take a look around to see if Ginny left behind any hints about where they might have gone?"

"That'd be fine."

Corrine was riffling through a drawer in the kitchen that most people would call a junk drawer. Two notepads, but no relevant notes. Owner's manuals, pens, a screwdriver and a hammer, a spare Honda key. "Did Ginny leave you her car, too?"

The Powells had sold their Audi, but according to the DMV, Angela's mother still had a current-year-model Honda Pilot registered in her name. Corrine hadn't seen it in the driveway.

Lucy was finishing her sandwich on the sofa. "I assume she took it."

Or, Corrine thought, she paid someone to scrap it so it couldn't be searched for Kerry Lynch's blood.

*

It all came back to that one nagging question: How had Jason Powell gotten to Long Island and back the night of Kerry's murder?

Every time Corrine pictured it, she saw him in a car. She made a list of all the possibilities and started checking them in her spare time. When the taxis, rental car companies, car services, and every other way of scoring a ride from the city were exhausted, she circled back to the Audi.

She called the Manhattan dealer and asked the service department to pull up the Powells' account, hoping a mechanic might have noticed a device used to protect the license plate from the view of automatic cameras.

The garage manager told her that Marty was the last person to work on the car. "Doubt he remembers much from a job that came in on June 6. Not exactly an Einstein."

Corrine sat up straighter at the mention of the date. It was the last day Kerry was seen. "Do you happen to know if you gave them a loaner?"

She heard tapping on a keyboard. "Yep, the new S6. Out for three days, a hundred and sixteen miles."

It hadn't taken Corrine long to find the loaner in the plate-reader data from the night of the murder: outbound on the Williamsburg Bridge at 7:41 p.m., then inbound at 10:53. The time and the mileage would cover the round-trip between the Powells' house and Kerry's, but it didn't get Jason all the way out to where Kerry's body was found.

She called the Nassau County prosecutor with the evidence, but ADA Rocco was unpersuaded. She planned to argue that Jason hid Kerry's body somewhere near her house before going back out to Long Island and moving her again. Corrine was convinced Rocco was refusing to see the truth because she had screwed up by subpoenaing Angela to the grand jury, automatically giving her immunity.

Corrine remembered what the East Hampton detective said about Angela: *When push comes to shove, she trusts her mother more than anyone.* Angela would have left the house shortly after the phone call from her son, and started streaming the movie as soon as she got back, while her mother was driving Kerry's corpse to Ocean Beach. It was the only explanation.

Angela might have immunity, but Ginny didn't, which meant Corrine might have an angle, if she could only find them.

*

She had searched every drawer in every room of the small house. The only hint she had gleaned came from the family photographs on the walls, nearly all of them on the beach—but the world had a lot of beaches. Her final, desperate step was to flip through each book on the built-in shelf of what had once been Angela's bedroom. A hollowed-out book was still one of the best do-it-yourself hiding places.

A photograph slipped from a dusty, dog-eared copy of *Flowers in the Attic.* Two teenage girls stood on the beach, their arms around each other's waists. Angela's sandy-blond hair was pulled into a ponytail at the top of her head. She was wearing a high-leg one-piece that would have been trendy in the late

1990s. Her friend had short, blunt-cut dark brown hair and was wearing a bikini top and baggy, low-slung cutoff jean shorts, exposing a tattoo of a rose vine on her right hip.

Corrine was about to tuck the photo back in place when she did a double take. The location of the tattoo matched. So did the size. And something about the girl's face seemed vaguely familiar. She looked like someone. Corrine clicked through every possibility: Angela, Jason, Kerry, Rachel, Colin, Spencer. Spencer. She remembered thinking he looked more like Charles Franklin than his mother.

She finished her search, found Lucy in the living room, and held up the picture. "Do you know who this girl is with Angela?"

Lucy made a *tsk* sound. "Trisha Faulkner. Those two were inseparable back in the day." She did not make it sound like a good thing.

"Do you know where she is now?"

"Nope. She used to come and go as she pleased, even as a teenager. She up and left for good right after high school. Can't say I blame her. That whole family's full of criminals."

Corrine's gaze drifted back to the photograph, wondering if it was possible. She ran the dates in her head. "So she's been gone for about fourteen years?"

"Well, she was a year ahead of Angela, so, yeah, I guess that's right. Time sure does fly."

The timing couldn't be a coincidence. And the longer Corrine studied Trisha's features, the greater the resemblance she saw to Spencer Powell.

Corrine's mind was pinging with possibilities, but she was certain of one thing: this girl deserved to be claimed. She could call the Pittsburgh Police and suggest they compare the DNA of Franklin's unidentified victim to one of Trisha's family members. Depending on what she learned about the Faulkners, maybe she would keep her suspicions about Spencer's biological lineage to herself, at least for the time being.

When she got to her car, she called ADA King. "I want you to get me a meeting with Olivia Randall."

He knew she was annoyed that the Nassau County DA had blown her off about the mileage on the loaner car, but he had talked her out of going to Powell's defense attorney directly.

"You're not letting this go, are you?"

"No way."

"Fine. I'll make the call."

Corrine had asked Angela how well she knew her husband. Now she was going to find out how much Jason knew about his wife.

# Acknowledgments

One of the loveliest perks of completing a new book is the opportunity to thank the many generous people who helped along the way.

I am grateful for the valuable expertise and sage advice of Matthew Connolly; Kenneth Crum; Roseanne DeLaglio; Dr. Jonathan Hayes, associate medical examiner for District 20, Naples, Florida; Dr. Jill Hechtman, medical director of Tampa Obstetrics; Shannon Kircher; Michael Koryta; NYPD lieutenant Lucas Miller; Miriam Parker; Don Rees, Multnomah County chief deputy district attorney; Anne-Lise Spitzer; and Dr. Elayne Tobin, clinical assistant professor, New York University.

My editor, Jennifer Barth, has been my trusted sounding board and closest reader since she acquired my first novel more than fifteen years ago. I consider myself lucky to work with a person of her talents and integrity. She and the matchmaker who introduced us, Philip Spitzer, *aka* the Jerry Maguire of literary agents, remain my biggest champions. I'm not kidding: Speak poorly of one of their writers near them, and I can't protect you.

I am also thankful to Amy Baker, Jonathan Burnham, Heather Drucker, Jimmy Iacobelli, Doug Jones, Michael Morrison, Katie O'Callaghan, Mary Sasso, Leah Wasielewski, Erin Wicks, and Lydia Weaver at HarperCollins; Lukas Ortiz and

Kim Lombardini at the Spitzer Agency; Angus Cargill, Lauren Nicoll, and Sophie Portas at Faber & Faber; Kate McLennan at Abner Stein Ltd.; Giulia De Biase at Edizioni Piemme; and Jody Hotchkiss.

To my loving friends and family, especially my extraordinary husband, Sean Simpson: thanks for believing I deserve you.

Last, but never least, thanks to my incredible readers, especially the longtime "kitchen cabinet" crew. Some days, simply knowing that someone other than my parents is enjoying my work and waiting for the next story is what keeps me at the keyboard. Happy reading.

*Also by Alafair Burke*

ff

## All Day and a Night

When psychotherapist Helen Brunswick is murdered in her Park Slope office, the entire city suspects her estranged husband – until the District Attorney's office receives an anonymous letter and the case is linked to convicted serial killer Anthony Amaro.

NYPD detectives Ellie Hatcher and JJ Rogan are tapped as the 'fresh look' team to reassess the original investigation that led to Amaro's conviction. The case pits them against both their fellow officers and a hard-charging celebrity defence lawyer.

As they search for certainty among conflicting evidence, their investigation takes them on the road – and it soon becomes terrifyingly clear that someone involved has gotten too close to the truth.

'Compulsively readable.' *O, The Oprah Magazine*

'Whip-smart and emotionally deft, it delivers all the way through to its final pages.' Megan Abbott, author of *The Fever*

'The story is packed with surprises and cunning plot twists, leading to an explosive finale.' *Irish Independent*

ff

## The Ex

What would you do?

Olivia Randall is one of New York City's best criminal defence lawyers. When she gets a phone call informing her that her former fiancé has been arrested for a triple homicide, there is no doubt in her mind as to his innocence. The only question is, who would go to such great lengths to frame him – and why?

For Olivia, representing Jack is a way to make up for past regrets and the hurt she caused him, but as the evidence against him mounts, she is forced to confront her doubts . . .

'Highly addictive.' Karin Slaughter

'Packed with plot, *The Ex* rocks.' *New York Journal of Books*

'Burke's writing has always been intelligent and often funny, and her female protagonists sharp and engaging – *The Ex* is her best yet.' *Guardian*